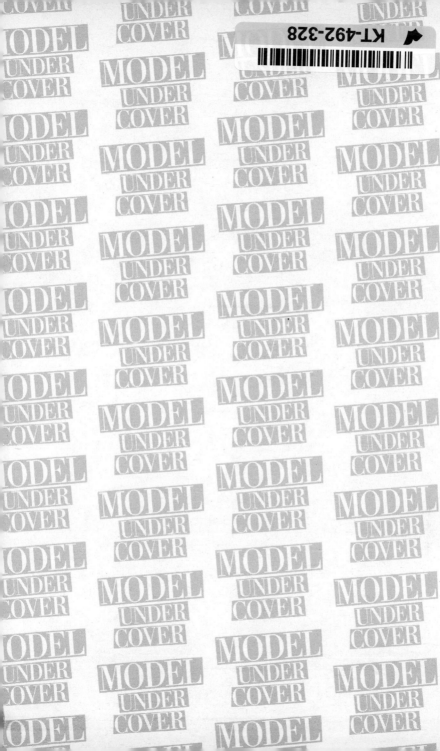

MODEL UNDER COVER

After zipping my dress, the stylist helped me step into a pair of high-heeled snakeskin sandals and gave me a thumbs up. I launched myself down the length of the room towards Claude. As I teetered past him and turned, Claude's phone rang. "What now?" he answered.

I was trying to hear what Claude was saying while concentrating on not tripping. Walking on heels is definitely easier said than done...

Remembering Ellie's command to "feel" the shoes and to "trust" myself, I lifted my eyes and as I was about to walk past Claude again, I tried to concentrate on what he was saying...

"Do you actually think I'd kidnap my own sister?"

To Gustav, as promised, and with love...
And a huge, sparkly thanks to the
ever-patient and super-fab, Jenny Savill.

First published in the UK in 2014 by Usborne Publishing Ltd., Usborne House, 83-85 Saffron Hill, London EC1N 8RT, England. www.usborne.com

Copyright © 2014 by Carina Axelsson

Cover illustration by Yusuf Doğanay

Author photo by Anne-Marie Mulot

The right of Carina Axelsson to be identified as the author of this work has been asserted by her in accordance with the Copyright, Designs and Patents Act, 1988.

The name Usborne and the devices ♈ ☻ are Trade Marks of Usborne Publishing Ltd.

A CIP catalogue record for this book is available from the British Library.

ISBN 9781409563686 JFMAMJJA OND/14 02990/4

Printed and bound by CPI Group (UK) Ltd, Croydon, CR0 4YY

MODEL UNDER COVER

A Crime of Fashion

CARINA AXELSSON

USBORNE

*S*he was being pushed up a stairwell – of that much Belle was sure.

"Come on, faster," urged the gruff voice behind her. "Do you think we're window-shopping at Chanel?"

She couldn't have answered the question if she'd wanted to – the tape on her mouth made sure of that. Up, up, up they climbed. It was a tight, steep, stone stairwell – an old one, judging from the worn edges and uneven steps she kept tripping over. But, then, buildings in Paris were full of old stone stairwells – if they were still in Paris, that was. The tightly bound blindfold was preventing her from confirming what the rest of her could only feel.

Suddenly they came to a halt. From behind, an arm reached out along her side and a key was worked roughly into a lock. There was a raspy scrape, then a click, as the lock was opened.

"This is it, gorgeous – your ivory tower."

Her blindfold was removed and the tape on her mouth was pulled off, but, before she could cry for help, she was unceremoniously thrust onto a musty bed, its metal springs squeaking loudly in complaint as she landed on it.

"Get some rest," she was told, as her captor retreated, "and we'll negotiate later."

She lay face down with her wrists tied. Seconds later she heard the key turn.

Belle was locked in.

SUNDAY MORNING

Unfashionable Beginnings

There was no backing out now, I thought as I slipped the two tickets out of their envelope for a last look before putting them into my tote bag. They looked harmless enough. Although why shouldn't they? It was hardly their fault I was being shipped to Paris.

AXELLE ANDERSON
London St. Pancras – Paris Gare du Nord
Train 3309 Departure Time 15h05
Coach 12 Seat 35

Nope. No getting out of it – that was definitely my name printed there.

"Axelle, hurry up, would you? We don't want to be late!"

And that was definitely my mum's voice.

"Axelle?"

"Coming!" Quickly I lurched across my room to the wardrobe opposite my bed. I didn't care what my mum said – I was taking it. As far as I was concerned, I needed all the good vibes I could get. From the back of the bottom drawer I pulled out my lucky jumper and shoved it into my tote.

"Your father has started the car!"

"Coming!" With a last look around my room and a quick kiss on the top of Halley's furry white head, I bounded down the stairs.

It was sunny and bright that afternoon; a brisk spring breeze whistled through the St. Pancras terminal as, thirty minutes later, I waited for the boarding call for my train with Mum and Dad.

"Axelle, did you pack your new jumper?"

"Don't forget to charge your phone."

"And did you have to take your old tote bag? After I've just bought you a new one?"

"Forty-four, Axelle! Don't forget to put a +44 before dialling any English number."

"And for goodness' sake, DO brush your hair while you're away, Axelle. Every day."

No, I hadn't packed my new jumper, I'd packed my old and lucky jumper, but there was no point admitting to that now. Like, how old did they think I was? And hadn't I been to Paris often enough that I knew how to dial out?

Parents. Honestly.

"And remember, Axelle," said my mum, "this is *your* week. Enjoy yourself!"

Right, I thought. If this is *my* week then why am I going somewhere I don't want to go to do something I absolutely don't want to do?

"You might end up liking it so much you'll never come back!" my dad said.

Yeah, ha ha, Dad.

The final call for my train was announced over the loudspeakers. I gave my parents a last hug, then turned, stepped through the automatic doors and queued for security. Minutes later I climbed into my carriage on Platform 5, one floor up from the entrance level. I could just see my parents near the Searcys bar next to the platform. My mum was walking along, looking into the carriage windows. She saw me just as the train began to pull out of the station.

I waved goodbye to my family as the train began its two-and-a-half-hour journey to Paris. I kept waving until they were nothing more than pinpricks of colour on the now distant platform and then, with the final turn out of the train station, disappeared from view altogether. I leaned back deeply in my seat and stretched my legs out in front of me, careful not to hit the stockinged ankles of the lady sitting across from me.

This wasn't my first trip to Paris – I'd been many times before. But this was my first trip alone...and, contrary to what probably happens to most sixteen-year-old girls, I was being sent to Paris for Fashion Week as *punishment*.

I'll start at the beginning: what I love most in this world is a mystery. Getting to the bottom of a story, finding a secret, following a riddle, solving a puzzle, that's what makes me buzz. Discerning the differences between what people do and what they say is fun, a never-ending game of find-the-motive. My mum likes to say sleuthing is my "hobby", but that's like saying Lady Gaga likes to sing in her spare time. And despite my mum's many delusional attempts to push me to do something else, all I've ever wanted to be is a private detective.

"I blame your gran," she always says. "Every time I turned my back she'd switch off *Sesame Street* and pop in one of her Agatha Christie DVDs. Instead of Elmo and Big Bird you had Hercule Poirot and Miss Marple."

Then I always say, "It hasn't done me any harm!" which makes my mum roll her eyes. "Besides," I continue, "what's so wrong with wanting to be a private detective?"

"Axelle, detective work is for old men shuffling around in trench coats," she likes to remind me, "although, mind you, Burberry has some nice ones out right now – but, still, Axelle, is that really what you want to be?"

"What about Nancy Drew? She's not an old man in a trench coat."

"True. But she didn't get that convertible by solving mysteries."

"Maybe she didn't, but I will."

"Right." Then, at this point there is always a short pause, after which my mum invariably starts with the one idea I'm absolutely allergic to: "Axelle, why don't you give modelling a try?" This is my mum's big wish, that I become a model (failing that she'd love me to take over her successful interior design business – but modelling wins by a long shot). "Your Aunt Venetia could help you and with your long legs—"

"I'm short, Mum, remember?"

"You're not *that* short, Axelle, and if you cut your hair…" Blah, blah, blah.

It's always the same, round and round we go. It's the one story I never seem to get anywhere with.

At least my best friend Jennifer Watanabe is supportive – up to a point.

"I mean, you *are* good at finding stuff out, Axelle. Remember how you found Mrs Singh's missing mail? And remember my mascara?"

"Halley found your mascara in the garden. That hardly qualifies as great detection."

"Still. I wouldn't have found it without you – I mean, she's your dog."

"Thanks, Jen."

"Anyway, my point is, even if you are good at figuring

things out – and you are – what could be the harm in, you know…trying to *improve* yourself a little?"

The problem with Jenny's ideas for my self-improvement is that they always involve my appearance. Lying on her bed as we had this discussion for the hundredth time, I watched as she looked at me through half-closed eyes, like an artist before a lump of fast-drying clay. "Your silence is becoming ominous, Jenny," I said.

Jenny herself left no room for improvement – she was perfect, as far as I could tell. Her straight black hair fell in a shiny sheet to the middle of her back, her face was devoid of pores and her delicate build never failed to make me feel gangly by comparison.

"If you'd just let your hair—"

"Don't start with my hair, Jenny."

"And your glasses—"

"I like wearing my glasses!"

Jenny shrugged her shoulders. "Fine. Have it your way. But you could easily look totally amazing. You'd have everyone at school eating out of your hand. I mean, look at you, Axelle, you're slim and you've got the longest legs of anyone I know. Lots of people think you're a model…"

Jenny left the rest unsaid – namely, that lots of people think I'm a model…*until I turn around.*

"It's your hair, Axelle. It's too overwhelming. And those glasses – do they have to be so big? And so *heavy*? And why can't you let me do your make-up instead of—"

"You know why I do what I do. I mean, how am I supposed to be a detective if I walk around looking like some supermodel? Then I'll have everyone staring at me and I'll never get to the bottom of anything. As a private eye I'm supposed to blend in, remember?"

"You sort of have a point..."

"I *totally* have a point."

Sometimes talking to Jenny could be scarily similar to talking with my mum.

For the most part I think I've always managed to combine my detective work with school and home quite well. The investigative column I write for the school magazine gives me some good cover when nosing around and as long as I keep my grades up – which I do – there isn't much my parents can say. *But* there have been a few incidents lately that, for whatever reason, seem to have exploded out of all proportion, like mushrooms after a rainy day. And, unfortunately, the worst one had to happen when I was with my mum...

A few weeks ago Mum and I went shopping together at her favourite department store. She loves shopping there so much that I would actually count it as a hobby of hers. Anyway, we were at a cosmetics counter and my mum was being given a facial by a woman with dark hair scraped back into a hard bun. She wore lots of jewellery and enunciated her words v-e-r-y c-l-e-a-r-l-y. She was telling my mum that she knew the products worked because just last night she had celebrated her fortieth birthday and see how fresh and youthful her skin looked. Needless to say that got me thinking because, honestly, her complexion did look fresh and youthful – suspiciously so. While my mum told her, "Wow, you look amazing for your age," I slipped behind the counter and took a look around. Within thirty seconds I'd found what I was looking for.

"Excuse me," I said, "but is your name Leanne?"

"Why, yes," she answered, surprised. "How did you know?" I saw one of my mum's eyes slowly open, panic beginning to register in it. With that green stuff slathered all over her face and her hair pulled back into a hairnet, she looked like an angry turtle. Anyway, I was hot on the trail of truth and wasn't about to let my mother stop me.

"Right. So, Leanne, why did you just lie to us about your age?"

Underneath its layer of powder, the saleslady's face turned white. My mum's second eye opened, the panic changing into outright anger.

"According to your employee card you're actually only thirty-two – or is that a lie too?" I didn't want to get her in trouble or anything – I simply wanted the truth – but no sooner was it out of my mouth than a tight-lipped silence filled the air. The saleslady was not amused. Neither was Mum.

We had to cross the entire cosmetics floor and then walk along a good length of Knightsbridge in the glare of broad daylight with Mum's face slathered in a bright green face mask. As Mum drove out of our parking space (a bit too quickly, I thought), she seemed stressed, so I said, "Mum, calm down. I'm sure that with a lot of warm water and some elbow grease that green guck will come off your face."

Suddenly the car swerved, narrowly avoiding a few pedestrians and a bus. I thought Mum was about to have a heart attack. But no. "This has nothing to do with the mask on my face, Axelle! It has to do with you! You should calm down and STOP STICKING YOUR NOSE INTO OTHER PEOPLE'S BUSINESS." Mum was wiping furiously at her face with a tissue she had found in the glove compartment but she wasn't having much luck – the mask had dried to a pretty hard consistency.

"I don't do it intentionally – it just kind of happens. I get a feeling about something and then I need to follow it to its natural conclusion."

Mum gave me a look that even the hardened streaks of the face mask couldn't disguise the meaning of.

"'Just kind of happens'? This time you've gone too far, Axelle, really TOO FAR. You have no limits when it comes to snooping around. None. Zero. You've got to start going out more, doing more, seeing more... I mean, you've spent more time in the last year working on your 'cases' for your school column or spying on our neighbours than most girls your age spend in the bathroom."

"But, Mum, she was lying to you!"

"And so what, Axelle? Who cares? It was only a facial and the poor woman was only trying to do her job. She's not Mrs Peacock in the conservatory with the candlestick! Life isn't a game of Cluedo!"

"I was only trying to help. It's not my fault if I felt something was off with what she said – and, by the way, I was right!"

"Axelle, that 'I felt something' line doesn't work any more. It's time you discovered there's more to life than solving mysteries which don't even exist."

Needless to say, the ride home was quiet after that, although as we drove past Marble Arch my mum let slip (in the same way one lets slip a lion from its cage) that perhaps it was time that she and my dad helped me "take full responsibility for your actions". Well, as time would prove, it wasn't an empty threat. The seed of the idea must have already begun to sprout, and by the time we turned out of Hyde Park at Bayswater, I've no doubt that her plan was fully formed.

Four nights ago (and three weeks after the face mask incident) it was my birthday. And because it fell on a school night, we were to have dinner at home. Mum was going to make pizzas and Jenny and her parents were coming round. "We have a special surprise for you tonight, Axelle," Mum told me that morning.

My mum's idea of a special surprise tends to have sleeves.

But maybe I'd get lucky and my parents would give me the periscope I'd been asking for. ("If they don't give you one," said Jenny, "then we can make one with mirrors from my supply of make-up freebies.") Anyway, I crossed my fingers and hoped this was the surprise my mum was so mysteriously alluding to.

After dinner the cake was brought out. As the birthday girl I had the privilege of cutting it. Now all I had to do was sit back, eat my cake, and wait for my present.

WRONG.

As I was scraping up the last bits of cake with my fork, my dad decided to drop the bomb. He pushed his chair back and cleared his throat. "Axelle, your mother and I have a wonderful gift for you. We've put a lot of thought into this and we feel sure we've found a gift that will mean something special to you…"

Can I just say that at this point all of my alert systems were *on*. Any time my parents start using words like "wonderful", "thoughtful" or "special", I get nervous.

My dad cleared his throat again before continuing. "For your sixteenth birthday we have decided to send you – alone – to your favourite city…the city you know so well…" My dad paused, hand frozen in mid-air as he smiled at me and waited.

Paris was the only city besides London that I knew well. My aunt lived there. I'd grown up going regularly with my mum to visit her. I even had a French name. And while I liked Paris – *really* liked it, even – there was something about my dad's frozen smile that made me nervous. "Uh… Paris?" I carefully asked.

"Exactly! Paris! And you'll be there for Fashion Week."

A haze of silence descended upon me as I digested this surprise. As if from the end of a long tunnel, I heard my mum say, "And you'll leave on Sunday."

How did we go from periscope to Paris? HOW? Even a surprise with sleeves would have been better.

I was in shock. My mouth just kind of hung limply open. My hair hung, too. I mean, PARIS? And FASHION WEEK? ME? Surely this was some kind of joke?

"And," my father continued, "thanks to your Aunt Venetia, you will be spending your time there working as her personal fashion assistant at *Chic: Paris* magazine!"

Right. It wasn't a joke.

After this last cruel bit, I was in a state of such anger and stupefaction that, honestly, it's a miracle my hair didn't spontaneously combust and just disintegrate off the top of my head. To make matters worse, the Watanabes (yes, *et tu*, Jenny) were oohing and aahing and making all kinds of aren't-you-the-lucky-one comments.

"But I don't want to go to Paris! I know nothing about fashion nor am I even the least bit interested in it! I LIKE WEARING A SCHOOL UNIFORM PRECISELY BECAUSE I DON'T HAVE TO THINK ABOUT FASHION!!!"

"Axelle, calm down, please. It's only for a week and,

besides, this is an opportunity any girl would love," Mum chirped brightly.

"But I am not any girl! And I don't want to go to Paris or work in fashion! And I don't want to work with Aunt Venetia! She's a dragon!"

"Listen, Axelle," my dad said, "you know we wouldn't ask you to do this unless we felt it was important. We feel you've been going a bit overboard with your 'detective work' lately, and, well, this could be a wonderful opportunity for you to see new things, expand your horizons…"

ARGH! PARENTS. How corny can they get? "Yeah, but—"

"No buts, Axelle," my dad said sternly. "If you don't go to Paris then Aunt Venetia is ready to set up a week-long internship at one of the magazines here in London."

"I wonder if *Vogue* would have you…" my mum chimed in.

I felt my mouth fall open again. "You can't be serious?"

"Actually, Axelle," my parents answered in unison, "we are."

"You decide," my mum finished for them both. "Paris or London."

I slumped into one of the living-room armchairs and closed my eyes. I couldn't believe this was happening! Jenny must have wisely decided I needed a bit of time to myself because she stayed at the table. Suddenly I felt claustrophobic. I heaved myself out of the armchair, grabbed my dad's cardigan, climbed the stairs up to our tiny roof terrace and gave in to my anguish on my own. The one person in the world who would have understood how I felt – and who no doubt would have vetoed the entire Paris idea – was Gran. And she wasn't here. How I missed her.

Wrapping the cardigan tighter around myself, I lay down on the chaise longue, looked up at the sky and took a deep breath. I told myself that a week wasn't for ever. I'd go to Paris – that much was sure. There was no way I'd stay in London and submit to Mum's daily interrogations on everything I'd been doing at *Vogue* or wherever. Besides, with a bit of luck my workaholic Aunt Venetia just might forget about me for long enough to let me do some exploring on my own. Seven days in Paris with my fashion editor aunt couldn't be that bad…could it?

Actually…

Yes, it could.

I know I was angry when I called my aunt a dragon, but, honestly, my Aunt Venetia really is a dragon – and a dragon of the worst kind. She's a fashion dragon – which means that instead of breathing plain old flames, she breathes silk and patent leather and address books filled with unpronounceable names.

I admit that after years of listening to my aunt bang on about fashion I know quite a bit about it. But still…that doesn't mean I want to be a part of it – not even for a week!

I lay outside for some time, looking at the stars. Eventually, I heard Jenny and her parents leave, after which the house went quiet. Thankfully, I was left alone. Even Halley wasn't scratching at the door to join me.

You decide: Paris or London.

My parents' ultimatum continued to ring in my ears. Again my thoughts switched back to my gran. She would have known just what to tell me, how to make me see the bright side of things (is there a bright side to fashion that doesn't involve sequins or neon lycra?). Of course, more often than not, Gran's favourite solution consisted of a pot of tea and the latest episode of *Midsomer Murders*. "Come sit with me, Axelle," she'd say with a twinkle in her eye. "It'll do you good to get your mind off school" (or my parents or whatever the problem of the moment was) "for an hour." And she was right – I always left feeling better.

Anyway, my decision was made – Paris it would be. Quietly I made my way to my bedroom, undressed, and slipped into bed beside Halley's snoring warmth. Her sweet little West Highland White Terrier eyes were shut tight. Halley, I thought ruefully, had been a much better birthday gift (for my 10th) than Paris Fashion Week. My last thought before closing my eyes was a silent prayer that I'd manage to survive both Fashion Week in Paris and my aunt – and that one day soon I'd find a case to solve that was so interesting, so big, so undeniably juicy that my parents would finally bow to the inevitable and give up in their efforts to change me.

That wasn't asking too much, was it?

SUNDAY AFTERNOON

The Dragon in the Flesh

"Mesdames et Messieurs, dans quelques instants, nous arriverons à Paris..."

The train had slowed; we were on the outskirts of the city, gliding into our final destination, and I'd been dozing. By the time I was fully awake, half the passengers in my carriage were already standing with their luggage, forming a queue at the exit doors. Catching sight of my reflection in the large window, I quickly ran my hands through my bushy, brown hair (actually, without the aid of a wide-toothed comb or large fork, that's an impossibility – let's just say I made a last desperate attempt to artfully arrange my hair), and brushed the chocolate biscuit crumbs off my jumper.

The conductor kindly helped me with my suitcase. I followed with a quick hop and alighted on French soil – my Fashion Week had officially begun. I turned to thank the conductor and relieve him of my baggage – but his head was swivelled to the side, a delicate smile of appreciation curling his lips. "*Merci, Monsieur,*" I said as I followed his gaze.

It seemed everyone on the platform was gazing in the same direction as the conductor and, to be fair, it wasn't surprising. My eye, too, was drawn to where the crowds were parting before the most impeccably tailored silhouette of black I'd ever seen. As this apparition made its unhurried way along the platform, I stood immobile. The jaunty set of the soft felt hat, the contrast between the deep black of her expensive-looking tweed coat and the white pallor of her skin, the long bare legs ending in an amazing pair of deep violet crocodile-skin platform stilettos, and the fine wisps of platinum hair framing her face, all conspired to serve the intended purpose of setting the wearer off to her best advantage. It also conspired to make anyone within her orbit feel hopelessly unstylish. And, while I've never been one to give much thought to the way I look, even I could sense, all the way down to my unpolished toenails, that compared with the vision on the platform, what I was wearing was nothing more than Neanderthal.

Great… I hadn't even made it out of the train station yet and already I was feeling fashion-impaired.

Why couldn't I just go back home? Couldn't I just promise to be more discreet? I felt myself leaning in the direction of the long queues at the ticket booths, desperate to melt into the crowd and get myself on a train back to London. I could feel a sharp longing for the safety of my fashion-free cave on Westbourne Park Road coming on. Suddenly the thought of a week at London's *Vogue* offices seemed like a cosy idea, my mum's daily interrogations like fun.

Too late, I sighed, as I locked eyes with the apparition and raised my arm in a quick wave.

She was my aunt, Venetia White, fashion editor supreme...and she was here to pick me up.

The distinctive scent of her perfume heralded her imminent presence (she'd been wearing the same perfume since before I'd been born), the click of those amazing stilettos confirmed it. But before she hugged me or asked me how the journey had been or even how I was feeling, out came the question that had haunted every visit with her since my childhood, the question I never had a suitable answer for, the one question she *always* asked. Like a rabbit caught in her headlights, I waited...

"Axelle, darling. What *are* you wearing?"

Ten minutes later, Aunt Venetia's driver was zooming along the streets of Paris at a speed that would have made my parents think twice about sending me here. Furthermore I was sweating – an inevitable by-product of sharing a small enclosed space with Aunt V. I found myself suddenly wishing that I did have short hair – if only to keep me cooler in situations like this. I was feeling so hot, my glasses were beginning to steam up. I took them off and wiped them on my sleeve.

"Axelle, darling," she tut-tutted. "Eww. Honestly. We've got to do something about those dreadful glasses. And they're filthy. How can you possibly see anything? Anyway, one thing at a time. So how was the ride? I hope you were sitting on your own. There's nothing worse than being surrounded by ghastly-looking people for two hours." From underneath the soft black brim of her hat, Aunt V's arctic blue eyes focused intently upon me. "Axelle, are you all right?" Her voice was low and smoky, nearly growling.

No, I wanted to say, *no I'm not all right. Even my suitcase is probably sweating in the boot right now.* Anyway, for once discretion got the better of me. "I'm just a bit tired..." I answered.

"Frankly, Axelle, you're looking a bit pale. I certainly hope your mum didn't send you here with a cold. If that's the case, I'm sorry to tell you, but you'll just have to remain quarantined in your bedroom. Carmen can take care of you. I cannot risk catching even the slightest cold during Fashion Week. We'll take your temperature as soon as we're home."

"I don't have a cold, Aunt V, nor do I feel unwell or ill in any other way..." *Great, this is getting off to a good start,* I thought. I mean, needless to say, while I'd love to get out of trailing behind my aunt from one fashion show to the next, the thought of being quarantined in my bedroom for a week was even worse.

"Yes, well, all forms of mass-transportation are chock-a-block with strange germs. You may have caught something, you know. Anyway, we'll see."

Out of the corner of my eye I stole a look at my aunt, while with my left hand I carefully reached into my tote bag and took out the notes for the story I was working on for my school magazine, *The Notting Hill News*. Aunt V had a pair of black professor glasses on. She was perusing her printed schedule for the upcoming week. Without looking up from her schedule, she said, "What are you doing, Axelle?"

"Just taking out some…uhhm…homework, actually…"

Taking her glasses off, she turned to look at me. Her hat was off, the black stripe that ran through the middle of her platinum hair prominent. My very own Cruella de Vil. "That homework wouldn't happen to have anything to do with your school column, now would it? What is it this time? The Case of the Missing Lab Rat?"

I knew it – I should have opted for the London internship. My mum was beginning to seem cute and fluffy – harmless, even – compared to Aunt V.

"I'm joking, Axelle. Don't look so frightened," she said curtly. Then, leaning her head back, she sighed. "Listen, Axelle…your parents have sent you here because they feel you spend too much time obsessing over your dream of being a private eye, and, after hearing about your latest transgression at the department store, I must say I am inclined to agree."

"But, I promise you, the saleswoman—"

"Axelle, calm down. Forget about the saleswoman and

forget about being a private eye, okay? You're sixteen now, Axelle. Sixteen! It's time you put your notebooks, lock-picking devices, endless theories and everything else you fool yourself with to rest. And this is the week to do it. You'll be very busy as my assistant."

"That's fine, Aunt V. I'm more than happy to be your assistant, but, the fact is, I'm just not made—"

"Axelle, that's enough. Your parents have wisely entrusted me with the broadening of your horizons – so let's concentrate on that. I repeat: it's time you left your childish fantasies behind. Here," she said, handing me a slick folder made of black patent leather. "I've had the office put together brief biographies of the designers whose shows we'll be seeing. A copy of our schedule is also included. You can start reading about the designers now – I'll quiz you later. This information will come in handy after the shows, when we go backstage. I can't have *my* niece not knowing a thing, now can I?"

Then, silence. I couldn't believe it. Was that all Aunt V was going to say?

"And, by the way," she said, as she slipped her glasses back on and turned a page in her notes, "if one day you really do become a private detective...you'll *definitely* have to do something about your outfit."

I had been waiting for that. As Gran used to say, with Aunt Venetia life is very circular: everything always comes back to clothes.

I leaned back against the plush cream-coloured leather seat and pretended to read the proffered notes. But actually I was still thinking about Gran.

It had started innocently enough. Quite simply Gran just loved a good mystery and thought it natural to share her hobby with me. "You're going to become the best private detective this city has ever known, Axelle," she'd tell me. Then, turning to my father, she'd add, "Don't forget, Tom, it's in her blood." And with this last comment she'd end the discussion before it had even begun.

It was true. The bit about the blood, I mean. My grandfather (Mum's father and Gran's husband), whom I couldn't remember, had worked out of Scotland Yard. He'd even solved some famous cases, but he'd died before I was old enough to speak – although that didn't stop Gran from being convinced that his sleuthing blood coursed through me.

It also explained my mum's resistance. "Your grandfather turned me off trench coats for ever, Axelle," she'd say. "He was always away on some case. And so *secretive*. Trust me, it's not a life for a woman."

"So what do you think? Interesting, no?" Aunt V said, breaking into my thoughts. She didn't get any further, however, before her phone rang. It had been ringing non-stop since she'd fetched me. "This time I have to answer," she said, as Jean (her driver) handed Aunt V her phone. "Yes, Marie... Yes... Is that an elephant I hear in the background? Good. How light is its skin colour? I said light, remember. If they're too grey, send them back to their tent or wherever they came from... Remember: think grey like light rain on the Normandy coast, NOT grey like a Kansas thundercloud. Okay? Good. And, by the way, I want more colour in the backgrounds. And I mean saturated colour – not just bright colour. Any questions?"

Just so you know, when Aunt V says "Any questions?" she doesn't actually expect you to come up with any. She uses the phrase in the same way most people use full stops.

Turning to me as she cancelled the call, she said, "That was Marie calling from India. She's there on a reshoot. Let's hope they get it right this time around. Anyway, Axelle, we have a busy week of shows ahead of us. Dior, Chanel, Lanvin, Givenchy..."

As Aunt V reeled off more names, I slumped further into my seat. I'd only just arrived and already Aunt V had mentioned the names of about a dozen designers I'd never heard of – at this rate I really would have to read the notes she'd prepared for me! How was I supposed to survive the week as her assistant?

As if in answer to my silent question, she said, "And don't worry – there'll be plenty for you to do. For instance, as you're so good at taking notes, I thought you could write something about the shows we'll be seeing. If it's good, I'll feed it to *Teen Chic*. 'Fashion Week Through The Eyes of a Teen Fashionista'. Something like that. Anyway, by the time this week is over," she continued, "you'll be more concerned with skirt length than you ever were with *The Hound of the Baskervilles*. Speaking of which, Axelle, you're covered in white hairs. I thought terriers weren't supposed to shed. Are you sure Halley is pure-bred?"

"It's spring, Aunt V," I answered as I watched her flick some hairs off the seats. "Halley's changing into her summer coat."

"Well, at least she has that much sense. Many people use the same clothes year round. Oh, good. We're nearly home." We were heading towards the Left Bank, which is where Aunt V lives and works. The *Chic: Paris* magazine offices, where Aunt V has been editor-in-chief for the last twenty years, are on the Rue de Furstemberg, a tiny, tree-filled square fifteen minutes away (by foot – not that her red-soled stilettos ever tread pavement) from Aunt V's apartment.

As we made our way around the Place de la Concorde, the open square was suffused with the last of the day's golden light. Everything glowed, from the well-worn cobblestones to the gilded tip of the obelisk adorning the middle of the square. On our left, the treetops in the park were ablaze with colour and far beyond I could see the Louvre museum. I turned quickly towards my right to catch sight of the Champs Élysées; looking this way I had the sun's fading brilliance full in my face. Through the crimson haze I could just make out the clipped horse chestnut trees lining the boulevard, leading up to yet another monument.

"Cheesy samples," my aunt said, as she folded her glasses and slipped them into their case.

For as long as I can remember my aunt has always carried an anagram puzzle book with her in her handbag. And *cheesy samples*, I quickly figured out, was an anagram of Champs Élysées. I was just about to say so when a loud siren bore down upon us from behind. Jean swerved the car hard to the right and stopped just short of the yellow stone balustrade of the bridge we were crossing. I saw Aunt V's glasses fly out of their pocket in her handbag and land on the carpeted floor, as two black sedans, blue lights whirling on their roofs, sped past us.

"Jean, turn the radio on, would you, please?" Aunt V said. "It looks serious..." Jean duly found the news channel and just as he managed to untangle us from the other cars on the bridge, Aunt Venetia took a sharp breath. "Turn it up, Jean," she demanded impatiently as she leaned forward, left hand held high to silence me. I listened just in time to hear the following announcement: "BELLE LA LUNE, FASHION'S TOP DESIGNER, IS MISSING!"

"Jean," Aunt V commanded, "I don't care what you have to do – just get us home. Now!"

I don't know when Carmen had last seen her boss run, but it must have been a long time ago judging by the way her mouth dropped open when Aunt V bounded through the opened door at a gallop, flung her tweed coat at her and raced into her study to put the television on.

As I trained my ears to the rapid cadence of the newscaster, I silently thanked my mum for all of the private French lessons she'd insisted upon. "BELLE LA LUNE, FASHION'S FAVOURITE YOUNG DESIGNER, IS MISSING!" ran the news. "Belle, only twenty-three and already considered a fashion genius by her legion of young fans, was officially declared missing this afternoon. Last night – Saturday night – the La Lune family had dinner together with two family friends," the newscaster continued. "However, since this morning, there has been no sign of Belle La Lune and no one in the family has seen or spoken to Belle since dining together last night. Her disappearance comes at an especially delicate time for the La Lune family and for Belle in particular. As overall creative director for the La Lune brand, Belle designs the brand's fashion collections, the latest of which will be shown at the family's fashion show this Friday. Furthermore, the family is launching their next handbag – the 'Juno' bag, also designed by Belle – on Wednesday evening, in the most anticipated event of this spring's Fashion Week. The family is counting on successful sales of the Juno bag to help retain its position at the top of the cut-throat fashion world. More news as we receive it…"

Even I know who the La Lunes are – they're the poster-family for French fashion: glamorous, colourful, and sophisticated. My mum can never resist asking Aunt V about them. And I actually met Belle a few years ago, here in Paris, at a show Mum dragged me to. Aunt V introduced us to Belle and I think Mum had hoped Belle would inspire me to dress better. But when my mum asked her what advice she could share with me, Belle said: "Just do what you love to do – nothing else is important." Ha! Thank you, I said, and I told her I was planning to be a private eye, at which point Mum said we had to move on or we'd be late for the next show.

And while I don't remember anything else about that show, I *do* remember Belle leaning in, blue eyes smiling, her long blonde hair catching the light as it tumbled over her slim frame. But that was only the half of it – you see, she'd actually seemed human (for a fashionista!) and so *nice*... Besides, as far as I'm concerned, that whole "just do what you love to do" thing was spot on.

"I cannot believe it," Aunt V said as she flopped into a large armchair. "And I'm one of the 'family friends' who had dinner with them last night..."

I couldn't believe it either. The only other time I'd seen Aunt V this much at a loss for words was at a family wedding when my father had worn brown loafers with a dark suit.

"She's missing. Unbelievable. How is her family going to cope without her? It's Fashion Week, for goodness' sake! *And* they have to launch their new handbag this week too..."

Before Aunt V could say more, the normal broadcast was interrupted by another newsflash. The newscaster introduced Belle's oldest brother, Claude La Lune, head of public relations at the family's fashion empire. The camera panned to him standing in a vast, airy, white room. Tanned and slim, Claude was dressed in tight black jeans and a crisp white shirt, the cuffs poking out from a fitted black jacket. He was dark, with black eyes and dark brown hair that curled along his jacket collar. Forty seamstresses dressed in white uniforms stood silently behind him, their eyes swollen and red from crying. He was obviously in the La Lune atelier. As the camera panned back, the soaring ceilings of the design studio seemed to dwarf them.

"My family and I are devastated," he began. "Unfortunately, the stresses of the fashion world can sometimes lead even the strongest among us...to..." Here his voice caught before he managed to squeeze out the word. "...*disappear*." He looked down and pulled on his cuffs before continuing. "We ask anyone, anyone who could have any information on the whereabouts of my sister to please, please, contact us."

He stopped again to collect himself before his emotions overtook him – at least, that's presumably what it was meant to look like, although, to be honest, the entire gesture didn't seem genuine to me. He held his right hand over his eyes for a moment while the seamstresses behind him all pulled white handkerchiefs from their sleeves and held them to their eyes. Then he turned back towards the camera, dropped his hand and carried on. "And I would like to add that my family has agreed to offer a reward of half a million euros for any information leading to the safe return of my beautiful sister..." After that the programme returned to the rest of the news.

If they had returned to showing Bigfoot, Victoria Beckham, and the Little Mermaid all doing a song and dance number together, I wouldn't have cared. Because there was only one thing ringing in my ears at that moment: Belle La Lune was missing.

Now, finally, after following an endless trail of missing mail and lost pets, a real case had come my way. A case big enough and juicy enough to turn my mum around to my way of thinking. A case with enough glitz factor to forever banish the thought of even a hundred dirty trench coats.

And the case was mine for the taking.

Well, mine and the French police force's.

I was going to solve this mystery before they did.

I didn't know how...

But I was.

*B*elle had no idea what time it was – whether it was even day or night. She was hungry, thirsty and cold. But above all, it was fear she felt. Fear of her captor, fear of not being found, fear of dying in this dark, damp space – wherever it was.

She knew her family must be looking for her.

But how would they ever find her?

MONDAY MORNING

<u>A Morning of Surprises</u>

Belle La Lune's face was all over the morning news. Where was she? Was she alive? And how had she, or her kidnapper, so far eluded all investigative efforts to find her?

Somehow, I needed to get near the La Lunes...

"Axelle, what *are* you wearing?"

Jeez! That scared me! I nearly dropped the mug I was filling. It was Aunt V. I was making myself a cup of tea in her sleek white kitchen, but don't think that my aunt was in the kitchen to do the same thing. No way. She NEVER leaves her bedroom until she is public-ready and she'd certainly NEVER deign to do anything as plebeian as boil water. Her breakfast had been taken to her on a tray at 7.30 as usual. It was nine o'clock now.

"Uhhh..." How did Aunt V always manage to reduce my communication skills to Neolithic levels? "Ummm...Well, I'm wearing my favourite pair of jeans and my lucky jumper."

"What could that jumper and the concept of luck possibly have in common?" asked Aunt V, glancing at a *Figaro* newspaper article on the La Lunes. "Axelle, let me make myself clear: you are my niece and I love you." She paused to apply a touch of lip gloss to the middle of her bottom lip. "I would even go so far as to say I find your whacky sartorial ways *nearly* bohemian, and even, on occasion, quaintly endearing. I prefer to think of your sense of style as being eccentric, as opposed to...just strange. However, as long as you are here working with me, you are representing...*me*. And *I* represent *Chic: Paris* magazine, which means that by association, *you do too*." Here she paused again, giving the words a chance to sink in as she rose and walked to the kitchen window. The clear lacquer on her perfectly manicured nails caught the morning light as she brushed her fingertips over the tops of her lush and immaculately potted kitchen herbs and inhaled their fragrance.

Fleetingly I wondered whether thyme could be fatal if inhaled too deeply.

"Axelle, are you listening? Therefore," she continued, "for the duration of your stay, you will dress in what *I* deem to be an elegant, fashionable, and stylish manner – lucky jumpers and favourite jeans simply will not do." Glancing at her elegant gold watch, she continued, "Unfortunately, we don't have the time to change what you're wearing. We're due at Miriam's in a quarter of an hour and I don't want to be late – she'll know everything about Belle's disappearance."

She scrutinized me one last time through narrowed eyes, then turned on her python-skin heels and said, "We'll just have to say that you came in on the early train this morning and that I've only just fetched you from the station. That way it'll be obvious to everyone that you dressed yourself – on foreign soil. We cannot have Paris believing that a blood relation of mine left *my* house looking as you are now." She was quiet for a moment as she checked her make-up. "I'll see you downstairs in two minutes," she said. "We'll go straight to Miriam's. She'll be able to sort you out."

Then, with a click of her gilded powder compact, she was gone.

Miriam Fontaine owns a modelling agency and is Aunt Venetia's oldest friend in Paris. They met at a party held by mutual friends when they were both new to the city (Aunt V from London and Miriam from the countryside south of Paris). That was well before they'd both been married and divorced or had even started in their respective fields. Through thick and thin their friendship has endured and rare is the week when they don't see each other. This morning Aunt V was desperate to get to Miriam because Miriam hears everything. She's gossip central in the fashion world. And sure enough, as we made our way into the agency, the first words out of her mouth were "Can you believe?"

Then: "Ah! Zee little niece Anglaise! Hallo, Axelle," she said embracing me with air kisses. As she air-kissed my aunt, I heard her say, "She looks so serious, *non*?"

Turning to me, my aunt said, "Axelle, Miriam and I have a few matters to discuss. We'll be in Miriam's office, so now is your chance to begin writing your article for *Teen Chic*. Look around, absorb the ambience, and write something interesting about it all. I'll be back shortly."

No! I knew they were going to talk about Belle La Lune. I couldn't let this chance for some inside information just pass me by! "But wouldn't it be a good idea if I were to begin by taking notes on your conversation?" I asked.

"No, Axelle, not now."

"But I'm sure your readers would like to know what you have to say about the world of fashion this morning. Come on, Aunt V, share with me!"

"Axelle, darling, I will not share and you will not listen. Now go, *absorb*," she commanded with a wave of her wrist. "In the next room. Okay?" and she turned down the corridor, arm in arm with Miriam.

"But I promise to be a fly on the wall! You'll forget I'm even in the room!" I called out to no avail. They turned the corner and a second later I heard Miriam's office door firmly close.

I shuffled off to "absorb" for Jenny's sake – she'd want to hear every detail about everything. Jenny loves fashion. It started last year when Mrs Watanabe told her she could wear mascara and lip gloss to school. What Mrs Watanabe didn't know was that Jenny had mastered the "no make-up" make-up look. In other words, what Mrs Watanabe took to be a bit of mascara and lip gloss was in reality foundation, concealer, powder, eyeshadow, eye pencil, blush, bronzer, eyebrow gel, and, yes, mascara and lip gloss. Jenny's dream is to be a make-up artist. She's always working on different looks, and once she has a new look perfected, of course she wants to try it out on somebody. That somebody is me. I'm her life-sized guinea pig.

"The only problem is that once we release your hair and you put on your glasses, my work is all covered up. No one can see that you have a lick of anything on," she'd say, appraising me through narrowed eyes, head tilted to one side.

Gee, thanks, Jen. It's nice to know that an hour's worth of make-up applied to my face doesn't make a difference.

Anyway, let me tell you what being in a modelling agency is like: it's like being on ANOTHER PLANET. A planet of long-legged, flawless-skinned inhabitants sporting abundant hair and practically see-through silhouettes.

Even the conversation had nothing to do with my world:

"My mom is at my apartment in New York right now stocking my refrigerator with goodies. I'll fly out tomorrow. I can't wait to eat at home – for once!"

"I have to fly to South Africa in two days. Is it, like, summer or winter there right now?"

"Cool bag! Balenciaga?"

"I've been travelling non-stop for two months. I am so desperate to sleep in my own room for just a few days..."

"Your boots are amazing! Whose are they?"

"They want me to cut my hair short for the Elle shoot. But, I'm talking like, really short..."

"Did you know you're on the sides of all the buses in Milan right now?"

"Do you think I can eat this croissant?"

"My new chihuahua puppy scratched my face this morning and tomorrow I have to shoot beauty for W! Do you think they can cover it with make-up?"

I made my way to the room with the so-called "booking table". Around this table sat the "bookers", each facing their own computer screen. Each booker is assigned a number of models to look after. Which models they get to handle is dependent on how long they have been on the job and how good they are at "booking" a deal. The better the booker, the higher on the fame scale the models they handle will be.

I perched myself on a chair in the corner, pulled my notebook out, and listened as the whirlwind of activity grew around me. Since I'd arrived there'd been a gradual crescendo in the amount of telephone-ringing and computer-clicking going on. Like a jet reaching its expected flight altitude it would soon level off, then continue unabated until the end of the day. The bookers sat like air-traffic controllers, earphones on, computers facing them, taking instructions, giving directions:

"Maggie is not available on the 10th – she's doing Dolce & Gabbana's ad campaign that week. But I could give you a second option for the 15th."

"How late are you? Okay. Okay. Listen, I'll call the airline then I'll call you back."

"No, no, it's not that studio – you're supposed to be at the one further up the street at number 7. Go now, I'll call to say you'll be there in a minute."

A steady stream of models came in and out, stopping to get appointments or discuss their next career move with their booker. Some had just landed from New York or Tokyo, others were coming in from a nearby casting, small dogs in tow. Several of the models were deeply immersed in updating their "books".

A model's "book" is her portfolio. And the newer the photos in it, the better it is, because it clearly shows you've been working recently. The most prestigious photos are those which are known as "tear sheets". These are pages which are literally torn from magazines. The most in-demand models have the kind of book all new girls dream of: page after page of the glossiest, most prestigious (and recent) magazine work, shot by the best photographers in the business. I suddenly realized that I knew a lot more about all this stuff than I'd thought. It must have seeped into my brain during previous trips to see Aunt V – Mum would be thrilled.

My phone suddenly vibrated. It was Jenny. *I heard the news and I bet you're on it. Any leads yet? Where are you? X J*

I'm at Miriam's. No leads yet. FYI: Tiny jackets and tiny dogs are in. Got to go. Someone's talking about Belle La Lune!

Pricking my ears, I'd noted one of the bookers to my right reading an article on the internet about Belle. Over her shoulder leaned a tousle-haired guy who'd just come in. He looked only a little bit older than me but in his leather jacket and biker boots he was better dressed for a quick getaway than for a modelling agency. What was he doing here? He didn't seem pretty enough to be a model…in fact, he didn't look like a fashionista at all – not even a part-time one. Maybe Miriam had a son I'd never heard about? I couldn't tell, and his wicked grin gave nothing away, but by the way he and the booker were pointing at the computer screen and exchanging whispers, they obviously knew more about Belle's disappearance than I did. Quietly I got up and tried to get close to where they were now standing. Maybe I could pick up a bit of information…

As I was thinking, the most stunning model I'd seen so far that morning walked in. The effect when she came into the room was palpable. All the bookers simultaneously looked up and beamed. Her booker (Hervé, as I was to find out), wiggled with excitement in his seat and mouthed that he would be with her in a moment. As soon as he ended his call he jumped up and bounded over to the model, giving her a hug and air kisses. "My beautiful one, how was zee trip? Zee islands look so beautiful on zee photo you sent me." And then, stepping back from her: "You look splendid."

"You really do look ravishing," the other bookers cooed. "And so tanned and relaxed."

"So, my beautiful one," Hervé continued, "this morning you'll go to Madrid for Spanish *Vogue*. You'll shoot this afternoon and evening then fly back early tomorrow morning to shoot the La Lune Fall/Winter campaign. The La Lunes know you'll be coming straight from the airport. Tomorrow after the La Lune shoot you're doing the Christian Dior and Louis Vuitton shows. You're on option for all of the big shows this week. They should all confirm later today. Next week, after the shows, you go to London to shoot the new Burberry campaign and from there New York for a week of *Vogue* and more advertising. And more shows, of course. Oh, and I think I'll be confirming a Guerlain perfume commercial for some time next month. I just have to find a free day in your schedule. As of now, you are completely booked for the next six months."

"And when am I leaving for Madrid?" she asked in an English accent. And somehow she looked familiar...

"Your flight leaves in two hours and twenty minutes. I have your details here waiting for your confirmation," Hervé answered as he waved a printed email in his hand. "And I have all of your details for the La Lune shoot tomorrow. Like I said, you'll go straight there from the airport tomorrow morning."

She stifled a yawn before asking Hervé, "Do I have to go? I'm exhausted. I've been travelling non-stop since Christmas and from what you've told me it doesn't sound as if I'll have a day off for another six months…"

"Ellie, my beautiful one, when zee big God gives you *le* grapefruit, you must make zee juice, *non*?"

Like a rolling snowball, a small idea began to form itself in my mind, gathering momentum with each second that ticked… She speaks English, she's booked to work with the La Lunes tomorrow, she seems nice… She could be just the person to introduce me to the La Lunes and then I could solve the mystery of Belle's disappearance! But how? She was about to leave for Madrid and if I wanted her help I'd have to get to know her now, today, this morning. I had to convince her to take me to the La Lune shoot with her tomorrow. How could I do it if she was about to catch a flight to Madrid?

"I'm all for making *lemonade*, Hervé – but do I have to get so tired making it?"

"*Ma chérie*, you are too young to get tired! So," Hervé continued, "departure at 11.55 on Air France. Or would you prefer the next flight? It's a half an hour later."

"No, 11.55's fine," she answered.

No! No! That was NOT fine. I had to stop her. I needed her help and she needed my…my what? What could I offer her? How could I convince her to stay?

"Good, I'll just call to confirm." Hervé rapidly dialled a number on his phone.

Ellie yawned again, this time not bothering to hide her open mouth. Then she stretched her arms up over her head and said, "After you've confirmed, Hervé, we need to talk about giving me some time off."

Hervé rolled his eyes at her as he waited for his call to go through.

"I'm serious, Hervé. I'm worn out working and I'd like some time off – just a few days."

While talking to the travel agent, Hervé mouthed the words, "*Next year.*"

"You're joking," the model said.

Hervé shook his head. And that's when I had my idea.

"So, 11.55?" Hervé asked.

As Ellie answered, I said "You can't go!" – or at least, I thought I did. But only a dry little croak came out of my mouth. Thick and dry, my throat felt as if I hadn't swallowed since breakfast.

"And Seat 1A?" continued Hervé. "Yes, yes, no problem, I'm still here," he said to the travel agency, "and, yes, we'd like to—"

But before he could say anything else I jumped up and yelled, "YOU CAN'T GO!"

Complete silence descended upon the room. The bookers all looked at me, frozen in action. Even Mr Leather Jacket, still bent over the same booker's computer, forgot about Belle for a moment and stood up.

"Yes, just one second, please," Hervé said, putting the

travel agent on hold. "Ellie," he said calmly, giving me a look usually reserved for annoying insects, "would you like a vegetarian meal?"

"Say no," I whispered, "please."

"Why?" she mouthed. "Who are you?"

"Because I need your help! I'll explain later – promise." She was hesitating – and why wouldn't she? She'd never seen me in her life. "Take the day off! Have some fun. Forget them," I added under my breath, with a nod towards the bookers.

She visibly perked up at the thought of some free time.

"Ellie?" Hervé said. "Vegetarian meal?"

The model flicked her long honey-blonde hair behind her shoulder, smiled at Hervé and shook her head, NO. "Get rid of the travel agent, Hervé. Tell them we'll call back." Hervé looked confused. "I can't go, Hervé," Ellie said, looking at me.

"But—" Hervé protested.

"But nothing, I can't go because…" It took me a moment to realize she wanted me to give her a reason. Out loud. I began to sweat under my lucky jumper. My lips felt thick and my throat was going dry again. Furthermore, I'd just realized why she looked familiar: Jenny had photos of her taped all over her bedroom walls and all the girls at school were constantly dissecting her latest magazine pictures. She was none other than Elizabeth Billingsley, otherwise known as Ellie B, the hot new English export and rumoured to be the next "big thing". And I was about to stop her from flying to Madrid to shoot for Spanish *Vogue*. Visions of my mum, her face an angry bright red under the cracking green face mask, filled my mind.

"Well?" she asked.

"You can't go because you've agreed to a *Chic: Paris* magazine interview," I said in one quick breath. "A big spread with photos... Remember?" Desperately I looked at her, silently pleading with her to play along with me. "So you can't fly to Madrid because *Chic* magazine would be upset. You agreed to the interview last week. Directly with my aunt. I guess the magazine forgot to call," I added with a shrug of my shoulders as I looked at Hervé. If I planned on living long, I thought, I could only hope that my aunt never heard what I'd just said. At the very least, she'd force me to wear polyester for the rest of my life. Quietly I stood and held my breath as I watched Ellie decide whether to join me or not.

"Yes... Yes, I remember now," she finally said. I let out a long sigh.

Hervé was rolling his eyes. "Ellie, please, we have to confirm this trip."

"I am not going on the trip. Cancel it, Hervé."

"But, Ellie, my beautiful one, you cannot cancel. Everything has been booked around you! Please."

"No buts, Hervé. I'm not going and that's final. The client will have to forgive you – and me. Tell them we've made a mistake – a computer error. *Chic: Paris* booked me first. But we can reschedule the *Vogue* for next week. I'll fly out on my way to New York. And you can drop the news that I'll be on the cover of next month's British *Vogue*. They'll want me more than ever after hearing that." She gave Hervé that million-dollar smile of hers and flicked her hair some more. It was as if she was turning down nothing more than a last-minute reservation at a neighbourhood restaurant.

At that moment Hervé's telephone rang. "Ellie," he said, as he put the caller on hold and openly scowled at me, "Chanel wants to know if you'd do a fitting today – as you're not going to Madrid now, you could fit that in, couldn't you? They know you've just gotten off the plane and are tired, but they'll have your favourite green tea and you can order whatever you'd like for lunch. Oh, and Christine," he added, turning to the booker in charge of the "new faces" division, "they'd also like to see anyone new."

"Yeah, I'll go, but…" Ellie turned to me. "What's your name?" she whispered.

"Axelle," I answered in a clear whisper, accent on the second syllable (like the verb *excel* – and *not* like the car part!).

"But *Axelle* should come with me."

"Fine." Hervé gave me a snooty look. "As long as she stands quietly and waits patiently – your fitting could take some time. Better yet, she could wait across the street at the Ritz and have a milkshake," he said with a smirk.

"No," Ellie said. "I mean 'come with' as in she can go as one of the agency's new faces. You know: me, her, two models from this agency going together to Chanel for their fitting. Here, let me talk to them." And before Hervé knew what was going on, Ellie had snatched the earpiece off his head and was speaking to the person on the other end of the phone.

"Oh my gosh, you have to meet this new girl. Yeah… yeah…okay." Turning to me, Ellie continued, "And she looks just like…" *Please be kind* I thought, *please be kind.* "Well, she looks…interesting…and…unique! She has very long legs… Okay. Great! See you later!"

Hervé was glaring at me and the rest of the bookers were looking at me as if I were a plate of rotting leftovers that they'd just found shoved in the back corner of their refrigerator. Only Mr Leather Jacket with the wicked grin seemed to find the whole thing amusing. I could see his smile playing at the corners of his mouth as he fiddled with his phone.

"Ellie, honestly, that kind of decision can only be made by Miriam! In case you have forgotten, this is her agency!" Hervé was apoplectic with rage. Only the thought that the agency could not afford to lose Ellie kept him in check.

"Well, I think she looks great," Ellie said with a shrug of her shoulders. She knew full well I didn't, and she also knew exactly how to irritate her bookers by throwing her weight around. "I think it could be fun," she said turning to me. "We could model together for as long as you're here. How long are you here for?" she asked.

"A week."

"Fantastic! Then please say you'll model for the week. We'll have fun together – I know it. Besides, at this point I could use a new adventure to keep me going. You can be the holiday the agency never lets me take!" Here she paused to smile at the roomful of angry grimaces directed our way. "Besides, fashion loves a new face – especially an interesting one. And don't worry – I'll teach you everything you'll need to know. So, what do you say?"

My mind was racing. I began to think about the fact that I hadn't worn a dress since that cheesy family portrait my mum had insisted we take two years ago. Plus there was my hair and glasses... I'd been living for so long behind the wall of anonymity they afforded that the thought of being shorn of my "disguise" was nearly terrifying. Then again, Ellie had inadvertently given me the best possible disguise for this case, the one I never would have thought of: fashion model.

I stood transfixed, surprised and anxious in equal measure at the idea of modelling. Visions of high heels and lip gloss whizzed through my mind. I'd never tried modelling before. Could I do it? Could I make the leap from being Jenny's makeover guinea pig to the pages of *Vogue* (as if I'd ever get that far)? And, more pointedly, could I really use this opportunity to get close to the La Lunes? The last thing I wanted was to get stuck modelling for a week with no pay-off for the case.

I didn't hear the ringing phones and non-stop chatter. I stood in a cloud of indecision, waiting for some kind of signal to drop from the sky. Yes? Or no? Ellie was waiting. Now she was the one silently pleading, her eyes willing me to join her for a week of fun. Before any kind of fear bit back at me, I said… "Yes!"

You could have heard a pin drop in the agency.

"Good, that's settled then," Ellie said.

Hervé looked as if he was going to go straight home from work to stick long sharp pins into the little voodoo effigy he would surely make of me during his lunch break.

At this moment Aunt Venetia and Miriam strode into the silent room.

"What's settled?" Miriam asked breezily.

Within two seconds the story was out. I stood next to Ellie, saying nothing.

Unlike the bookers, Miriam seemed to find the entire situation amusing. "Don't worry about Spanish *Vogue*," she said, "I'll speak with them. And Ellie deserves to stop jetting around for a couple of days, don't you think?" Miriam then turned to me and, cupping my chin in her hand, turned my face this way and that. "Hmm… Well, perhaps…why not? Since Kate Moss, the industry also wants girls who aren't conventional… Look at all of these London 'It' girls – they can hardly be called beautiful in the traditional sense. And, *petite* Axelle, you do have nice cheekbones."

"You cannot seriously expect us to push her," Hervé cried in exasperation, unleashing a torrent of criticism from the other bookers:

"I mean, she couldn't hope to fit into a sample size – look at how short she is."

"Short? That's the least of our worries. What about the glasses and that hair?"

"Everyone is going to think she's the make-up artist or the stylist's assistant when she arrives on location!"

"Are we supposed to open a new division called Short and Strange?"

"How about Little and Odd?"

"Or Weird…and More Weird?"

"Axelle, I'd like to have a word with you – alone," my Aunt Venetia interrupted.

I could feel her glaring at me from behind her enormous black sunglasses. All my previous fears came back as she motioned me to follow her into an empty meeting room. She shut the door and stood, hands on hips, lips pursed, ready to launch into me at once.

"You told me to write an article for *Teen Chic* so I thought an interview with Ellie B could be a scoop!" My aunt's eyes narrowed as she made a step towards me. "And I had nothing to do with the Chanel fitting – I promise! It all happened so fast…"

"Axelle, from what I have gathered, nothing just 'happened'. You told Ellie B she should cancel a job because of an interview – AN INTERVIEW WHICH I KNEW NOTHING ABOUT. Do you have any idea how much prestige that job was worth to this agency? Do you even have any idea who Ellie B is? And since when do you want to be a model? Correct me if I'm wrong, but aren't you the girl who CHOSE to wear a stained jumper this morning?"

To say she was furious was to put things lightly. I felt her eyes laser into me from their perfectly made-up sockets. Finally, after a long pause, she broke the heavy silence with the one question I didn't want to answer.

"This is all about Belle La Lune, isn't it?"

I wanted to hold fast, stay cool and play the *what are you talking about?* card – but this meant too much to me. Before I could collect myself, a wave of anger and defiance washed over me. When would I be left alone to do what I wanted to do?!

My aunt leaped at my silence. I should have known I'd never be able to hide anything from her – she was too sharp.

"It is! It is about Belle! I saw how you watched the news report last night – you were absorbing every detail! You actually believe you can find Belle, don't you? And why? Why? Because your grandfather was a detective? Because my mother brainwashed you with years of playing Cluedo? Or is it time to move on from finding missing cats?" She paused for breath. "Axelle, I've promised your parents that

for one week I will steer you away from potential trouble –
and that is what I am going to do. You will not be modelling
or spying on the La Lunes and you will apologize to
Miriam."

"Aunt V, please, I—" At that moment, Aunt Venetia's
phone rang. It was the *Chic: Paris* office.

"Yes," she answered curtly. Within three seconds Aunt
V's face had drained of colour. "*What?* Is Ivan on it? Right.
Well, get moving. We want damage control now." She hung
up and collapsed into the nearest chair.

What was going on? I waited as Aunt V slowly stood up
then paced up and down the length of the room a few times,
her hand held out to silence me. Finally, after a deep breath
at the opened window, she spoke.

"Axelle." Aunt V hadn't quite yet regained her full
composure, but, as her mind began to move beyond the
shock, her colour slowly revived. Finally she seemed to
come to a decision. What she said next took me completely
by surprise. "Axelle, do you really believe you can find Belle
La Lune?"

I was sure it was a trick question.

"Well?" she asked again, turning to face me.

I looked at her closely and saw that it wasn't a trick
question. Her gaze was steady, not a trace of irony or
sarcasm played upon her features, her jaw was clenched.
She was serious. "Well...yes, I do believe I can find her,"
I answered.

"Good, then do it – quickly." She paused again as she struggled with what she was going to say next. Then, "I'll help you as much as I can. And I'll start by telling Miriam that you really do want to model – after all, the best way for you to infiltrate this world is to become one of us." She quickly reapplied some lip gloss then snapped her purse shut. A long angry breath escaped her before she said, "The police have just called my office. You remember Blossom Ing, my assistant?"

I nodded.

"Well, last night Blossom was at a party at an art gallery in the Marais district...and copies of Belle La Lune's drawings – *Belle's drawings!* – of the new Juno bag fell out of her shoulder bag. And it's just my luck that Harlan Forbes – European editor-at-large for my biggest rival – found the drawings!" My aunt could barely contain herself. She resumed pacing the room as she told me the rest.

Harlan had, of course, immediately recognized Belle's distinctive handwriting and understood the importance of what he held in his hand. As a consequence, Blossom had been held at the police station for questioning and safe-keeping until early this morning. Of course, she denied having ever seen the drawings – let alone having stolen them – but this was the first clue anyone had found concerning Belle's disappearance; the police were not going to let her go just like that. It was being said that Blossom must have ties to a ring of Chinese counterfeiters to whom she was going to feed the drawings. It would be worth millions to counterfeiters to have the drawings of the bag before the bag itself was even launched. They could have the fake article out on the streets just as the genuine ones were hitting the shops.

The fact was, as long as Blossom was considered a possible accomplice and suspect in the disappearance of Belle La Lune, and no matter how discreetly the entire matter was dealt with, no amount of perfume would cover up the scent of suspicion which now clung to Blossom's employer: Aunt V and *Chic: Paris* magazine.

I stood in shock as Aunt Venetia gathered her scarf and handbag and headed for the door.

"Come on, Axelle," she said, "we haven't got a moment to spare." Then, as she placed her hand on the doorknob, she stopped and turned to me, her voice deep as she coolly said, "Oh, and, Axelle, this will remain between you and me. I'm afraid your mother's well-laid plans are about to take a detour."

Back at the booking table, everyone was waiting to hear what punishment I'd been given.

You should have seen the looks on their faces when my aunt smiled gently and announced, "My niece and I are delighted that you have offered to represent her as a model."

Talk about a stunned silence. And it looked as if smoke was coming off of Hervé's head – but that might just have been the light.

Suddenly a loud clapping pierced the still air. It was Miriam. "All right, everyone, get moving! We have a new girl and she has to be at Chanel in two hours. We don't have one minute to waste! And, Hervé, you can be Axelle's booker."

My new status brought everyone to attention. I was quite probably a first for the agency, in that I hadn't even been modelling for a day and already one of the world's leading fashion houses wanted to see me. Actually, not just see me, but to actually try clothes on me!

"Let's start with Axelle's hair," Miriam said, as she looked me over. "Hervé, get Victor on the line. She needs a cut." I could hear some snickering about needing pruning shears. "And a bit of colour."

"Yeah, but—" I tried to catch Hervé's attention, but to no avail.

"And clothes, she's got to wear something else. What *is* she wearing, by the way?"

"Oh my goodness! Those glasses! *Quelle horreur!* Call *Docteur* Douai now!"

"Yeah, but my glasses—" Again I was cut off.

"And shoes! We need to get her a pair of heels and she has to learn how to walk properly before seeing *anyone*."

"And, Hervé, make sure you book a manicure and pedicure at Victor's too!"

"Axelle, these are the numbers for the agency: this is Hervé's and this is the general number. I'll give you Miriam's too, just in case."

"Oh, and this is the address for your casting. It's around the corner on the Rue Cambon. You'll go with Ellie."

I tried one last time to explain the truth about my hair and glasses – about the little secret I'd been keeping – but I wasn't given a chance. With a last, *"Au revoir et bonne chance!"* I was pushed out the door.

Ellie laughed when she saw my look of shock and confusion. I followed her into the lift as I tried to make sense of what was happening. "Axelle, you didn't seriously think the agency would send you on a casting without polishing you up a bit first, did you? Let me just tell you that no matter how gorgeous or stunning a girl is, when she signs up to be a model, she gets polished."

"Yes, but what I've been trying—"

"Axelle, there are no buts. You have to have a makeover – or the fashion machine will spit you out before they've even had a proper taste."

At that moment the first of two things happened. As we descended in the old-fashioned cagelike lift, Mr Leather Jacket whizzed past us on the stairs, stopping at the bottom to open the door for us. Catching my eye, he gave me one of his wicked smiles. Then, as I stood there grinning stupidly back, I could have sworn he paused for a second, almost as if he wanted to say something but then thought the better of it. Whatever. He turned quickly and left the building. As I pulled opened the large entrance door and looked out onto the busy street, I caught sight of him speeding off on a scooter.

Then, as I stood holding the door open for Ellie while she fished her phone out of her bag, the most gorgeous guy came heading directly towards me. I continued holding the door until he walked through it – not that he acknowledged me. He simply walked through and didn't stop chatting on his phone until he saw Ellie, at which point he hurriedly put his phone away and stopped to greet her. Ellie introduced me and, with a vague look in my direction, he acknowledged my presence with a curt nod. They chatted for a moment and Ellie mentioned that Miriam had just taken me on as a new model. "Good luck," he said as he turned to leave – and as he stepped away I heard him mutter, "You'll need it," under his breath.

As Ellie and I walked away from Miriam's, she said, "Dom La Lune is gorge, isn't he? He has the most amazing green eyes."

"Is he from *the* La Lune family?"

Ellie nodded. "He's Belle's younger brother. He's a photographer. He works a lot with Miriam's agency. In fact, he's on his way up to drop off some test shots he did for Miriam of a new girl. He told me his whole family is upside down because of Belle's disappearance. I mean, who can blame them?"

I didn't say anything else. And while I was excited that I'd just brushed shoulders with a La Lune, I'd have to get a lot further a lot faster if I wanted to crack this case before leaving on Sunday – or before the police solved it. I could only hope that the other La Lunes were easier to engage with.

"Sorry to distract you from your daydreaming, Axelle," Ellie said, as she linked her arm through mine and pulled me in the direction of Victor's, "but we have a lot to do before we go to Chanel. And, more importantly, you promised to explain to me why you need my help – and I want to hear everything because, whatever it is, you made it sound important and mysterious..."

I forgot all about Dom's eyes and Mr Leather Jacket's cryptic smile. Looking up, I let the sun hit my face for a moment. Even though I'd only just met Ellie, I instinctively knew I could trust her. So I told her about my desire to find Belle. I told her everything, starting with my being dispatched to Paris as punishment, as we made our way to Victor the hairdresser's on the Rue du Mont-Thabor.

Standing at an exclusive-yet-discreet-looking doorway we rang the bell and waited until we were buzzed into an inner courtyard filled with potted trees of varying size and shape. On the far side of the courtyard was a glass door with a simple V etched into it. Large floor-to-ceiling windows were to the left and right of it. Music and laughter echoed round the courtyard walls. Victor himself came to the door to see me in; his curiosity was palpable. "Miriam says you are the next big thing!" he said loudly above the din of the hairdryers.

"Although," he continued as he slowly looked me up and down, "I have to say, *ma chérie*, you're actually more of a small thing. But, no matter – small can be beautiful. And it certainly will be by the time I've finished with you!"

I'd never been in a salon like Victor's. It certainly made a change from the local hairdresser's I occasionally (and grudgingly) visited at home. High ceilings and gilded mirrors gave the space an undeniably glamorous feel, yet Victor's funky touch prevented things from becoming too elegant or stiff. His receptionist clucked round me like a mother hen before taking my jacket and helping me into a crisp white dressing gown. Then I was whisked away to sit behind the privacy screens at Victor's station.

Just as I sat down, Aunt Venetia arrived – after sorting things out with Miriam, she'd come to oversee my transformation. "Victor, it has to look natural yet sophisticated, not too trendy but edgy," she said.

"Yes, exactly," Victor said, as he searched for the right brush to tackle my growth with.

"Before you start I have to tell you that my hair—" Once again I was cut off. Did anyone in fashion let anyone else speak?

"Axelle, this is no time to tell us about your hair. Victor's the best, people are waiting, and we haven't got much time," Aunt Venetia said crisply.

"Yeah, but—"

"No buts!" Aunt V and Victor said in unison.

Frustrated, I ducked the brush Victor was about to take to my hair, slipped out of my chair, and dashed to the loo I'd spotted near the entrance. In one swift movement I jumped in, shut the door and turned the lock.

I took a deep breath then adjusted the light, turning the dimmer up as brightly as it would go. I wanted to take one last good look at myself. I'd been hiding behind my glasses and thick hair for so long that sometimes I forgot what I looked like underneath it all – not that Jenny ever did, but she was under oath. Anyway, I loved the anonymity my disguise gave me – after all, no one ever looks twice at girls with bushy hair and big glasses.

Slowly I took my glasses off and folded them, before setting them on the side of the sink. My eyesight was just as sharp without them – I'd never needed glasses. Then I lifted my hands to my "hair" and gently searched through the teased mass for the clips I used to stick the extensions on with. Another couple of minutes and they were all out. Gently, I ran my fingers through my real hair. Soft and brown, it fell in jagged chunks to my shoulders.

"*Hallo?* Axelle? *Petite chérie?*" It was Victor knocking on the door. "We aren't going to do anything drastic to you – promise! – we just want you to look your best!" Then, after a pause: "Your aunt and Ellie have left to pick you up some new clothes. Why don't you step out and we'll go over everything together. There's no need to be frightened. I won't do anything you don't agree with. I promise."

Taking another deep breath and a last look in the mirror, I gathered together my glasses and hairpieces. Then I opened the door and watched as Victor's face registered the change. It would be an understatement to say I'd surprised him.

By way of explanation, I handed him what looked like a brown angora rabbit with glasses on top of its head. Then, without waiting, I walked past him.

"*Ma chérie*," Victor said, once we were back at his station, "you're the only girl I've ever met who intentionally disguised herself so that she looked worse than nature intended."

"I had my reasons," I said and left it at that. I wasn't about to get into any explanations.

"Yes, well, it's a surprise – but an enjoyable one," he said, applying some kind of honey-brown-colour-gloss-shine-something-or-other to my scalp with what looked like a special plastic paintbrush. "Your hair is in good condition considering, and actually your cut is okay. Later Chrystelle will shape it a bit, but I like the jagged edges. It suits you to have hair that isn't too pretty, if you know what I mean. You look good a bit boyish and wild. I'm adding a gloss to give it some shine and a touch of colour to darken the lengths a bit. That's it."

Victor is very tall and energetic. As his hands flew in all directions, working their magic on my hair, a steady stream of assistants came by, asking questions or seeking advice.

According to *Chic: Paris* magazine, which my mother is forever quoting at me, Victor is nothing less than "*the* Hair Colour Oracle". He is what is known as a colourist. Victor doesn't cut hair – he only colours it. His was the first salon in Paris to specialize in colour alone. Ten years ago, Victor arrived in Paris, sixteen and penniless, and today is consulted by every A-list actress and top model in the world.

He was wearing a pink T-shirt with *FIND BELLE* scrawled across the front. On the back was a drawing of the famous "Feather Dress" she'd designed five years ago. As its name suggested, it had been made entirely of feathers. So great was its impact in turning fashion back from grunge to glamour that Italian *Vogue* had dedicated an entire issue to that dress alone.

"Do you know Belle well?" I asked Victor.

"Yes, *ma chérie*," he answered. "She was one of my first clients and very young when we met – about fifteen or sixteen. I met her backstage at a La Lune show. I was there to put streaks of colour in the models' hair. Pink, blue, and orange. Anyway, she wanted blue streaks – so I did them. You should have seen her mother's face! Fiona, Belle's mother, is very elegant and formal – she was not amused. But we were! I've been working on her hair ever since.

"In the beginning she would come to my flat when I did her colour – I had no salon then. I could barely afford my rent! Anyway, Belle is so sweet and so loyal, not only did she come to me but she sent every one of the models she worked with – she still does. Thanks to Belle, many top girls became my clients and friends. Then she started sending me the actresses who bought her designs. Of course, we started as friends, and that has carried on…" His voice began to quaver. "I just hope they find her…I hope she's alive."

"What do you think has happened to her?" I ventured.

"Ah, *ma chérie*, that is the question!"

"But surely there must be some theories about why she's disappeared? Yesterday her brother Claude suggested that her disappearance is due to too much stress."

"*Humf!*" he snorted, but he didn't elaborate. In the mirror, I watched Victor. I couldn't tell whether he was studiously ignoring me or just concentrating really hard on my hair.

"Maybe the stress of the business got to be too much for her and she decided she needed a break? Maybe she's taken off to Mexico or Bali or something?" I persisted.

"*Ma petite* Axelle, you are very curious, *non?*"

"Yes – but it's odd. Why would she disappear now, during Fashion Week? If she really disappeared for personal reasons then this is the worst time to do it. Any designer would instantly draw massive amounts of attention to themselves by disappearing at a time like this. So I can't help but think that it isn't just stress…despite what the family claims…"

As my probing didn't seem to be getting me anywhere,

I decided to change track with my questioning. "What wa— is she like?"

"Beautiful, talented, charming. And, like I said earlier, loyal and sweet. Everything you read about her is true." Victor was now bending over me with a comb in hand. I watched as he carefully used the back of the comb to scrape off some of the goop on my hair. "Hmm...another two minutes and your hair will be more shiny and soft than since it first grew out of your head."

"What about the rest of the family?" I asked, bringing him back to Belle.

Victor shrugged his shoulders. "The others I only know a little. Her mother, Fiona, is *très chic* and formal. Her oldest brother Claude is smooth and sophisticated – he does the company PR. And Rose, she's a year or two younger than Claude, is in charge of the company's accounting. Honestly, I don't know her at all. Rose has always been the shy, awkward one in the family. Darius is number three – the sandwich child; very nice, also shy, and the family intellectual. He writes about fashion history. And then, of course, there's Fiona's favourite, Dom. He's a photographer. Handsome – and he knows it."

Dom's green eyes came to mind. "Why is he his mother's favourite? What about Belle?"

"Dom is Fiona's favourite because he's good-looking and charming – and the youngest. As for Belle, she's always been her father's favourite. Patrick La Lune has always believed she's the most talented of his children. I'm sure if he wasn't so ill – he doesn't go out in public any more, he can hardly breathe let alone leave his bed – this never would have happened. He used to watch over her like a hawk. Anyway, despite their many differences, the family is very close – in any case, that's the impression they've always given."

"Impression? So you don't think they really are close?"

Again Victor shrugged his shoulders. "They all live together in a large mansion."

"Couldn't living together make them *less* close rather than *more* close – I mean, them being so different and all...?"

Victor was ignoring me again. Why? As if in answer to my unspoken question, he said, "*Ma chérie,* you are too curious."

"But I'd like to find her."

That comment caught Victor off guard. He stopped moving his hands and looked into the mirror, catching my eye. He had an eyebrow lifted quizzically.

"I'm serious," I said.

"Well, then, *ma chérie,* I must wish you *courage.*"

"Courage?"

"Yes, *ma chérie, courage* – and lots of it – because in order to solve this mystery, you'll have to go up against a..."

I waited for him to finish his thought, but he didn't. His lips were firmly shut.

"A what?" I asked.

"No, I'm sorry, *ma chérie*, I won't say it. It's only an old rumour – and, anyway, this isn't the moment for such a dark matter," he continued. "Right now we must concentrate on getting you ready for Chanel."

Then he asked me to tilt my head back into the wash basin and began washing the colour-gloss out with the most amazing-smelling lemon-lavender shampoo (from his own brand). I shut my eyes and let all kinds of questions float through my mind: *What was he talking about? What old rumour? And why was it such a secret? Somebody else must know. Who?*

"*Voilà!*" announced Victor, waking me from my reverie as he stepped in front of me. "Now we cut and dry your hair, then we must start make-up… Hmmm…although, first we must tackle those eyebrows of yours," he said holding my chin in his hand and turning my face this way and that. Then he held out his hand like a surgeon at the operating table, and his assistant Maxi handed him a pair of tweezers.

"Ouch! Hey, that hurts!"

"*Ma chérie*, stop complaining. This thick monobrow isn't doing you any favours – unless you like caterpillars. Today an eyebrow should be thick but tamed. Ah…like this!" he proclaimed finally, handing me a mirror. But I hardly had a chance to look before Victor began to apply the make-up and Chrystelle started trimming my hair.

I couldn't wait to tell Jenny how little was painted on me. "As a model, there is no point in wearing much make-up – if any," explained Victor. "Remember, the photographers, editors, and clients you will be meeting are all experts in beauty. They will be looking at your profile, bone structure, skin condition, teeth and smile – not your make-up. Hair is important too, of course."

He was dabbing everything on by hand in light feathery movements. Apparently I didn't need concealer or foundation. Instead, a light dusting of loose powder was brushed onto my face with a large, thick, pillow-soft brush. I shut my eyes and breathed deeply as the sable hairs flickered gently over my skin. Next, Victor dabbed a bit of Nars blush over my cheekbones. "The creamy texture of this blush looks *soooo* natural," he cooed.

Suddenly a gust of spring wind burst through the opened door, blowing the sound of familiar voices over the top of the privacy screen.

"Just wait till you see what we've picked up for you!" It was Ellie. She and Aunt V had returned from their shopping trip. "You're going to look amazing," she gushed.

"I have to admit," Aunt V added, "we were lucky. Now let's try some of the stuff on. I think we should start with the Karl Lagerfeld jeans and the H&M jacket and top."

But before my aunt and Ellie had any hope of getting into our screened-off corner, Victor took the situation in hand: "I'll take the clothes," he said as he sprang out to stop them from looking. "No one is to see my latest creation until I say she is ready!"

He returned with what seemed like half of the Paris shop windows in bags. Bags from Chloé, A.P.C., H&M, and Isabel Marant left barely enough space for us behind the screen.

"This is just like Christmas!" Victor said excitedly as he looked through the bags, pulling out a jacket and a pair of trousers.

I was just unpacking a navy pea coat when I realized Victor was trying to undress me!

"Hey, what are you doing?" I asked as he tried to pull my trousers down.

"*Ma chérie*, we must get you dressed and out of here. You are expected at Chanel in twenty minutes."

"That may be, but I can undress myself, thank you!"

"From now on you are a model. And models, while on the job rarely dress themselves."

"What?" I mumbled as he pulled my lucky jumper up over my head.

"Get used to it, because as a model you will be helped into and out of everything by a stylist."

"But why? I can dress myself." We were now getting me into the pair of Lagerfeld jeans.

"Well, trust me," Victor said, as he helped me into the H&M jacket, "half the things you'll be asked to dress in you absolutely will not be able to get in and out of alone. Plus the clothes will all be ironed and steamed just before you wear them and you'll wrinkle them beyond recognition if you twist and turn half as much as you did just now. So unless you want to sabotage your new career," he continued as he tugged and adjusted the jacket at my shoulders, "I suggest you get used to being helped... Ah! *Et voilà!*"

Smiling, he stepped back to admire his handiwork. He pushed his enormous vintage Yves Saint Laurent glasses up his nose and peered at me from every angle. Finally, he spoke. "You look amazing – *éclatant* – that's glowing, I think, in English. Now let's go and surprise your Aunt Venetia."

We did. Big time. Keeping her eyes glued on me (at least, I imagined they were glued on me – as usual, she was wearing her sunglasses), she looked me over top to toe. Then I watched as she reached one arm out to the dainty cup filled with sugared almonds that lay on the reception table and her long fingers uncurled to delicately pick one up.

"My goodness, Axelle, you certainly do wash up well," she said, before popping the pink sweet into her mouth.

Ellie was more forthright. "You look fantastic!" she squealed. "Your hair – and, oh my gosh – your glasses are gone too...wow! A good haircut and contacts can make such a difference."

I didn't say anything.

Truth be told, I'd been frightened I'd be given a horribly short haircut. The result – thank goodness! – was a dark jagged mop that brushed my shoulders.

As far as the clothes went, Aunt V was right – style is in the details. I mean, basically, I was wearing what I always wear – jeans and jumper and jacket with flat shoes. But the cut and fabric of the jacket, shape of the jeans, and colour of the jumper made it all so much more. And my dainty new ballerinas and the rock-star-ragged long skinny scarf Ellie had wound around my neck tied everything together nicely.

The entire salon was now standing around staring at me. At that moment Hervé burst through the door and made his way to Aunt V. "Where is Axelle?" he asked her, standing right in front of me. "She has to sign her contract – and I have a new appointment for her."

All eyes turned to me as silence descended. Hervé's eyes followed suit and slowly a look of disbelief spread across his features. *"Non!"* he exclaimed as he stepped back with shock. For a moment or two he stood gulping for air like a big carp out of water. *"Mon Dieu!"* he finally said. *"Quelle différence!"*

"I've read through the contract, Axelle, you can sign it," Aunt V said as I was handed a pen.

"And word travels fast," Hervé said excitedly. "Thanks to Ellie, everyone wants to meet you – Lanvin has already called. They'd like to see you this afternoon, and if they like you they'll book you for their show. You'll go straight there from Chanel. And after Lanvin, you have another new appointment at La Lune with Claude La Lune. Ellie can go with you. She has fittings at both," he said with a smile (yes, a *real* smile) as he handed me my copy of the contract and slipped his copy into his folder. "I think you'll be pretty busy this week, Axelle."

There was no time to celebrate my new look, though. Hervé quickly ushered me out into the courtyard and asked me to stand against one of the cream-coloured walls so that he could take my picture. "I'll make you a temporary zed card which you can use until we get you some nice pictures," he explained as he tried various angles. (As I knew from Aunt V, a zed card is a large card made of thick paper with a picture of the model, the name of the agency representing her, and personal information such as height and hair and eye colour.)

"It's a bit dark here," he said as he snapped the first shot. "Hmm...more to the right... Ah! Yes, that's it! Good." He continued to click away. "Chin down a bit. More to the left. No, your left. Hmm. Okay. Now don't smile. Good. Now a smile. Great! Take a look," he said, as he came to me holding out his camera so I could look at the little screen on the back. Excitedly he scrolled through the photos he'd just taken. "Not bad for a first shoot."

"Right! Axelle, time to go." Aunt V had just stepped out of Victor's. She took a quick look at the new photos, then kissed me goodbye and wished me luck. "I'll tell you about all I hear later tonight," she said with a knowing look.

While Hervé had been taking my picture, Victor had been busy emptying the contents of my old, worn tote bag into my new Prada shoulder bag – a gift from Aunt V. Slouchy and big enough to hold the "book" I would eventually be lugging around, it would be a necessary accessory to my new career. "You'll see, by the end of the week it'll be holding your entire life," Ellie said as she untwisted the bag straps on my shoulder.

I was now officially a model. Or, more precisely, a *model under cover.* The secret thrill of it coursed through me as I said it silently to myself. I was on my way to solving this case!

MONDAY AFTERNOON

High Heels and High Hopes

Located on the Rue Cambon, directly opposite the back entrance of the Ritz Hotel, the Chanel boutique and showroom are housed in the building Coco Chanel herself chose. And upstairs, so they say, her grand apartment is still exactly as she left it.

If I'd thought I'd be able to quietly follow Ellie in, I was mistaken. She waltzed into the boutique like an urban glamazon, commander of all she surveyed. As she exchanged hellos, she introduced me to everyone as her new friend and as a new model with Miriam's. Finally, Ellie and I climbed Coco Chanel's famous mirrored staircase and turned down a corridor that led us to the showroom.

"Are you ready for your first casting?" she asked, pushing open a pair of tall double doors. "I have a good feeling about this, Axelle. I think he's going to like you and that you and I will go down the runway together on Wednesday." *As long as it brings me closer to finding Belle, then I hope so too*, I thought, as I followed her into the showroom.

The atmosphere was buzzing with energy, models were in various states of undress, and long racks of tulle, lace and tweed dresses stood at the end of the room. The head designer and various assistants and stylists stood near a large trestle table. At least three different languages were being spoken at the same time, as rapid-fire commands and ringing telephones punctuated the frenzied air.

"Fashion can never move too quickly." Ellie smiled as she saw me staring.

At that moment one of the stylists came to lead me away and Ellie moved off to say hi to the rest of the team. Ellie had briefed me on what to expect on the way over, so I knew that I was here to try a few outfits on from the new Autumn/Winter prêt-à-porter collection. The fashion calendar is always far ahead of the rest of the world so, for instance, even though spring had only just begun, it was the Autumn/Winter collection that would be shown at Fashion Week, as usual a good six months before the clothes would hit the stores. Anyway, if the outfits I tried suited me (or, rather, as the designer would phrase it, if I suited the clothes), and if I managed to walk without falling, I just might get booked to walk down the runway.

The first thing I put on was a deceptively simple-looking dress made of cream-coloured tulle overlaid with delicate strips of cream silk. As I slipped it on over my head, Ellie came to join me. She crinkled her nose as she eyed me.

"We forgot to get you some new underwear. I'm afraid white cotton just won't do, Axelle – it shows through everything. Remind me to take you to Le Bon Marché for some flesh-coloured undies, would you? But first," she whispered as the stylist walked away to find some ornament that was missing from the dress, "I'd better give you a few pointers on how to walk."

We both looked down at the eight-inch heels I was perched on. Even with their thick platform soles they didn't exactly fill me with confidence.

"I get vertigo just looking at them," I said.

Ellie rolled her eyes. "Don't exaggerate. And don't worry – it's easy," she said reassuringly. "What you have to do is *feel* the shoe. Trust yourself and you won't fall. And, look, hold your head high, like this." Imperceptibly she lifted her neck. I can't tell you what she did exactly, but I could note the results: her torso was immediately elongated and her legs looked longer. "Yeah, like that. Good. Now, to walk, just do as you'd normally do. No, relax, Axelle, like normal."

She watched as I walked in little circles behind the clothing racks. "Don't try to prance or exaggerate anything, just relax and let your arms swing. Feel your legs, hold your head high and trust yourself to keep your balance. Yeah, yeah, like that. Don't think about what you look like – remember: *they* asked *you* to come here for a fitting. They want you to walk well. They want to book you. So just relax and don't think too much about it."

By the time I'd taken that information in and done a few turns behind the racks, the stylist had returned with a large enamelled camellia that she pinned on my dress. "You can go out now, Axelle. They're waiting," she said.

Right. Move, Axelle, move, I told myself, *because the longer they wait, the more they'll be focused on you when you step out.* Gathering my courage, I took a big breath and stepped out from behind the clothing rack.

I stepped forward with a bit of a start, but, remembering what Ellie had instructed me to do, I concentrated on advancing one step at a time until I'd carefully walked to the end of the long room, stood for a few seconds before the scorching scrutiny of the design team, and then, before fear got the better of me, I turned and walked back to the safety of the clothing rack – which I quickly ducked behind. "Well done!" Ellie whispered. "You did great!"

With a huge sigh of relief, I fell onto a pile of discarded dresses and lay there with my face buried deep in lace. I stayed like that until I heard a crisp cough from just above me. I turned my face and pushed a velvet ribbon out of my eyes.

"Axelle, you'd better get back up." The stylist smiled as she offered me her hand. "They want to see you in another dress."

"What? In another dress?"

"*Oui*. It seems they may want to book you for Wednesday's show."

Ten minutes later, Ellie stifled a squeal as she high-fived me behind the dress rack. The fitting was over, Chanel wanted to confirm me. "I told you I had a good feeling about this! And watch – I bet you they'll have us walk down the runway together – maybe we'll even get to open the show together!"

I wish I could have matched Ellie's elation, but, honestly, I was exhausted after the stress of being scrutinized (how did models go through that day in and day out?) and, while I was thankful that I'd been booked, I was also feeling a good deal of anxiety at the thought of walking down Wednesday's runway under the collective gaze of fashion's elite. Then again, maybe now that Chanel had booked me the La Lunes would too (Aunt V always says fashionistas are like sheep). In which case jittery nerves were a small price to pay for the chance to get close to the La Lunes – and the possibility of picking up Belle's trail.

Ellie and I changed back into our own clothes and left. As we stepped out of the building my phone began to ring.

"Bravo, little Axelle! Amazing! Amazing! Amazing! You are zee hot zing in Paris this week!"

It was Hervé. After hanging up, all I could think was that fashion really was a fickle world. This very same morning, Hervé would have gladly banished me from Paris for ever, and now, six hours later, frizz-free and spectacle-less, I was "zee hot zing".

While Ellie didn't find anything strange in this turn

around, she did find my imitation of his accent hilarious. "Don't worry," she said through her laughter, "the bookers are always stressed and often insecure. But once they like you, they fight like lions to keep you happy. I admit that Hervé was not showing his prettier side this morning, but in fashion a model is only as good as her latest booking."

"No wonder modelling careers are so short," I said.

Ellie shrugged her shoulders. "It's the same in football: a player is only as good as his last goal. Don't get me wrong: I'm not saying it's right – I'm only saying that it is what it is and the quicker you approach it with that attitude, the better you'll be able to protect yourself."

She had a point – but this wasn't the moment to discuss it.

Then, speaking of people changing their opinions of me, my phone rang. It was Mum calling.

"Axelle, darling, I always knew you were a star!" A frenzied stream of words gushed over the long-distance line. "I'm so proud of you, my darling! Dad is too. I'm so sorry, but I can't come out to see you do the Chanel show or be with you at the launch of the new La Lune handbag on Wednesday night because a very important client will be flying in from Brazil to see my plans for their new pied-à-terre. But Hervé says there is a good chance you'll be booked for the La Lune fashion show on Friday – and that one I definitely plan on making it out for. I've already reserved a ticket, leaving Friday morning. Then I'll stay the weekend and we'll go home together – that is, if you *can* come home. Who knows what other jobs you'll have booked by then! Maybe Lancôme or a new perfume or *Vogue*! Oh, darling, it's *too* exciting. Anyway, I have to go. We'll talk later – and don't worry, Hervé is keeping me posted on absolutely everything!"

Thanks, Hervé.

"Oh, and Axelle…?"

"Yeah, Mum?"

"Dom La Lune is so handsome. And I've always thought he seems like such a nice young man…"

After that cheeseball comment about Dom, I pretended I'd lost the signal and hung up.

"Was that your mum?" Ellie asked.

"Uh-huh."

"Is she coming out? And does she know that you're trying to find Belle?"

"Yes, she's coming out. And, no, she doesn't know that I'm trying to find Belle and I have to keep it that way. She'd be furious if she knew what I'm up to…"

"Well, obviously I won't give anything away. But then we'd better get cracking on the clue-gathering because, basically, you won't be able to do any investigating once your mum gets here."

"Don't remind me." Feelings of frustration and impatience rose to the surface as I thought of Belle. Would I find her? And would I be able to get to her before it was too late?

* * *

The Lanvin offices were a short walk from Chanel along the Rue du Faubourg Saint-Honoré. But with so much on my mind – my new booking with Chanel and impending casting with La Lune – my appointment at Lanvin went by in a blur. But, despite being distracted, the casting went well. Ellie said as much as soon as we were outside. "I'm sure you'll get booked for Lanvin, too." Then she put her arm through mine and led me towards the Champs Élysées and Avenue Montaigne. Ellie and I decided to walk to La Lune from Lanvin, as we had a little time before my appointment and Ellie's fitting.

We arrived just as the sky darkened and the first raindrops fell. The security man sitting at reception recognized Ellie and, after asking us to sign in, he waved us through. I followed Ellie up a vast stone stairwell with a delicate balustrade of gilded bronze. A plush dark green runner muffled our footsteps. Soaring above us was a cupola, its ceiling painted to look like the inside of an aviary. Jewel-toned birds flitted across the blue sky or sat silently twittering on the branches of exotic flora. An enormous crystal chandelier hung from the cupola, its soft light reflected in the gold mosaic tiles embedded in the walls of the stairwell.

We stopped on the second floor and Ellie pushed open the first pair of double doors that gave onto the landing.

The scent of lilies and tuberose wafted out. The room ran the entire length of the back of the building. One side of the ballroom-like space was lined with windows overlooking a small garden. Fantastic silk curtains in a cool shade of lilac/blue (La Lune lilac) echoed the colours of the clouds outside, while the gilded panelling throughout the room glowed as it caught the last of the day's light. Overhead, four large crystal chandeliers were ablaze with real candles. Music played loudly although there were no speakers to be seen. I did notice about six iPods lying on the large table, though.

Ellie quickly said hi to the two other models in the room, then, taking me by the hand, made her way to Claude La Lune, Belle's oldest brother. I recognized him from the television last night. His dark eyes were as intense as they had been on screen, but, in contrast to yesterday's televised announcement, today he seemed completely absorbed by the work at hand. In fact, if I hadn't known, I would never have guessed that his sister was missing. *Brotherly* and *sad* were not words that could have easily described him now. Furthermore, I learned, as Ellie whispered to me while we waited for him to finish speaking to one of the designers, "Claude's never normally here for the castings – Belle is. *He* just does the company PR – although to watch him now you'd think he's the one who always runs the shows! I've heard it said he's jealous of Belle – perhaps that's true after all."

Ellie was obviously surprised by the authority with which Claude was commanding the small army of assistant designers, stylists, and secretaries. Normally, she told me, it was Belle these people all reported to: she was the creative director of the entire company. Not only had she designed the clothes we were about to try on, but she'd also designed all the handbags and other accessories sitting on the tables near the clothes racks – not to mention the new handbag the family was launching on Wednesday night. Yet Claude, from PR, had seemingly slipped into Belle's role of star designer quickly and with great aplomb.

When Claude eventually finished with the designer, Ellie introduced me to him and the La Lune team. They asked after my aunt (news travels quickly in the fashion world), asked how long I was staying in Paris, and then a stylist led me behind a screen to help me into my first outfit. I changed into a deep-purple-coloured ballgown while listening to Claude talk about the storyboard for the next day's shoot for the Autumn/Winter advertising campaign. Ellie was the star of the campaign and they would be shooting at various well-known Parisian landmarks – starting at the Eiffel Tower. But they were still looking for another girl to book for the shoot, so if they liked me, there was the chance I might not only get booked for Friday's fashion show – but for tomorrow's advertising campaign too.

After zipping my dress, the stylist helped me step into a pair of high-heeled snakeskin sandals and gave me a thumbs up. I launched myself down the length of the room towards Claude. As I teetered past him and turned, Claude's phone rang. "What now?" he answered.

I was trying to hear what Claude was saying while concentrating on not tripping. Walking on heels is definitely easier said than done. The music had suddenly changed – the volume had been turned up and an energetic dance beat throbbed through the room, nearly bringing me to my knees when the first loud note shot through the speakers. Remembering Ellie's command to "feel" the shoes and to "trust" myself, I lifted my eyes and as I was about to walk past Claude again, I tried to concentrate on what he was saying – he was clearly irritated and completely distracted, paying me no attention whatsoever. The room was vibrating with the music, but even over the pulsating sound, I could just make out his angry hiss: "I am telling you the truth!" he was saying. "Do you actually think I'd kidnap my own sister? Some friend you are!" He was sitting very still, his limbs tense. "Listen, I'm telling you once and for all: I was home on Saturday night – the whole night."

I added an extra turn in front of Claude before heading back to the waiting stylist. I wondered how I'd be able to double-check what he'd just claimed. Furthermore, who'd called him? Was it really a "friend", as Claude had said? And, if so, why did the friend doubt Claude's story? As I finished my walk, I turned around to see him set his phone down next to the pile of iPods lying on the end of the table.

Perfect! This was my chance. Claude and the others were already deep in a discussion concerning the hem length of another model's dress – I was forgotten for the moment. They had their backs to me and, before I'd even consciously made a plan, I grazed the table as I passed it and grabbed his phone. Hiding my fist in the folds of the ballgown, I made my way back to the rack of dresses. A quick glance reassured me that I was alone – the stylist had been pulled into the hemline argument. I took his phone and found my way to *Received Calls*. *Philippe de Vandrille* was the name of the last caller. Who was he?

I opened Claude's agenda setting and looked up last Saturday – the day Belle went missing. Claude had had meetings all day and into the evening. Then dinner at eight o'clock with his family at their house. The only other thing noted down on that day's entry was *CAT* at the bottom of the screen. What did that mean? Suddenly Claude's phone began to ring. I switched it to silent and saw that it was Philippe de Vandrille again. I let it finish ringing then switched the ringer back on. I had to get it back to Claude! At that moment the stylist returned – team La Lune wanted to see me in another dress – and I heard Claude asking if anyone had seen his phone. As the stylist moved behind me to adjust the fastening on a turquoise dress of layered chiffon, I erased the record of Philippe's missed call from Claude's phone. Then I stepped into a pair of sparkly heels, tucking Claude's phone loosely into one of the ankle straps under my long skirt.

I walked out, moving as carefully as possible, until, just as I passed Claude and his team, I gave my foot a swift flick to send the phone flying, and then stumbled as if I'd slipped on it. I watched as the phone skidded across the polished floor and stopped at Claude's chair. Without taking his eyes off me, he leaned down and picked it up.

Stay calm and keep walking, I told myself. *Ignore him, pretend you never took his phone. Remember: you want to get booked for Friday's fashion show – and for the advertising campaign shoot tomorrow – so you can spend as much time investigating the La Lunes as possible.* I walked the length of the room and by the time I turned back Claude was in another deep discussion.

Ellie joined me and together we walked back to the rack. "You took his phone, didn't you?" she whispered.

I nodded.

"Did you find anything?"

"I'll tell you when we're out of here."

The stylist helped me out of the turquoise gown and I dressed in my own clothes and ballerina flats. Then Ellie and I went back to Claude and his group to say goodbye. He really gave me the creeps – despite, or perhaps because of, his fashionably thin build and edgy suit. He was standing slightly apart from the rest of the team and as I shook his hand he looked at me through narrowed eyes, as if trying to decide whether I'd intentionally taken his phone or not.

He decided on the former. "Are you in the habit of taking other people's phones?" he asked quietly, a fake smile on his lips.

I flushed and shrugged my shoulders. "It fell off the table as I walked by." It sounded lame even to my ears but I couldn't think of anything else to say – and there was no way I'd admit I'd been snooping or my detective days would be over with this appointment. Clearly, all hope of getting booked for either Friday's show or tomorrow's campaign was rapidly evaporating.

"I bet." Then, before turning away he quickly said, "A word of advice, Axelle. Be careful. For a model, having greedy fingers is even worse than having a greedy appetite. And it wouldn't look too good for your aunt if her niece was found to be a...you know..." He left the last word unsaid but he'd made his accusation and threat clear: he would label me a thief and rat on me to my aunt if he so chose. I clenched my fists as I watched him walk back to the storyboard.

I swung my bag over my shoulder and turned to leave. What bad luck that he'd guessed I'd taken his phone! But why had he been so menacing? If he really thought I'd stolen his phone, why hadn't he just called me on it and kicked me out in front of everyone? I didn't know him well enough to guess, but it seemed likely there was something in his phone he wanted to keep to himself. And his veiled threat was engineered to make sure I kept my mouth shut in case I'd seen that something. But had I? At this point *CAT* and Philippe de Vandrille's name didn't mean anything to me. Besides, he couldn't have known I'd want to check his schedule for Saturday night. Then again, from what I'd overheard, it sounded as if Philippe de Vandrille was questioning Claude's whereabouts on the night his sister Belle disappeared. In those circumstances, maybe I'd feel edgy and distrustful too...

"I wonder if you'll get booked," Ellie said as we stepped outside. "He was looking at you so strangely when we left."

"I wonder too... It didn't really turn out as I'd expected, but, on the other hand, we have two things to follow up on: CAT and Philippe de Vandrille."

"What and who?"

"It was on his phone. I'll explain..."

It had rained while we were in the casting, but the sky had cleared now to a watery grey with patches of blue. There were no taxis to be seen at the end of the road, so Ellie suggested we wait a few minutes at the kiosk across the street. As we crossed the road, I noticed a black Peugeot saloon car – one like my aunt's – out of the corner of my right eye. It was moving slowly down the left-hand side of the road. In fact, it seemed to have been following us since we left La Lune. I mentioned it to Ellie. "But don't turn and look!" I said.

Of course, she did just that. As we stood in the middle of the avenue, she pointed up the road. "Axelle, look – there are loads of that kind of car lining the entire avenue. They are *the* car for business people who get driven around Paris."

She was right; there were at least eight of them within sight. "They are either waiting for a designer or for their super-rich shopaholic employer. Look at how many are double-parked outside the La Lune boutique alone," she continued.

She may have a point, I thought as we turned and walked away, but I still could've sworn that car had been tailing us.

It was crowded underneath the tented top of the kiosk. While Ellie pushed her way around to find the latest issues of French *Vogue*, American *Elle*, British *Vogue*, and *W* (she was featured in all of them and planned on sending these copies to her family), I quickly rifled through the pages of the French fashion magazines in the hope of finding some possible link to CAT. No such luck.

After a few minutes with no sign of a taxi, we decided to walk to Aunt V's. Ellie and I would have dinner together and work on my runway walk (ugh!). We turned back up Avenue Montaigne and then right at the Christian Dior boutique. It seemed to me that the same black Peugeot was still following us, but, as Ellie had pointed out, the street was thick with them, so I couldn't be sure.

From Christian Dior we headed down Rue François 1er until we reached the Seine. It wasn't the most direct route home, but a colourful sunset was beginning to tinge the sky, so we chose to walk along the river. After ten minutes we came to the Alexandre III Bridge. Looking far down as the river flows, I could just make out the Gothic bulk of the Notre Dame Cathedral. Closer to us, the glass roof of the Grand Palais Museum glimmered in the setting sun and behind us loomed the Eiffel Tower. Overhead, clouds were threatening more rain.

At the far side of the bridge, Ellie motioned that we should cross the large avenue in front of us. We waited for the green man to flash that it was safe to cross, then started on our way, but I stopped halfway to take a last look at the view behind me – and good thing I did, because at that moment a large dark shape came hurtling down upon us.

I felt the hair on my neck stiffen, yelled Ellie's name, and threw myself at her. I fell into her and together we rolled and landed on the sidewalk. In a blur I saw the menacing mass of a black Peugeot fly past, its heavy bulk smelling of hot oil and fuel. I coughed as a cloud of black exhaust fumes wafted over my head, all that was left of my near encounter with the speeding car. It was only then that I realized it had grazed my hand. In fact, it would have hit me if I hadn't suddenly stopped to look at the view one last time.

"What the...?!" Ellie gasped. Slowly we picked ourselves up, then stood in silence, leaning against the traffic light pole, as the cars sped past us. "We have to report this to the police," Ellie said. "Do you...do you think that could have been the car that you thought was following us?"

"Uh-huh..."

"But then…they must have done this…on…" Ellie looked at me, her eyes wide. She didn't finish her sentence but I knew what she was thinking, though I dared not say it either: someone had just tried to hurt me on purpose.

"I didn't see the licence number, did you?" Ellie asked.

"No, it happened so fast…"

"It must have been Claude La Lune! It must have been. You saw the car pull away from outside the La Lune headquarters!"

"I did see the car pull away from La Lune, but I didn't see the driver."

"Yeah, but who else could it have been? Claude was furious with you when we left! You saw the look he gave you— "

"Well, I did take his phone—"

"Yeah, but he's obviously worried about what you saw on it. He must think there's a chance you'll figure out who or what CAT is. And then, not half an hour later, somebody tries to run you over. I think the police should know that you're at risk."

"Ellie, honestly—" But before I got any further, she grabbed me by the arm and pulled me after her.

"We're going, Axelle. This morning I listened to you, now you're going to listen to me."

There was clearly no point in arguing with Ellie. After seeing how she'd tackled Hervé and Miriam this morning

– not to mention her cancelled booking and my future modelling career – I decided to follow her. Five minutes later we mounted the steps leading to the entrance of the police headquarters for the 7th *arrondissement* (that's French for district).

It was half past five and the station was winding down. The officer at reception seemed more interested in going home for the day than dealing with us – he didn't even bother to look up at first. But when he did, he took one look at Ellie's well-known face and led us straight to his superior.

Inspector Joaquim Witt was both large and small at the same time. Although not tall, he gave the impression of size due to his broad shoulders and thick torso. And while he didn't present himself as especially fastidious, he nonetheless looked...well, kind of chic. His lush moustache, elegant trench coat, and smart suit gave him an undeniable flair. We stood waiting as he filled his pipe with tobacco. Finally, with measured movements, he put the small pouch in a desk drawer and leaned back in his swivel chair to look at us.

"*Asseyez-vous, asseyez-vous, Mesdemoiselles,*" he said, waving his large hand at the two nondescript chairs facing his desk. "And don't worry, I've stopped smoking," he informed us as Ellie eyed his pipe. "But I still go through the motions of filling it. It calms me."

As we introduced ourselves, Inspector Witt's office door

suddenly opened. "Sorry, I didn't realize you were still busy," a voice said. "I'll come back..."

"No, no. Come in, Sebastian," the inspector said. "This is my son, Sebastian," he continued for our benefit. "He's here for a week of work experience – as a journalist, learning about crime from the police force's point of view. If you don't mind, he'll take a few notes as we chat."

When Sebastian came in, I found myself staring at a familiar face. The shock of recognition took a few seconds to wear off: it was Mr Leather Jacket with the Wicked Grin! From behind his father, he brought his finger to his lips. He obviously didn't want it known that we'd met earlier – or maybe he didn't want his father knowing that he'd been at Miriam's. Why?

Ellie and I started talking as Sebastian settled down in an armchair in the corner behind his father, notepad in hand. We began with the La Lune casting. The inspector didn't interrupt once but kept sucking on his unlit pipe, observing us through half shut eyes. Sebastian's outwardly relaxed demeanour, on the other hand, was betrayed by the lively spark in his light blue eyes as he followed what we said. I watched as his hand busily moved across his pad of paper, taking notes – or so I thought.

After a few minutes he held up his notepad to show me a very good cartoon likeness of his father. Stifling a smile, I shook my head at him. Inspector Witt looked at me. "I'm sorry you don't agree, Mademoiselle Anderson," he answered. Now Sebastian was smiling. "But," continued the inspector as he leaned far back in his desk chair and sighed, "there is nothing I can do."

"But whoever it was, they tried to hit Axelle," Ellie protested.

"Or perhaps they were simply driving dangerously and you are reading more into Claude La Lune's anger than is actually warranted." Inspector Witt stood up and carefully arranged a checked scarf around his throat. Obviously, the meeting was over.

"I'm sure Claude's lying about some things," I said.

"Ah! *Ma chère mademoiselle*, you will see as you get older that we all have things we lie about! Claude La Lune is hardly alone in that. However, I'm afraid I fail to make the same connection that you do between his anger and his possible lies, and the black Peugeot that you say tried to run you over." The inspector left his office and walked briskly down the corridor towards reception. Ellie and I followed him, protesting all the way. Sebastian was behind us.

"Listen!" The inspector stopped suddenly and turned to face us. "I am worried about Belle La Lune – very worried. I don't know whether she's alive or dead and so far the leads…well…" He shook his head. "I haven't a moment to spare. If you really do find something, please let me know. It has been lovely meeting you both. Mademoiselle B," he said as he shook Ellie's hand. "Mademoiselle Anderson," he said, turning to me – but he never had chance to shake my hand because at that moment his phone rang.

"*Oui*," he said gruffly into the phone. "*Quoi? Avec les mêmes suspects?*" And then after a pause: "*J'arrive tout de suite.*" He hung up and slipped his phone back into the breast pocket of his trench coat. "I'm sorry – I have to go. I'm afraid there has been another…*occurrence*…at the La Lune mansion. Sebastian, would you please see the ladies out," he said over his shoulder as he stepped out the door. And then he was gone.

Ellie and I looked at each other in shock.

Another occurrence? What did that mean? And he'd said *les mêmes suspects* – that meant the same suspects. But who was he talking about?

"Quick, we have to follow him!" I said as I caught the closing door and wrenched it open again. We ran out, but the inspector had vanished without a trace. Furthermore, there was no taxi at hand, and I certainly had no idea where the La Lune mansion was. Ellie knew it was nearby but she wasn't sure how to get there.

"I know where it is," said a voice we'd completely forgotten about. Sebastian motioned for us to follow him as he jogged past. This was no time to ask questions – Ellie and I exchanged glances then quickly fell in behind him. "It won't take us more than three minutes to get there if we run," he said over his shoulder. "It's on the Rue de Varenne. Come on!"

We ran up the Rue de Bourgogne until we dead-ended at

the Rue de Varenne. In front of us was the stone wall of the Rodin Museum, and just to the left an even higher stone wall adjoined it. It loomed over us in the evening gloom, blackened with age, imposing and spooky.

"This is the La Lune mansion – or, rather, it's behind this wall," Sebastian said. At that moment, the heavy wooden gates swung open as a police car slowed to enter. "Quick," Sebastian whispered, "this is our chance!" He motioned for us to duck down and follow. As the car eased through the opened gate, we crouched low and ran alongside it until we'd slipped past the gates and were in the courtyard. At that point the car turned left towards the main door and we...well, let's just say I'm sure the three of us could have won an Olympic gold medal in the long jump that night. Before the car had finished its turn to the left we jumped into the bushes on our right, just in time to avoid being exposed in the full glare of the house lights.

I lay on my back, panting, Ellie and Sebastian beside me.

"I was right," whispered Ellie as she turned towards me. "I'm having *much* more fun with you around. I mean, I haven't had this much excitement since the safari story I shot in Africa last winter. A mad elephant took our tent down. Of course, this is more serious. I hope we find Belle..."

I heard murmuring from the direction of the open front door, and the sounds of opening and shutting car doors reverberated around the courtyard. Slowly I turned onto my stomach and lifted my head above the low hedges. Police were coming and going, and about ten cars were parked in the courtyard – Inspector Witt's among them. More interesting, however, was the sight of so many members of the La Lune family rushing out of the house to greet Inspector Witt, who was getting out of his car.

"They're all there – except for Darius…and Patrick," Sebastian said.

"Darius is Belle's second brother. He writes about fashion history," Ellie whispered, confirming what Victor had told me earlier.

"And Patrick is Belle's father," Sebastian added. "They say he never leaves his bed any more."

Near the door stood a sticklike young woman with frizzy hair and flat shoes. She had to be Rose, Belle's only sister and the second eldest sibling after Claude. I remembered Victor saying Rose was shy and awkward – and tonight, at least, she certainly looked it. She was in charge of the company's accounting.

On the bottom step stood an aloof and silver-haired woman: Fiona, Patrick's wife. As Fiona Purseglove, she'd been a famous model in her youth and her icy beauty had graced many a magazine cover, according to Aunt V. Today she was better known as the driving force behind the La Lune Fashion Design Foundation, a family charity celebrated for its yearly fashion design competition for underprivileged students.

The black-clad figure with the camera I recognized as Dom. He repeatedly lifted his camera to his eye, capturing every moment of the unfolding drama. Even in the semi-dark he looked gorgeous. The lack of light only served to accentuate his pallor and green eyes. He looked like a runway vampire.

A tall, well-dressed figure was standing one step behind Fiona. He clearly wasn't old like Fiona but he was a bit older than Claude and Rose.

"Who's that?" I whispered.

"That's Philippe de Vandrille, the family lawyer," Sebastian answered.

Aha...so he was the one who wasn't sure about Claude's alibi.

Behind Philippe stood Claude. Even among this select group of fashionistas, his look stood out in a way that spoke of innate style – as well as long hours in front of the mirror.

"You know, they fell out a few years ago – Claude and Belle, I mean," Sebastian told us. "They had a struggle to see who'd be in charge of the company – and Belle won. They say his jealousy knows no bounds."

No surprise, then, that he'd stepped so quickly into his sister's shoes.

I became engrossed with watching the assembled cast on the steps. Their status and wealth seemed to seep from their pores, and, despite the present tragedy, each gave the impression of having only one thing on their mind: themselves.

Then another elegant shadow emerged from the house.

"Something must be done about these police uniforms," she declared, glancing about her. "They really are an embarrassment to French fashion." Aunt V looked, as usual, effortlessly chic. Her hat cast a wonderful elongated shadow on the wall behind her.

"By the way, I believe your story," Sebastian whispered, as I watched my aunt join the others. "Your hit and run story. Not that I'm sure the La Lunes would go so far as to kidnap one of their own, but—" We ducked as Sebastian's father walked right past us, talking on his phone. "But," Sebastian continued in a whisper, "I find their extreme closeness and glossy perfection a bit spooky. And thanks for not letting on earlier with my dad. He's known Miriam for ages through work – she's often passed on some useful tips – but if he knew that I'd been there to hear about this," he said, nodding towards the La Lunes, "a case *he's* in charge of, he would not be amused – especially not this week. I'm supposed to be at the police station all day for work experience."

Inspector Witt had finished his call and was greeting the group at the front door. It was the perfect distraction for our next move. Crouching low, we moved out from the cover of the hedge and crawled across a gravel path to the nearest car – a large 4 x 4. As quietly as possible, we slid under it and continued to watch the proceedings from this closer vantage point.

"So you were at Miriam's to find out about Belle?" I asked Sebastian.

He nodded. "I live just around the corner from here. I've known the La Lunes my whole life – Dom and I even went to the same school, although he was two years ahead of me. Anyway, it's an intriguing case and it's happened on our doorstep, so to speak. How could I not want to be involved?"

"And did you find anything out at Miriam's?"

"Not anything that hasn't been in the papers. I'd actually hoped to see Dom there – he's in and out of Miriam's quite often – but I had to get back to the police station. Like I said, it's work experience week."

As the La Lunes, Philippe, and my aunt slowly made their way into the house, we slid out from under the 4 x 4 and made a quick dash for the side of the house. Standing flush against the wall, we waited for Sebastian's dad and the other police officers to follow them in, until the door was shut and the courtyard silent.

"I can't believe I'm sneaking around the La Lunes' house," Ellie whispered to me. "If there is such a thing as a fashion god, I hope she's looking out for us."

Yeah, me too, I thought. My aunt would be about as thrilled with my trespassing as she was with cheap synthetic fabrics – in other words, not at all.

"You never told me your reason," Sebastian whispered.

"My reason?"

"Your reason for being brainwashed into modelling," he said with a flash of his grin. "When I first saw you at the agency this morning, you seemed like someone who had resolutely planned to stay at arm's length from fashion since birth."

I smiled. "Let's just say that using the modelling as a disguise while I look for Belle gives me much more freedom than the alternative."

"Which is?"

"Which is trailing behind my aunt with a laptop and fashion-appropriate outfit."

"And you think you can solve this?"

"I don't know – but I'm going to try."

"Well, as we're on the same trail, maybe we should join forces?" He was smiling at me, his eyes sparkling.

I was actually happy darkness had settled – because his suggestion didn't make me smile. I didn't know how to tell him that I wanted to solve this mystery solo – without a sidekick. I needed to do this on my own. It was my only chance of being taken seriously by my parents. And while I was appreciative that he'd led us into the La Lune compound, I didn't really want things going further.

Then, after a moment, he said, "By the way, you were right to lose the hair and glasses. You somehow look more like yourself, if you know what I mean."

Great. Now he was an admiring sidekick! I said nothing.

The high walls of the courtyard blocked out all street light. Overhead, the clouds swept quickly past, their undersides glowing against the black sky. Standing back from the house, half-hidden by shrubbery, I watched as a white-gloved butler moved from room to room, turning on lights and drawing curtains. But, even in the darkness, the house didn't fail to make an impression. It was huge and creepy, with a grandeur that felt oppressive. The vast garden – it was nearly a small park – surrounding the house was beautifully landscaped. I could just make out formal parterres and beyond those a large lawn that descended to a water basin and fountain. The lawn was flanked by wide flowering borders, all encircled by a high stone wall.

But, pretty as it was, it wasn't why I'd snuck in. I wanted to search for clues – and this was more than likely my one and only chance. "Is there any way of getting in?" I asked.

Sebastian flashed me his grin. "I was hoping you'd say that. Obviously, there's no way of going through the front of the house," he whispered. "But maybe around the back…"

"I've been in one of the La Lunes' shows here – sometimes they hold them in a tent in the garden or even in the house," Ellie said. "I know that at the back of the house the rooms all have doors that open onto a large terrace that overlooks the garden. If we're lucky, one of those doors might be open…"

107

It was worth a try. Keeping our backs to the wall, we began creeping round the house. The sound of our footsteps on the gravel was muffled by the splashing water of the fountain, and, luckily for us, the police were inside now – although I did notice that two guards were stationed at the front gate.

We'd gone halfway along the side of the house when I felt my phone vibrate in my pocket.

"Allô? Axelle?" It was Hervé, calling to tell me that I'd been booked by Lanvin and La Lune as well as Chanel. "Since I work as a booker never once have I seen a total newcomer be booked by three such prestigious fashion houses – and in the same day! *C'est incroyable!*" He told me he'd call me later with my job details for tomorrow's La Lune photoshoot. "By the way, where are you? It is very quiet. And why you whisper?"

Clearly I wasn't about to tell him that I was spying on the La Lunes after having snuck into their compound. "I'm uh…we're…we're watching videos of the shows from last autumn and I don't want to disturb Ellie. You know how you have to concentrate to catch every move the models make…"

"Good, Axelle! With this attitude you will soon hit the top!"

I said goodbye, then sat silently for a moment. I couldn't believe Claude had decided to book me – and I said so to Ellie.

"He must be desperate to know what you found in his phone," she whispered.

"What?" Sebastian said. "You looked in his phone? No wonder he's after you. You didn't tell my father that part of the story, did you?"

"No, I forgot," I answered.

"I bet."

"Shhh," I said, drawing their attention to the garden. Inspector Witt and Claude La Lune had just walked out onto the terrace, which we could just see from our hiding place.

"My father has known the La Lunes for a long time," Sebastian said. "He used to be Chief of Police for this district. Over the years he's worked quite a bit with them. They have a well-known art collection, a few pieces of which have been stolen in the past, although they're hardly the only designers in Paris to have had that problem. But beyond that, the La Lunes – mostly Belle, actually – have had the occasional run-in with fashion-obsessed fans. She's even had a couple of serious stalkers."

Ellie nodded. "I remember two years ago, the first time I did their show, Belle came with bodyguards."

"Well, it's too bad she didn't have them with her on Saturday night," Sebastian said.

Finally, Claude and Inspector Witt went back inside. Still keeping flush to the wall, we crept to the back corner of the house. From there we crawled onto the terrace and carefully manoeuvred ourselves between the various outdoor chairs and tables until we were close to the house. The moon was high overhead, and behind us the perfectly clipped lawn lay like a sea of silver in the evening light.

In front of us, soft lamplight shone through the glass doors, throwing squares of light across the flagstones of the terrace. The group was assembled in a large drawing room in the middle of the house. The room's high ceiling dwarfed them; like a forest of white and gold, the walls and columns sprang up at the sides to support a canopy of carved cherubs overhead. Large vases of lilies sat on gilded surfaces.

Inspector Witt, meanwhile, sat with his assistant in a small study just to the left of the drawing room and directly opposite the iron patio table I was hiding under. I panicked as I saw him suddenly get up from his chair and walk straight to the large window opposite me. Certain he'd see me, I began to back out from my hiding place, but, after opening the window, he put his pipe in his mouth and turned to lean with his back against the window sill.

"At times like this, Thomas," he said to his assistant, "I miss smoking." There was a pause before he said, "Thomas, would you please call the maid in?"

Like a snake, I pushed myself along on my stomach until I was behind one of the large potted shrubs just under the window, Ellie and Sebastian beside me. I didn't have a clear plan in mind – just to have a quick look around and hopefully stumble upon something interesting.

For now, I waited and listened, pushing my translation skills to the limit, as Inspector Witt's deep, melodious voice wafted out into the night…

Another *occurrence* was right! It seemed Darius La Lune, Belle's second oldest brother, had vanished too.

A meeting had been arranged for five o'clock between the family members, my aunt, and Philippe de Vandrille – the same group, minus Belle, that had met for dinner last Saturday night. Originally, the meeting had been scheduled to discuss the launch of the new La Lune "Juno" handbag – but, naturally, given Belle's disappearance, the question had become how to go forward without her.

Amazingly for a fashion meeting, everyone – with the exception of Darius – was on time and at the house by five. They started the meeting at approximately 5.10 p.m., without him. But Darius never showed up. By six, everyone was feeling nervous, the same unvoiced thought running through their minds: maybe he wasn't late – maybe he was gone. At that point Fiona had asked Philippe to call Inspector Witt.

According to the maid, everything in Darius's room was in order – nothing out of place, nothing suspicious. And he wasn't the type to seek attention with outlandish stunts. On the contrary, he always left a message if he went out, even if only for a walk through the garden. Serious and discreet, he'd been hard at work on a book about eighteenth-century fashion and style at Versailles. The maid had been the last to see him, in his bedroom, at approximately four o'clock.

"And did Darius say or do anything that struck you as unusual before he disappeared?" the inspector asked.

There was the slightest hesitation before the maid said, "No...no, not really..."

"Any little thing?" Sebastian's father pushed.

Again a short pause. "Well, Darius likes to write notes. He always has a notebook on him – a small La Lune leather one – and he also keeps blocks of different-sized Post-its on his desk and next to his bed..."

"And?"

"And on his desk upstairs is a note he must have written this afternoon – or in any case laid on his desk this afternoon – only..."

The inspector remained quiet while waiting for the maid to continue.

"Only this note wasn't written on a Post-it; it was written on the back of a used red envelope – and he's written his sister's name on it. It wasn't there when I tidied his room this morning – not that I make a point of looking at his notes, mind you..."

"Of course not," the inspector murmured smoothly.

"I left it on his desk. It might be nothing at all..."

"Sometimes the tiniest things are of the greatest importance," the inspector told her. "His bedroom is upstairs, is it not?"

"Yes, sir, directly above us."

"Good. Well, I have just a few more questions to ask you – pure formality – and then I'd appreciate it if you'd show me the note upstairs."

I didn't wait to hear the rest. If I moved quickly now, I had a chance of seeing that potential clue.

"We've got to get upstairs," I whispered to Ellie.

She was looking upwards. "Some of the windows are open…maybe we could climb up. It would be easier than trying to go through the house right now."

I followed her gaze. "You're probably right. And look at that," I said, pointing to a wooden rose trellis. It covered the entire back facade (excepting doors and windows, obviously), and nearly reached the upstairs windows. "If it can hold our weight, we could make it into that window," I said, pointing just above. The window was open a few centimetres and the room beyond was dark.

Sebastian crept out from behind a chair and carefully put his weight on the trellis. It held. Then he climbed a metre or so – it still held. "I think it's all right," he whispered. "Let's try."

Great. My charming sidekick was already trying to run the show.

Whatever. As long as he didn't touch anything until I got up there.

At the top it was tricky because he had to push the window open while keeping his balance. He had only the top of the trellis to stand on, a drainpipe to hold, and the window was at shoulder height. But, finally, he managed and the window swung open – hitting the wall as it did. I panicked for a moment, hoping the sound hadn't carried – but Rose, who was sitting close to the window in the drawing room, must have heard something, as she opened the patio door and stuck her head out. I held my breath and signalled to Sebastian to hold still while she looked to the left and right, and down the lawn.

"Don't be silly, Rose, it's only your imagination – as usual," I heard Claude say from inside. Finally, with a last look straight past Ellie and me, she went back in and locked the door. Whew! Ellie and I breathed out and Sebastian pulled himself in through the window.

Ellie was next. She climbed up quickly – it took her less than a couple of minutes to get in. Then it was my turn. I went up easily and at the top clasped Sebastian's waiting hand. He pulled me in and smiled at me. "That was a good idea," he said.

"Thanks, I have them all the time," I mumbled into my scarf, keeping my head lowered as I pretended to readjust it. *He's just being nice, Axelle*, I told myself. *He's not solving this case with you.*

The maid was right – Darius's bedroom was directly above the study Inspector Witt was using. We were in it.

And she hadn't been exaggerating – Darius loved to write notes. His bedroom left us with no doubt of that.

Differently shaped Post-it notes were layered over every flat surface – walls included. They covered everything. Some were in ink, others in pencil. All were written in his neat spidery scrawl.

"I wouldn't light a match in here," Sebastian said. "I've never seen so many notes."

While Ellie kept watch at the door, Sebastian and I quickly went through the room. Rapidly I scanned as many notes as I could, hoping to find something, anything, that might lead to Belle. Then I found the desk. I pulled my jacket sleeve down over my hand and switched the desk lamp on, and there, on top of a teetering yet tidy pile of papers, letters and notebooks, was the red envelope. There were four words written on the back:

Belle
Le Vau
passages

"Strange. Le Vau was a famous architect – but, like, three hundred years ago." Sebastian was peering over my shoulder. "And *passages* – what could that mean?"

I took out my phone and photographed it. "Maybe he found something that links them all together? I mean, have you noticed how precise his notes are? Every single one is very specific. Like, his whole personality seems to be specific." I pointed to a table at the foot of his bed. "Look, there are notes and books everywhere, but they've all been set down in a very orderly, neat way."

A door slammed downstairs. The inspector was on his way up. I switched the desk lamp off and slipped my phone back into my pocket. Drat! We needed to find somewhere else to hide so we could keep searching for clues.

"So...?" whispered Sebastian as we crossed the room.

"So I don't think Darius would've put those words together on the same piece of paper unless he had a good reason to..."

"Do you think that's maybe why someone got rid of him? Because he was onto something?"

"Maybe..."

At that moment Ellie called to us. "They're coming up the stairs now. We have to go!" Gently shutting the door behind us, we followed Ellie down the corridor and into the room next door. "It's large enough to hide in easily," she whispered. "I took a quick look."

We slipped in just as Inspector Witt reached the top of the stairs. A few moments later his footsteps passed us on his way to Darius's bedroom.

"Is this Belle's bedroom?" I whispered.

We opened the curtains to let in some moonlight. The room was large and light. A low bed was in the middle of the room and swathes of colourful fabrics, some patterned, some more muted, lay over every surface – much as the notes lay everywhere in Darius's bedroom. A chandelier made of feathers hung from the ceiling and an artwork of neon light shone over the bed. A guitar leaned against the desk. Even in the gloom, everything somehow seemed young and fresh and fun. A large photo in a silver frame caught my eye. It was Belle – with her father, Patrick, in healthier days, on a beach, turquoise water lapping at their feet. In the background I could make out her siblings Claude, Rose, Darius and, presumably, Dom, as a toddler, playing in the surf.

"It must be," answered Ellie. "She dresses exactly like this room looks. Oh my gosh – look at this! It's her dressing room."

I peered in through the door she'd opened. Belle's dressing room was enormous. Without the lights on it was impossible to make out the far wall. Sebastian switched them on. "No one will see the lights," he said. "There's no window."

Unlike the jumble of pattern, colour and texture in her bedroom, Belle's dressing room was ordered and neat to a fault. Everything hung according to colour and length. Shirts, dresses, skirts and jackets all hung in their own sections. Hats were overhead, and behind the cabinet doors her jumpers and jeans were presumably laid out in a similar fashion.

"And look at her shoes!" Ellie whispered. "There must be at least two hundred pairs!"

"Make that one hundred and ninety-nine *and a half*," I said, pointing to the first cupboard on the left. There was a dark hole where one shoe was missing – apparently one half of a pair of platform heels.

"Oh, I know that shoe," Ellie said. "It's from last year's La Lune Autumn/Winter collection. They weigh a ton – the heel is solid wood, you know," she added, as I lifted the shoe off the shelf. "I have the same pair in burgundy, although, I have to say, they look fab in this dark green."

"Why do you think one is missing?" I carefully wiped my prints off the heel of the shoe before placing it back on the shelf.

"Maybe it's getting repaired?"

"At this time of the year? Why would she be wearing dark velvet shoes in spring?"

"Hmm. You have a point. But maybe Belle does her shoe maintenance off season..."

Suddenly we heard the inspector coming towards the bedroom. I quickly flicked the light off in the dressing room with my elbow as Ellie and Sebastian hid in the racks of dresses. I joined them just as we heard Inspector Witt open the door to the bedroom. His voice carried easily to the open dressing room.

"We've been over all of her rooms, haven't we, Thomas?" he asked his assistant. "Good. Good. But would you please keep it as it is until further notice?" Then they left, shutting the door behind them. Slowly we stepped out of the layers of chiffon and silk.

"Axelle, I really need to get out of here – now," Ellie

whispered. "If I get caught in this house my career'll be over faster than you can say Chanel."

She had a point. Besides, my just-started career would also be over if I was caught here, and finding Belle by Friday would become an impossibility. Furthermore, it would only add to my aunt's woes if her niece was found sneaking around the crime site.

"You're right – let's go."

But just as we stepped into the corridor, a maid and Thomas, Inspector Witt's assistant, were coming out of a doorway at the opposite end. I'd thought they'd all gone back downstairs! Panic seized me – they were probably on their way into Darius's or Belle's bedroom. We bent low and quickly moved down the corridor to the next door along from Belle's. Hoping desperately that the room was empty and dark, I held my breath as I slowly turned the doorknob and slid inside, Ellie and Sebastian just behind me. I breathed a sigh of relief as I leaned my back against the door and heard Thomas pass by. Once my eyes had adjusted to the dim light, I saw we were in a library.

With the exception of the light made by small reading lamps mounted on the bookshelves, the room was dark. But it was smoky and warm and the embers in the fireplace were still glowing. The room was decorated in green, and shelves of books, all on fashion and art, lined the walls.

"The cushions are made from vintage La Lune silk scarves," Ellie whispered excitedly.

It was an interesting room, a muted contrast to the gilded extravagance elsewhere. We were just about to leave when we heard voices.

"Get down! Someone's coming!" I said as I ducked behind the nearest sofa.

Male voices, female voices – even my aunt's voice – echoed lightly around the room, coming from nowhere and everywhere at the same time. Even the way they sounded was strange – as if they were far away, yet nearby.

"I can't make out where they're coming from," Ellie said as she peered out of the keyhole. "The corridor is empty."

"Then let's leave now," I said, moving towards the door, "before our luck runs out."

"No. Wait!" Sebastian whispered. "The voices are coming from the chimney. Listen! They're travelling up the flue. We must be directly over the large room downstairs. If you get close, you can hear quite well," he said, crouching low and tipping his head towards the hearth.

I was torn between leaving now – I really did feel we'd pushed our luck – and staying. But, at this point I couldn't risk missing anything that could help me find Belle. *Maybe just two more minutes*, I thought, as I leaned down next to Sebastian. Carefully, I listened to the voices float up...

"Obviously, someone wants to make a fortune on the back of the Juno bag." It was my Aunt Venetia. "Counterfeiters are such a problem nowadays."

"You're right, Venetia," Fiona said, "counterfeiters are a horrible, bloodthirsty lot." Even after so many years in France she spoke French with a heavy English accent. "And to think they've taken Belle and now Darius – and how are they to know he has asthma and needs medication?" A short sob escaped her before she gathered herself and continued. "Listen, everyone. With your father being so ill, plus the launch of the bag this week, we must contain the potential scandal. We must find Belle and Darius. We must help the police in their search for the counterfeiters behind the theft. Everything else must wait...we can sort things out later...between ourselves."

What was she talking about? What must wait? And what did she want sorted out?

"You know," my aunt continued, as if Fiona had never spoken, "the Bulgarian mafia is very much into counterfeit handbags, and let's not even get started with the Japanese mafia."

"What about Darius's disappearance?" Rose asked – at least I surmised it was her: she was the only other woman in the group. "He didn't even know what the Juno bag looked like."

"Maybe he stumbled upon something he shouldn't have," Claude suggested.

"Darius and his silly books, which nobody except the occasional fashion nerd reads, are totally harmless," Dom answered.

"It could have been kidnap for money alone, you know," Claude continued. "It doesn't necessarily have to have anything to do with the Juno bag."

"Genius, Claude," Rose said. "If that's the case, then where's the ransom note?"

"For goodness' sake, can you stop taking photos for one second! All that clicking is getting on my nerves," Claude hissed. Presumably this was directed at Dom.

"Belle has always said that the only way to get away from fashion is to disappear altogether. Maybe that's what she's done. Maybe she's gone on holiday somewhere and didn't feel like telling us," said a deep voice. And that, I supposed, was the mysterious Philippe de Vandrille. "Although that still doesn't explain Darius."

"Changed track have you, Philippe?" spat Claude.

"That's enough, Claude," Fiona said. "Let's all try to remain civil with one another, please. I hardly think that Belle would have chosen to leave during the week of the shows and the launch of a handbag she's been working on for two years."

"Certainly not," my aunt said.

"Nor would Darius have gone on some mysterious holiday this week – at least not without telling us," Fiona continued. "He's been hard at work on his book and has hardly left his room these last few weeks."

There was a moment of silence before Rose spoke. "To be honest, I don't know why we're all trying to sound so concerned about these different theories, when really all we're thinking about is *It...*"

It? What was she talking about? The disappearances? But then she should have said *Them.*

There was another silence, this one swiftly punctuated by my aunt. With her usual lack of tact, she said loudly, "Rose, darling, what *are* you wearing? It's the same hue as your face. You seem a bit worked up, actually."

"Venetia has a point, Rose," Fiona said. "Perhaps you should go upstairs and change before dinner."

"Anything to change the subject, right, *maman*?" asked Rose. "If only everyone knew. Well, ignore it if you like, but a serious threat to our family is coming. Poor Belle and Darius are only the beginning! Can't you feel it? Haven't you heard it moving through the house like a ghost? It's closing in on us! The curse is closing in on us!" hissed Rose.

The curse? I looked at Ellie and Sebastian. Both shrugged their shoulders. This must be the old rumour – the "dark matter" – Victor had been referring to earlier!

Sebastian and I leaned further into the fireplace, concentrating as Rose continued in an eerie semi-whisper. "We all know what it says: *The day shall come when greed and deceit shall rip apart your family and destroy the success you stole from me. One by one, you and your family shall disappear as I have...*" With a sob, she continued. "It's happening, there's no use fighting! It's happening! The curse is coming alive! We're all greedy – and our greed is waking the curse!" Everything seemed to slow down as Rose's words cast a pall of fear over the room. A heavy silence hung in the air.

"Listen, everyone, please – let's stop all of this theorizing," Philippe finally said, his deep, firm voice cutting through the fog of fear. "It serves absolutely no purpose." We listened as a drink was poured – for Rose, no doubt.

"But Rose isn't fantasizing," Dom said. "There is a curse – and we've all seen it…"

"Yes, you're correct, Dom – there is something – we've all seen it. But it's nothing more than a harmless old letter, a childish threat written long ago."

"So you think there's nothing behind it?" Fiona asked Philippe.

"Absolutely nothing," he answered after a pause. "However," Philippe said, drawing breath before continuing, "whatever we may guess or believe or think…the fact remains that we were all present on the evening Belle disappeared – just as we were all present today."

"Are you saying it's more than mere coincidence?" Dom asked.

"I am."

"Which means…?" Claude asked cautiously.

"Which means that unless there really is a curse or a counterfeit gang…*then suspicion will fall on every one of us.*"

A long pause ensued as the room was again plunged into

total silence. Suddenly my aunt said, "Honestly, Philippe, I know we're in fashion but do you have to sound so dramatic?"

And then a knock at the door was heard. "Inspector Witt is finished for tonight, Madame," the butler announced. "He'd just like a word with Monsieur de Vandrille in the hall, please."

"Thank you, Gerard," Fiona answered. And then, after another pause: "I suggest we all have a drink before going in for dinner."

At that moment I rose to leave from my crouched position – or, rather, I tried to. But my legs had fallen asleep. I lost my balance and fell backwards. Instinctively I reached out, my arms flailing at the chimney mantelpiece, and my left hand found a handle that I clutched desperately. Pulling on it, I straightened myself back up.

"Coast is clear," Ellie said from her position at the keyhole.

But then, just before turning to go out the door, my attention was caught by a small flame flickering to life in the fireplace. Funny – when we'd come in, the embers in the grate had been smouldering, barely glowing. Leaning forward, I saw a book-sized bundle on the grate, small flames licking at its sides. It was tied with a ribbon and had definitely not been there earlier. It must have fallen when I'd pulled the handle by the mantelpiece. As if reading my mind, Sebastian grabbed a nearby magazine and threw it to me. I slapped the flames down and used a pair of fire tongs to retrieve the blackened bundle. I left it to cool on the marble floor in front of the hearth for a few moments before I carefully lifted it and carried it to the desk where Sebastian had turned a lamp on. Gently I pulled the burned ribbon away.

It was a packet of letters. They must have been jammed up behind the chimney damper – the moveable metal plate every chimney flue has for regulating airflow. The "handle" I'd grabbed wasn't a handle at all – it was the lever controlling the damper.

Varying in size and weight, the letters looked old. Some of the envelopes had no return address or postmark – they must have been hand-delivered. And in between some of the letters were postcards, tickets and other slips of paper. I turned over a postcard with an old sepia-toned image of the Eiffel Tower on it. Addressed to *Chère Maman*, it was signed *Violette*. Who was Violette? And why was she writing to her mother from Paris? (My mother was the last person I'd write to.) Who'd kept this postcard and the letters? And why were they important? Obviously someone in this house thought they were – otherwise why had they been hidden in the chimney flue?

Sebastian and Ellie peered over my shoulder as I bundled the letters back together with a rubber band I found on the desk. Trying to make sense of the thoughts racing through my mind, I whispered, "The fire died out not long before we walked in here, right? But judging by the amount of ashes in the grate, it must have been burning for some time before that…"

Sebastian nodded. "And you pulled the chimney damper *open*…"

"Exactly. And as it would have been open while the fire was blazing, the flue must have been shut after the fire had begun to die down. In fact, it was probably shut just to hide these letters…"

"Just before we came in."

I nodded. "So if the letters have anything to do with Belle's and Darius's disappearances, then Philippe de Vandrille has a point: the criminal must be one of the people we heard in the room downstairs."

I carefully placed the bundle of letters into my bag, then turned to leave, but remembered at the last moment to return the damper to its closed position. I pushed the protruding handle   and listened as it slid into its socket with a heavy thud, followed by the scratch of metal. The bang echoed down the flue.

Not good.

I stood frozen in the ensuing silence.

"What was that?" I heard my aunt ask, her voice loud, wary.

Panic engulfed us. We were upstairs, in a room with one door. How could we get out? The thought of my aunt watching as I was walked down the staircase in handcuffs was not a nice one. Plus I'd dragged Ellie and Sebastian along – and, if caught, neither would get away scot-free. I felt sick.

Then Rose wailed, Fiona told her to shut up, and Philippe's voice boomed up at us: "I think the noise came through the flue. Dom, call Inspector Witt. We need an officer up there now! In the library! Go!"

We ran to the opposite end of the corridor, turning the lights off behind us as we went. After trying a few of the doors, we came upon one that led to a service stairwell. Again, we turned the lights off and, using our phones as torches, flew down as quickly as possible.

After going down a flight we arrived behind a small door tucked underneath the soaring stone staircase in the hall. We opened it a crack to see Inspector Witt and two officers charge past us on their way up the stairs. After they passed, we crossed the hall and ducked through the first door we reached – and just as quickly turned around: two maids were setting the table. Back in the hall, the door to the left opened onto a small sitting room – with access to the terrace! We crossed the length of the room and slipped out through the door. From there we crept past the garden furniture we'd hidden under earlier and dived behind the nearest large shrub. We sat quietly for a moment before Ellie said, "Let me go first. I'll distract the guards and meanwhile you sneak out and get as close to the gate as you can. When it opens, run!"

True to her word, Ellie proved an admirable distraction to the two guards. Sebastian and I shadowed her movements as she walked along a side path until she was within calling range of the two beefy men.

"*Messieurs!*" she called, as she walked up to them. "Could you please tell me at what time the park closes? I see the gate is shut."

"The park? This isn't a park, mademoiselle. You're on private property."

"Isn't this the Musée Rodin? On my map it looked like..."

"The Musée Rodin is next door and it isn't open until tomorrow morning."

"Are you sure? Next door? But earlier there were so many cars and people going in and out of here, I thought..."

"Come. We'll show you," the shorter guard said as they led Ellie to the gate and pushed the button that opened it.

It felt like eons passed before the gate opened fully. When it did, Ellie stepped out with the guards. Sebastian grabbed hold of my hand and pulled me behind him. We jumped out of the shadows and into the street just as the guards turned to walk back in.

We were out.

MONDAY EVENING

Fashion History

Ellie flagged down the first taxi we saw. We squeezed into the smelly and sagging back seat, then leaned back and savoured a collective sigh.

"Oh my gosh, Aunt V – I was supposed to call her about dinner!" Quickly I pulled my phone out of my new shoulder bag and turned the volume back on. There were six missed calls. Who had been calling? Must be my mum.

But it wasn't. It was Hervé. I rang him back immediately.

"Axelle! Where have you been? I've been calling and calling. You are a model now and models must check in with their agencies every morning and every evening. It is just like brushing your teeth. Okay? And call in the afternoon too when you can. Anyway, I have your job details for the La Lune advertising campaign tomorrow. You begin at nine at the Eiffel Tower. There'll be a white Pin-Up Studio bus underneath the tower. Ellie will be there too. Maybe you can share a taxi. Please be on time and don't forget to call me tomorrow morning. I'll be in at nine. *Bonne nuit!* And get some beauty sleep!"

Beauty sleep? Who had time for beauty sleep when we had to find out about this curse?

Just as I'd finished with Hervé, my aunt called. She was still wound up after a day of drama. She ran all of her questions together into one long breathless sentence. "Can you believe? I'm finally heading home. What a day. Anyway, Axelle, where have you been? Have you found anything out? Belle's brother, Darius, has disappeared, so now the police are even more suspicious of us than before. This La Lune story is becoming even more convoluted than the Gucci family saga."

"Aunt V, I'm in a car with Ellie and…uhm…Sebastian." Great. I knew that now I'd mentioned Sebastian, Aunt V would invite him to join us for dinner. There was no way out – the sidekick was sticking.

"Well, bring Ellie for dinner if you'd like. Who's Sebastian?"

"Inspector Witt's son."

"Inspector Witt's son… How'd you meet him? Never mind, you can tell me when you're here. He's welcome too."

Yup. He was definitely sticking.

"Great. Thanks. We'll be with you in a few minutes. Oh, and we want to know all about the curse."

That made my Aunt V go silent for a moment. "Wow – that was fast. So you have been busy. And it seems you'll be having a busy time this week with work too. Hervé called. The agency is delighted – it seems Ellie has a good eye for new talent. Listen, I'll be waiting. I'll explain all over dinner."

I'd thought that was the end of that, but of course it wasn't. "Oh, and, Axelle," she managed to slip in before I hung up, "after dinner we'll have to work on your walk."

Some things never change.

The taxi arrived at Aunt V's and we made our way up the grand stone staircase in the entrance hall. As we reached the landing outside Aunt V's apartment, I caught sight of a brown-haired girl in one of the large mirrors lining the walls. Her hair looked messy but cool and her clothes suited her – she was dressed like a nerdy musician.

It took me a moment to realize I'd caught sight of my own reflection.

As I rang the bell I realized something else: for the first time ever, I was actually hungry for one of Aunt Venetia's super-sophisticated, minimalistic dinners.

After introducing Sebastian to Aunt V, we headed straight into the dining room. Dinner was laid out on the elegant sideboard against the wall opposite the two French windows. The street light glowed gently through the striped silk taffeta curtains, highlighting the gilded frames of Aunt V's collection of Dutch landscapes. (Have I mentioned that Aunt V's apartment is covered with paintings and she keeps buying more? My dad likes to say that in her next life she can be an art dealer.) Apart from that, the room was quite dark. The aubergine velvet on the walls absorbed the light from the candles on the tables and in the sconces. How Aunt Venetia was able to wear her sunglasses *and* still see what was on her plate was beyond me. She claimed that after so many years of being blinded by photographers' flashes during fashion shows she *had* to wear sunglasses to protect her sensitive eyes. I think she just liked the inscrutability they gave her.

We talked through the events of the day. Aunt V wanted to know *exactly* how my fittings had gone – no abbreviated versions for her. But I really got her attention when I told her about Ellie and me nearly getting run over.

"May they be denied cashmere in their next life – whoever they are! Although, like you, I wouldn't be surprised if it was Claude. Or Philippe, for that matter."

"De Vandrille?" Sebastian asked.

Aunt V nodded.

"Why?" we asked.

"Well, Claude, because he's always been a bit of a simmering volcano – I seem to recall there was some kind of eruption concerning Belle when they were younger – and because he must be hiding something or he wouldn't have become so enraged with you for taking his phone. You'd think he would have just brushed it off as the nonsensical action of a teenager."

"Thanks, Aunt V."

"You know what I mean, Axelle. Anyway, as for Philippe, he's always been something of a dark horse…and he's so… *connected* to the family. I mean, you'd think they were *his* family… Besides, imagine always being so close to such glamour and wealth and yet none of it is yours. He's an accessory to the La Lune lifestyle – nothing more. That would give some people an axe to grind."

By the time we got to the chocolate mousse, I'd started describing our trip to the police station.

"So that's where you met," my aunt said as she dipped her fork (yes, it's how the French do it) into her mousse with intense concentration.

"Exactly," I answered. Thankfully, she didn't remember seeing Sebastian at Miriam's. From across the table, Sebastian smiled at me and mouthed, "Thank you."

"And how did you hear about the curse? Not many remember it any more." I could feel her watching me from behind her dark glasses.

I'd been planning on divulging all to my aunt – honestly. I'd wanted to tell her how we'd slipped through the gates and had explored the house, and had heard her and the La Lunes in the drawing room. I was even ready to share my discovery of the cache of letters in the chimney flue. But now that I was faced with the actual prospect of doing just that, I hesitated. A quick look at Sebastian told me that he'd prefer I didn't mention our illegal break-in – and who could blame him, considering who his father is? Ellie, too, looked anxious, and I remembered her comment earlier at the La Lune mansion about her career being over if she were found in the house. I couldn't let them down.

Playing for time, I toyed with the mousse on my plate. Finally, the right answer came to me. "Well, actually, it was Victor who hinted at it – this morning, while doing my hair." Both Ellie and Sebastian visibly relaxed. "He said he'd once heard Belle mention it, but he didn't know any details."

"And what does your father think?" Aunt Venetia asked Sebastian.

Sebastian took his time in answering – as he had throughout dinner. I'd noticed that although he didn't say much, he missed nothing. He'd eaten quietly, but all the while his eyes and ears had been taking everything in. Ellie, on the other hand, was good at keeping the conversation rolling. She and my aunt had discussed Azzedine Alaïa's early bandage dresses all through the asparagus soup. Ellie's knowledge on vintage clothing seemed to know no bounds – she was more than a match for my aunt on *that* subject.

Finally, Sebastian set his fork down and said, "Well, I don't think my father has any solid leads yet – at least, none that he's shared."

Aunt V arched an eyebrow. "He's saying that it must have been counterfeiters…"

"True – for the sake of discretion. But, again, the problem with the counterfeit theory is that there is no solid lead. And if Belle was kidnapped so that she would hand over her drawings, fine – but then why kidnap Darius? He's not involved with the designing of anything."

"Maybe a fake bag will show up soon and then we'll have a lead," Aunt V said.

Sebastian shrugged. "Maybe."

"You don't seem convinced," Aunt V continued.

Sebastian carefully finished his mousse before answering my aunt. "No, I suppose I'm not convinced that the disappearances are the work of counterfeiters. I think this case is about money…money on a personal level."

"And how could you possibly have that impression?" my aunt asked. She was genuinely interested and leaned forward on her elbows, now gazing intently at Sebastian through her dark glasses.

"Because my father has always said that ninety-nine times out of a hundred any crime in a rich family is about money – regardless of how much the individual members may have. And even if they are in fashion, at the end of the day the La Lunes are like any other rich family."

"Only better dressed," Aunt V interjected.

"True."

"You might be right," my aunt said. "Time will tell – although I know this much: the entire La Lune clan is convinced the disappearances are due to the curse. Rose in particular was quite animated this evening. I nearly had to remind myself that she's an accountant. You should have seen her."

Little did she know that we *had* seen her. "What happened?" I asked. "I mean, in general, at the house this afternoon."

"Not much really," she said as she took the napkin off her lap, folded it carefully and laid it beside her plate. "We'd all agreed on Saturday at dinner that we'd meet again today at five o'clock to go over Wednesday night's Juno bag launch. So I went along as planned – we all did – and Darius never showed up. No call, no message, nothing – and this from a man who rarely leaves his desk, let alone the house. Needless to say, considering the present circumstances, it made us all nervous. Fiona was beside herself and finally rang your father," she added, with a nod to Sebastian.

"And where was everyone? Before the meeting, I mean?" Ellie asked:

"Oh, all in the house, reading the papers, talking on the phone, whatever. I'd arrived a little early so I was there talking to myself in fact – rehearsing a speech I'll have to make in New York next week at a fashion awards dinner. I'd locked myself in the small study downstairs for some privacy."

She was silent for a moment. "I have the sneaking suspicion that the police – your father," she said with a nod to Sebastian, "believe that one of us is responsible. It's horrible! I wish someone would get to the bottom of this thing right away. It's like a ticking time bomb and I feel as if *Chic* and I are attached to the end of the fuse. It's not amusing."

"Think of Belle and Darius," I said. "They've vanished and no one knows how to help them."

"True. But at least they don't have to go to the shows with this enormous accusation hanging over their heads."

I refrained from pointing out that they might never go anywhere again – let alone to a fashion show.

"Anyway, Axelle, maybe you'll find something out tomorrow while you're on the photo shoot. Something that could lead you to Belle. And Darius. Then the magazine and I can forget this ever happened." Aunt V got up from the table. "Right, well – why don't I tell you about the curse over coffee?"

We followed her to the sitting room. Once there, Aunt Venetia sipped her coffee in silence for a few minutes while Ellie, Sebastian and I stretched out on the low U-shaped sofa. The room was red, with heavily shaded table lamps and more paintings on the walls. Sebastian got up to light the fire and Ellie and I each took a chocolate truffle from the small silver bowl in the centre of the coffee table. Then we leaned back, replete and warm, and waited for Aunt Venetia to begin.

This is the tale as she told it.

The Curse of the Golden Handbag

In 1842, two best friends, Auguste La Lune and Maurice Merlette, established a saddlery shop in Paris. They were honest, hard-working and bright; their business flourished. For four generations the La Lunes and Merlettes passed down their respective shares of the business from father to son, calmly and quietly, without the slightest ripple of change – until Belle's grandfather, François, inherited in the 1940s. His father's business partner, Hector Merlette, presumably had no willing son of his own, as he continued to run the company alongside François. It was at this time that the company altered course for ever.

Ambitious, tough, and far-sighted, François La Lune was the one responsible for transforming Maison La Lune et Merlette from a well-respected but small family enterprise into a globally recognized brand. In order to make that happen, he realized that the family business would have to move beyond the old-fashioned world of horse tack and embrace the modern one of fashion. Slowly and carefully, François convinced Hector that they should begin to phase out the saddles and bridles (although to this day one can still custom-order a La Lune saddle) and then, just as slowly and carefully, they introduced wallets, suitcases, and leather diaries. The success of this strategy encouraged François to add a line of travelling clothes, and thus a fashion company was born. The Maison La Lune et Merlette label soon became synonymous with Parisian chic and exclusive luxury. And while they became famous for a wide range of products, the truth is that the company's lasting success was built on the back of a handbag. Not just any handbag, of course – this was the famous La Lune "Clothilde" bag. Ever since its launch in 1954, this handbag has been known to fashion insiders as the Golden Handbag, due to its status as the bestselling La Lune handbag of all time. In fact, those who know about such things say it is the bestselling handbag of all time (its only close rival being the equally famous Hermès "Kelly" bag). It is this handbag – the Clothilde bag – that gave the curse its name. Because what many don't know is that sewn within the elegant seams of this famous handbag is the story of a cruel deception…

One evening, while at a party on a private yacht anchored a stone's throw away from the palace in Monaco, François was seated next to a French princess. (By this time, François's winning combination of charm and success meant that he was beginning to lead the sort of life that many of his clients did.) But this wasn't just any princess…HRH Princess Clothilde of Bourbon-Condanza was descended from the last king of France. Lineage aside, she was beautiful and graceful. The first time the princess had topped the best-dressed lists she'd done so wearing a dress made of eighteenth-century curtains she'd found in the attic of her family's chateau – and from that moment on her unique sense of style had ensured she became a fashion icon. In short, she was the perfect client. And someone like François La Lune would certainly not allow such a prized opportunity to escape.

During the first course of the dinner, the princess didn't deign to even acknowledge François's presence. She continued to ignore him all through the second course as well. François, well aware that he had only two courses left in which to capture her attention, decided that drastic measures were needed. In a bold move that became legendary at the time (and is still quoted in nearly every magazine article or book written about the La Lune fashion empire), François accidentally – or so he claimed – spilled his glass of red wine into the princess's lap. Never mind – the desired effect was achieved. In the ensuing commotion, with many exclamations and offers of assistance he had managed to attract Clothilde's attention.

By the time the spilled wine had been cleaned up and the cheese course was served, Clothilde had visions of handbags dancing in her eyes. And when dessert came, François told her that his design studio had just recently shown him drawings of a new handbag that would be perfect for her. François promised to have the handbag made in a variety of colours – crocodile skins especially *dyed to match her favourite dresses – and different leathers to match her every outfit. He would even name it after her, he said.*

And that is how the Clothilde bag was born. It quickly became a sensation. The ensuing press generated by the princess – she wore the bag everywhere, from a private reception with the Pope to the Crown Prince of Sweden's wedding – ensured that the La Lune name became a byword for luxury; from then on the company flourished. Of course, over the following years the house of La Lune designed many other handbags, but none came close to attaining the mythical status of the Golden Handbag...

But now we must backtrack again: as we know, when François inherited his portion of the saddlery business he very slowly and very carefully phased out the saddles and phased in the diaries, agendas and fashion. So far so good. But François quickly realized that there was one major impediment to attaining the goal of becoming a well-known fashion brand: his father's old business partner, Hector Merlette. Not that Hector was especially meddling or aggressive, but he was there – a grey, grumpy presence, always banging on about how to improve this or that saddle. And saddles, as François saw it, were no longer the way forward. So he asked Hector if he could buy him out.

Now, Hector may have been conservative and stubborn, but, nevertheless he was not completely blind as to which way the wind was blowing. Even if he'd never admit it openly, he knew that the future of the company – if it was to grow as François intended – did, in fact, rest in fashion, and not just leather goods and horse tack. However, Hector was not the least bit interested in the many fabric samples and perfume prototypes that François bombarded him with. François's plans to create a fashion powerhouse did not stir much enthusiasm in Hector's old heart: what Hector loved was leather – and he had no intention of giving up this passion. To that end, he decided to sell his share of the company to François. And, he told himself, once the sale went through, he'd concentrate on making leather goods.

However, before leaving the company, Hector happened to show some of his designs to François and asked him what he thought. François didn't say much, although his eyes did seem to keep returning to the drawings of a particularly elegant handbag that Hector had designed. Hector didn't think anything of it at the time, but a year later, long after he had parted ways with La Lune, Hector was shocked to see François unveil the Clothilde bag. To say it looked suspiciously like Hector's design would have been an understatement: the bag was an outright copy of the very drawings he'd shown François before leaving the company, the very bag he'd been about to bring to market himself. The shape and size – even the gold metal handles – they were all his ideas! Furious, he called on François and demanded financial compensation, and a public acknowledgement that the Clothilde bag was his design. François declined. And to shut old Hector up for good, François decided to sue him for design piracy – and he won.

Somehow, mysteriously, all of Hector's original drawings had disappeared. François's design studio on the other hand, had drawing after drawing with which to prove the bag's provenance. Hector cried foul play, but by this time François was too powerful and, before you could say au revoir, Hector was penniless and relegated to the social backwaters. After a lifetime of hard work at the forefront of Parisian style (even if it was mostly for horses), his death didn't even warrant a one-line mention in the style section of the Figaro newspaper. In fact, apart from the Art Deco profile of the little blackbird that adorns every La Lune box and label (merlette means "blackbird" in French), there isn't the faintest vestige left of the hard-working Merlettes in fashion.

But don't think Hector went without a fight. On his deathbed he called for his lawyer and dictated a letter. In it, he cursed François's family and decreed that the La Lune fashion empire would not survive another two generations. Their greed, he said, would be the death of them; they would be helpless to prevent their inborn rapacity from tearing their family and business apart. One by one they would disappear under Greed's voracious *spell until there was nothing left of either them or their empire…*

"So that is the curse: that each La Lune will disappear, one by one, until every one of them has felt Hector's loss and humiliation," Aunt V said as she stood up to stretch.

"And they *are* disappearing one by one! No wonder they feel the curse has come alive…" Ellie whispered.

"What happened to Clothilde?" I asked.

"She died – on François's sixtieth birthday. It was quite horrible, actually. She'd been driving back to Paris early one morning after a party at the La Lune chateau in Normandy. On the outskirts of a small farming town she ran a red light and hit a tractor. In the police report it was written that she hadn't stopped – that she'd been unable to – because the golden handles of her Clothilde bag had become entangled with the gear stick… I've heard that from that moment on, François began to believe in the curse, that he interpreted Clothilde's tragic end as some sort of signal from Hector – and did everything in his power to keep the curse at bay."

"How? How can you keep a curse at bay?" Sebastian asked.

"Well, the curse clearly states that it is the family's inherent greed that will wreak havoc upon them, right? So, François figured that if he kept his family working hard, under his watchful eye, and taught them the value of money, they wouldn't have the time or inclination to want more."

"How did he do that?"

"He worked hard to make himself rich. Then he paid his son and daughter very good salaries as long as they worked for the company *and* lived under his roof. That way he could control them. If they asked for anything extravagant – anything he considered 'greedy' – he made them work for a soup kitchen instead. Of course, everything is relative and François's idea of what constituted extravagant was more generous than most."

"And they complied?" Ellie asked. "I couldn't imagine anyone wanting to live with their parents for ever – no matter how much is on offer."

"François's son, Patrick, was extremely spoiled from birth. He wouldn't have survived for more than a minute outside the family cocoon – although, having said that, he was a good businessman. And François was delighted when his daughter became a nun. Locked away, she was impervious to greed. She died some time ago. And Patrick, in turn has applied his father's policy to his sons and daughters. He's always believed in the curse – don't ask me why."

"And what about Hector?" Sebastian asked. "Didn't he have any family at all?"

"Good question," Aunt V answered. "I don't know...but perhaps—" She stopped to pick a minuscule ball of lint from her black cashmere jumper.

"Perhaps what?" I asked.

"Perhaps it would be interesting to find out if there are any Merlettes still alive. By rights, they are owed something – remuneration for Hector's stolen design, a public apology, something. Although I don't know how they'd prove that François stole Hector's design…"

I was silent for a moment as I mulled my aunt's idea over. "You mean, there might be someone – someone directly related to Hector Merlette – who knows about the theft of Hector's drawings and is now desperate for revenge? And maybe even a bucket of cash from the company?"

My aunt nodded.

"It's worth a look," Sebastian said.

"Yes, it is – tomorrow," Aunt V answered. "Right now, it's time someone got ready for their first photo shoot. Oh, and, Axelle, you can stop doing that, you know."

"Doing what?"

"That. What you just did. Pushing your glasses up your nose. You don't have them any more, remember?"

I thanked my lucky stars (yet again!) that I was out of Aunt V's grasp for most of this week. Her powers of observation were inhuman.

Ellie called for a taxi, and when it finally came she and Sebastian got up to leave. Ellie would drop Sebastian off at the police station where he'd left his scooter, then carry on home. Tomorrow morning she'd swing by and pick me up on her way to the shoot. My sidekick, meanwhile, would begin his morning following the trail of Hector Merlette at home on his computer, then, later perhaps, at the city records department. We'd meet after the shoot.

He wanted to help – had helped a lot already, in fact – and with all the modelling Hervé was piling onto my schedule, I knew I could use the extra hand...

"And remember: if you have any questions, call me. And stick together – safety in numbers and all that. And don't forget to help Axelle with her walk," Aunt V called out as Ellie and Sebastian ran down the stairs.

What a day: hair and glasses gone, another disappearance, a new friend, a sidekick, a modelling career, a narrowly avoided attempt on my life – and a cache of letters to read through.

I took the first letter from the bundle with me to bed (after carefully hiding the rest in my room), but sleep overtook me before I could even open it. My eyes were shut quicker than you can say Dior.

Belle was no longer alone.

Someone else had been dragged into the room. Not that she had any idea who was sharing this rat-infested prison with her. They were refusing or unable to speak and there was no light: no window, no candle, no lamp.

Darkness engulfed her.

She'd tried to find out who the other captive was, had attempted to question her jailer when she'd been brought her daily ration of thin soup. But a hard slap across the face had silenced her.

She'd stick to silence.

TUESDAY MORNING

My First Shoot

"Why so early?" I asked as I yanked my jumper over my head, croissant in mouth, and climbed into the back seat of the taxi next to Ellie. We had said 8.45 a.m. and it was now only 8.35.

"I like to be early."

"But I thought models were always late."

"Not any more – those days are over. I'm a businesswoman, Axelle. I have to be professional. Besides, you'll see – I become troublesome at lunch: no milk, wheat, red meat, or white sugar. By showing up at the job on time, I feel I've earned whatever trouble the client and crew have to go through to find me a lunch I can eat. Plus I love charging for overtime – and that only goes down well when the client can't say I arrived late. You know, clients love to complain to the agency. They think they'll get some kind of price break or something."

"Clients do that?"

"Absolutely! Give them a chance and they'll do it every time. Especially when you're just starting out. They'd be much more careful complaining about me now."

After I'd popped the last bit of croissant into my mouth, I opened the day's *Figaro* newspaper, which Aunt V had put in my bag. *Are The La Lunes Cursed?* screamed the headline.

"Did you see this?" I asked Ellie.

In answer she took her phone out of her bag and scrolled through it. "Here," she said, handing it to me, "look at this. I get goose pimples just reading it. It's from *Le Monde*. '*Jamais deux sans trois!*' It's an old French expression, meaning 'never a second without a third'."

"So they're predicting that a third La Lune will disappear?"

Ellie nodded. "It's all over the morning news. Everyone's saying the family must be cursed – although at this point the media is only guessing. Old François and Patrick have done a good job of hushing up any known facts about it. It's amazing your aunt knows as much as she does."

"Yeah, well, my aunt knows everything." Mentally, I made a note to ask my aunt later *how* she knew so much.

Our taxi pulled up at the base of the Eiffel Tower. As we climbed out, the driver asked Ellie for her autograph. With a smile she obliged, then wished him luck. He waved goodbye to us as we walked towards the bus.

As per Hervé's description, it was big and white with *Pin-Up Studios* written in bold black letters on its side. The driver stood outside, smoking a cigarette. Inside, the make-up artist, Thierry, was unpacking his equipment. Croissants, coffee, tea, and a large basket of fruit were laid out on a small table, and thick puffs of steam and a loud hissing sound emanated from the back of the bus, where the stylist's assistant was busy steaming the wrinkles out of the clothes we'd be wearing later.

Our arrival was followed a minute later by that of the hairdresser, Gilles, and the stylist, Murielle. They knew Ellie, of course, and had already heard about me. They were friendly and charming, but as they took off their black coats and set down their assorted bags, I could feel them looking me up and down, silently checking how well I measured up. I found their scrutiny unnerving. At home I was a nerd and everybody knew it. Nobody (except my mum) expected my sartorial sense to rise above that. But being in fashion meant I should *look* like I was IN FASHION, because, let's face it, fashion is all about the clothes.

While Gilles began straightening Ellie's hair with a pair of hot tongs, Thierry sat me down in a chair next to Ellie. We faced a large mirror surrounded with oversized light bulbs, just like in those clichéd dressing rooms they show in the movies. Laid out on the worktop just beneath the mirror were Thierry's tools. About twenty different make-up brushes and a large assortment of foundations, powders, eye shadows, blushes, pencils, and other tricks of the trade lay neatly arranged on a clean white towel.

"Today we're going for a very strong feminine look –

almost retro," he said, as he took a chunky black diary out of his bag and opened it to a double-page spread of drawings and collages. "We want something mysterious, almost dark, but we'll add bits of colour – like here, for instance," he said as he pointed to an old black-and-white photograph of Audrey Hepburn dressed in a black turtleneck jumper, but with pink flowers – they looked like orchids – drawn across one of her eyes, and then in a diminishing trail from there to the edge of the page. I really couldn't tell you what it was supposed to look like or symbolize, but it did look pretty. There was an added flash of glitter on her eyelids too. "See – soft but strong. Hard and dark but still light and feminine. Contrast."

I didn't really see, but never mind – I was here to see the La Lunes. Speaking of whom, Rose had just stepped into the bus completely out of the blue.

"*Quelle surprise!* I haven't seen her at one of these shoots in years," murmured Thierry.

"Hi, Axelle," Rose said shyly, her voice girly and slightly strained. "I'm Rose La Lune. Great to meet you. Is this your first shoot?" Her eyes were swollen and red – she'd obviously been crying. Why was she here, talking to me?

"Yes," I mumbled as Thierry massaged moisturizer onto my face.

"Dom is really looking forward to meeting and working with you," she continued. "He really pushed to have you booked after he heard all the buzz about you at Miriam's yesterday... Well, anyway, I just wanted to say hello... I'll let you get to work."

Dom was really looking forward to meeting me? But he'd met me yesterday as Ellie and I were leaving the agency. Although, then again, I could have been an extension of the wall for all the attention he'd given me. Anyway, if I'd been booked at Dom's insistence, perhaps that would explain why I was here, despite all that had happened at the showroom yesterday with Claude.

"Axelle, you must hold your head still," said Thierry as he concentrated on applying a foundation he'd mixed together on the back of his hand. He'd used about four different bottles of coloured liquid to make it, but what was especially interesting was that he applied it with light, feathery strokes of his *fingers* – not the usual thick sponge my mum and Jenny used. I couldn't wait to tell Jenny about that.

Next came a few dabs of concealer. "Not that you have any shadows or dark circles under your eyes," he said, "but the photographer's lighting can be so strong that even flawless skin ends up looking blotchy and grey." Then he applied a fine dusting of a yellowish powder – *not* the pink stuff the girls at my school used – with a large soft brush. I couldn't help but sigh as he flicked it gently over my face. It felt wonderful...

It felt less wonderful, however, when a few minutes later, as Thierry was applying eyeshadow with a long handled brush, Murielle the stylist decided it was the perfect moment to hang various earrings in front of my ears to see how they looked on me. Then Gilles, the hairdresser, began to twist and hold my hair this way and that as he studied my reflection in the mirror. As if that wasn't enough, my hips were twisted to the side so that Murielle's assistant, Coco, could slip different pairs of shoes onto my feet to see how they fitted. I felt like screaming. I was being poked, prodded, pulled and painted all at the same time. I was starting to understand why models got such generous pay cheques: patience does have a price.

This was supposed to be glamorous?

I stole a look over at Ellie. She was sitting, cool as a cucumber, her hair wound round the largest rollers I'd ever seen, giving Hervé orders over her phone like an army general. Suddenly she began to wave her hand furiously towards us. Once she had our attention she began to pucker her lips like a hungry carp (and she was still on the phone). I had no idea what she was doing. Maybe it was some kind of model warm-up for all the pouting she was expected to do later?

Murielle, however, understood immediately what the fishy-lip-puckering was about. In a panicky whisper, she cried, "*Mon Dieu!* Quick, Thierry – she needs some gloss!"

"*Ah non! Quelle catastrophe!* Dry lips!" he said, as he threw the eye-shadow brush down and grabbed the gloss.

Both Thierry and Gilles leaped to Ellie's rescue. I watched, fascinated, as she turned her chin up towards Thierry, lips perfectly pouted and positioned for the careful strokes of his lip brush. Then (and she was *still* on the phone), as Gilles gently swept back a few loose hairs with his fingers, she closed her eyes. She looked as if she were praying.

There was no point asking her how she felt about the incessant prodding. I might just as well ask a fish what it thought about water.

"Hi! You must be Axelle." Dom bounded into the bus, camera in tow. "You look even better in life than in the composite Hervé sent me," he said.

Thierry was hard at work applying some dark brown pencil to my right eyebrow which meant I had only my half-opened left eye to look through – although even that did nothing to diminish Dom's hotness.

"Actually, we met yesterday. You're Dom." While I realized there was a difference between the Axelle of yesterday morning and the one of today, still...did I look that different? Sebastian, after all, had recognized me immediately.

"If we met yesterday then I must be suffering from a major case of short-term memory loss," he laughed.

I wanted to answer him, but Thierry had begun to apply mascara to my top lashes.

"Now, Axelle, you must hold still and look downwards. Exactly, like that...good. Dom, she'll have to talk to you later." Then, as Dom moved off to chat to Murielle, Thierry whispered to me, "He has to talk to every pretty girl that crosses his path." Two minutes later he said, "*Et voilà!* Now I'm finished. You may stretch your legs."

"Ah! It's you," Claude greeted me as he stuck his head through the open door of the bus. I turned round and saw that while he sounded pleased enough to see me, he didn't look it. Despite his breezy manner, he seemed tightly coiled, like a snake about to strike.

Was I starting to get paranoid about the La Lunes or was there something odd about Rose's overly – in my eyes – warm greeting and now Claude's mildly sinister one?

They couldn't possibly know I'd snuck into their house yesterday...could they?

Before I could answer Claude – let alone start asking him about the disappearances – Dom and the rest of the crew surged forward to greet him and a discussion began about the day's shoot. Thierry brought out his collage book to show Dom and Claude the same pages he'd shown me, Murielle asked questions about the clothes, and Gilles twisted and held Ellie's hair to show his various ideas. My questioning would have to wait.

I poured myself some iced tea and then slipped out of the bus for a bit of fresh air. Carefully I sipped from the glass with tiny slurps; I was under strict orders from Thierry not to smile, laugh, or basically move any facial muscles. This was to stop the foundation and powder carefully layered on my face from cracking. Great. I was finally within talking range of the La Lunes, but, because of all the gunk on my face, I couldn't even move my lips.

At least I could still read.

I found a quiet corner near a neatly trimmed hedge at the bottom of one of the tower pillars and sat down with my iced tea. Then I reached into my shoulder bag and pulled out the bundle of letters I'd found yesterday. I couldn't wait any longer – I was too curious – and now seemed as good a time as any. Besides, the crew probably wouldn't be finished fiddling with Ellie for another half an hour. Carefully I took the first one in the pack – the one I'd meant to read last night before I conked out – and unfolded it. Fortunately, my French was up to the task. Now if these letters would only give me some clues to help find Belle...

> *Paris, 5th August, 1930*
>
> *Dear Adelaide,*
>
> *As you know, my delicate constitution prevents my family and me from joining you in Normandy, but I have a new-found reason to be thankful for this otherwise deplorable enforced stay in Paris this August. I am positively trembling with excitement: my darling daughter Giselle has a suitor! And it's all thanks to you, Adelaide!*
>
> *Tall, dark and handsome, and a businessman – well, I'll stop as I have no need to describe him to you. You see, Giselle's new suitor is none other than your dear friend Monsieur Pierre Roux. He has charmed us all and Giselle*

has rapidly developed a soft spot for this most gallant cavalier.

Thank you so much for the letter of introduction you gave him. By coincidence, he met Giselle straight away. Giselle had been walking back from the park with Hector (whom she'd miraculously persuaded to join her for a walk – you know how her brother loves being in the office, even in this stifling heat), when they saw Pierre standing just outside your gate. To say he was baffled at seeing your house closed up is an understatement – he'd expected to drive up together with you to Normandy! Obviously there's been a misunderstanding about the dates – although I confess that at this point I feel nothing but gratitude for this!

Of course we invited him to dine with us that very evening and now he's decided to stay on in Paris for a few more days! Now what do you think of that? As I always tell my dear Monsieur Merlette: a young man who makes a spontaneous change of plans can be motivated by one thing only – his heart!

Happily, I find my constitution has rallied sufficiently to allow me the pleasure of writing to you with this news. I believe Pierre plans on joining you at the end of next week. And, if my motherly instincts are anything to go by, dare I say that you may need a new hat by spring?

With a big hug,
Thérèse

I read through the letter twice more. The trail of a drunken spider would have been easier to follow than the extravagant flourishes of Thérèse's handwriting. At least the vocabulary used was straightforward (if breathless) – and, fortunately, the name on the back of the envelope was clear: *Merlette.*

Logically then, Thérèse was Thérèse Merlette; and Thérèse Merlette was the mother of Giselle and Hector – who were siblings. And, from what I could gather, a love story was unfolding, its principal players being Thérèse Merlette's daughter Giselle and a tall, dark and handsome stranger called Pierre Roux.

But what had me humming with quiet excitement was the brief reference to Giselle's brother, Hector. Could this be the same Hector Merlette of the curse? The letter was written in 1930. Hector Merlette worked with François La Lune in the forties and fifties – so the timing could easily fit. Plus, his mother, Thérèse, made that cryptic comment about how he loved to work. That definitely chimed with the image my aunt had painted last night of the old-fashioned, methodical and office-bound Hector.

I looked up quickly at the bus. Through the open door I could see Gilles's back as he wielded a hairdryer over Ellie's head. I folded up the letter and reached back into my shoulder bag for the packet, slipped the first one back under the rubber band, then took out the second one...

Dear Thérèse,

My dearest friend, the news you send me is of the most worrying kind. I'm afraid I will give you a terrible shock with what I must say, so pray do sit down before reading any further.

Unfortunately, I must emphatically state that we have never made the acquaintance of Monsieur Pierre Roux. Furthermore, we never invited anyone to join us on our journey north. I'm truly perturbed to think that someone – an imposter – has used our name to infiltrate your good graces. Please don't believe a word he says! On the contrary, if I were you I'd immediately report him to the police! He may be a part of this ring of thieves that break into people's homes when they're away. Oh, Thérèse! I'm truly sorry for such a troublesome, worrying business. Unfortunately, I fear the police may be your only recourse at this late date...

I anxiously await your next letter...

Yours,

Adelaide

I took a deep breath and folded the letter back up. I didn't need to read it again; the drama was all too clear: Mr Pierre Roux was not who he claimed to be!

Okay. But so what? It was Hector that interested me – I needed him to resurface. Hopefully he'd make more than a cameo appearance in the other letters. *In the meantime,* I thought, as I reached again for the bundle of letters, *I'd better keep reading.*

Suddenly my phone rang, making me jump. I'd been so absorbed by the letters that I'd forgotten about the outside world. I shook the spilled tea from my hand and reached for my phone. It was Sebastian.

"Did I call at a bad time?"

"No." I wiped my hand on my jeans, slipped the bundle of letters back into my bag and stood up. "I've just been reading the first couple of letters."

"And? Do they have anything to do with the disappearances?"

"Not that I can see, but I've only just started...although I've come across Hector's name."

"Sounds promising..."

"I'll tell you all later. Where are you?"

Sebastian was across town at City Records, searching for a trace of Hector Merlette's family. It sounded like fun – certainly a lot more fun than having my face and hair pulled in every direction, not to mention the fact that I wasn't even allowed to crack a smile. I said as much to him.

"You've only been working for an hour and already you've become one of those models who complain about the unglamorous working conditions," he said with a laugh. "Remember: for you, it's a disguise. And you couldn't have a better one for finding out about the La Lunes."

That's what I'd thought too – until this morning. Thanks to my make-up, I was reduced to mumbling, and even if I'd been able to talk properly, it wasn't as if I'd had chance to pull a La Lune aside for a one-on-one chat. Some disguise!

"Anyway," Sebastian continued, "so far you're not missing anything. Wiki had one sentence on the Merlettes – most of it false – and I couldn't find a lead anywhere else. If I do find something interesting I'll call you. Promise."

"Okay, okay," I sighed. "Just remember: any little thing could be important, so get it all down, will you, please? And send it to me?"

"*Bien sûr, mademoiselle.*" I could feel him smiling down the line. "Anything else?"

"Yes. If you happen to come across anything on Le Vau, let me know."

"You still think there's something to that?"

"Yes, I do. Remember Darius's room? It was messy, but his notes were all very precise. He wasn't isn't the type to just mention something casually."

"Right. I'll keep it in mind – promise. And I'll call you later after I've done more digging."

I slipped my phone into my bag and tilted my head back as far as I could. As the sun broke through a few fast-moving clouds, I closed my eyes and breathed deeply, basking in the fleeting warmth. A few seconds later I opened my eyes. Thinking of the clues in Darius's room had made me remember the missing shoe from Belle's wardrobe. Why was *one* shoe missing? The thought wouldn't let go. I had to find an answer...

By the time Ellie and I were needed on set it was nearly noon. According to Ellie this was normal. "But don't worry," she said, "we're only doing four shots today. We'll be finished by six. They know I have to be at my first show for hair and make-up at six-thirty." Ellie would be walking for Louis Vuitton and Dior tonight in the opening Fashion Week shows, so, despite the relaxed start, we were on a tight schedule.

Apparently, on some busy catalogue shoots models could be expected to do over twenty shots per day. But on a sophisticated advertising shoot, the norm was more likely to be around four or five.

We began on the second level of the tower, at the Jules Verne restaurant. We waited while Dom and his assistants took light readings and checked equipment. Thierry, Murielle and Gilles, meanwhile, were doing their frenzied best to make every last hair, thread, and bit of glitter adorning Ellie look perfect. Claude hovered around the set, jittery and jumpy, pacing in an endless loop from Dom to Ellie to the storyboard. (A storyboard is a series of drawings or photographs put together to illustrate the "story" the shoot should be telling – a sort of navigation system for the entire crew.)

Rose stood in a corner, talking on her phone, her back to us as she looked out at the view. I, too, turned to look at the view; from this height Paris looked like a toy city. As I watched the tiny tourists far below, a black Peugeot saloon car identical to the one that almost hit me drove into the parking lot. A tall, lean figure stepped out, then stood and tilted his head back and looked up before making his way to the nearest lift. I wondered if it could be Philippe de Vandrille.

Finally, Ellie was ready and led to a table. Freed of their main star, Murielle, Thierry and Gilles came to work their frenzied magic on *moi*. Once I was deemed photo-ready, I, too, was led to the table and asked to sit beside Ellie. This was it! I was about to be photographed for the first time as a fashion model. I sat perched in position, trying not to breathe too hard or look nervous. Dom's face was completely hidden behind his enormous camera. One of his assistants, meanwhile, was holding a large flexible disc of metallic gold fabric – a reflector – underneath Ellie and me to soften the light.

To be honest, I wasn't really sure what was going on. Everyone was quiet and Dom was moving around, changing positions every few seconds, as if he was trying to find the right angle to begin shooting from. Ellie wasn't saying anything but I could see her making minute movements with her lips, neck, and hands. *This time*, I thought, *she really is warming up.* Then, a moment later, Ellie elegantly picked up a freshly fried *pomme frite* between her manicured fingers and put it into her perfectly painted mouth. *Fantastic*, I thought, *we can start with lunch while we're waiting. I'm starving!* That was all the encouragement I needed: leaning over in front of her, I grabbed two handfuls of fries and greedily began wolfing them down.

Then all chaos broke loose.

"Hey, stop! Axelle, we're shooting the picture, not eating lunch!" Dom yelled. "Thierry, would you check her make-up please?"

Thierry was at my side within seconds and carefully began wiping salt off my lips. *"Oh non, oh non!* My lipstick!" he cried. At the same time I heard Ellie giggle and Claude order a new plate of fries.

"But I saw you eat one," I mumbled through my fry-filled mouth.

"Axelle," she said, through a bout of the giggles, "I put a fry into my mouth, but I didn't eat it. It's a prop. See, like this." With a quick flick of her wrist she plucked an unsuspecting fry off the plate and popped it into her opened mouth, but she continued to hold it with her fingers. I watched as the fry hovered over the best known teeth in fashion. After a few seconds, she pulled it back out.

"Axelle," said Dom, as he walked up to where Ellie and I sat, "the fries are a prop, Okay? They're not lunch. So, please, pay attention to me and try not to eat the props, all right?"

Like a hamster at snack time, I looked up at Dom with bursting cheeks and startled eyes. I swallowed hard and nodded yes as the lump of half-chewed potatoes made its way down my throat.

Thierry quickly retouched my lipstick while Ellie instructed me. "The camera doesn't make much noise, but it was clicking all the time. Didn't you see me moving?"

"I thought you were doing some kind of model warm-up exercises."

Ellie rolled her eyes.

"Well, now I know."

A fresh plate of fries was brought out and Dom resumed shooting. This time I made sure to listen for the camera. It was like a faint humming in the background – I was soon able to tune in and out of it. In fact, I learned by watching Ellie. She reacted instinctively to the camera and seemed to have a sort of sixth sense which told her when she should be "on". Keeping her movements to an elegant minimum, she continued to hold a fry to her mouth, only now I knew she wasn't actually eating it. All the while she managed to keep her eyes wide open like a kitten's. Sometimes she'd look up or down, other times left or right; only occasionally would she deign to flatter the camera with a direct look – and whenever she did Dom would yell, "Beautiful! *Très jolie*, Ellie! *Très belle!*"

Meanwhile, I sat beside her. I wasn't even sure how much of me was in the photo, but sometimes Dom would yell out, "More profile, Axelle. Yes, like that. Okay, now more to the left. Right. Left. *Super!* Beautiful! Beautiful!"

Wistfully, I waited for him to yell out, "Eat the fries, Axelle! Eat the fries!" But he didn't.

Every few minutes, Gilles, Thierry and Murielle would dash in and check our hair, make-up, and clothes. After a while I ended up tuning out of the proceedings altogether. I thought about the disappearances, or, more specifically, the *timing* of the disappearances. Why now, during Fashion Week?

And if it wasn't counterfeiters or the curse, then Philippe was right: surely it had to be one of the group who'd been at the La Lune mansion, both Saturday night and yesterday. But which one of them? And why?

"Axelle? Axelle – you can relax now."

With a start, I snapped to attention as I heard my name. Ellie was standing by me, smiling. "We're finished with this shot and we're going to have lunch now. You looked beautiful and you did really well. I know Dom, and I can tell that he's really pleased with the way you worked."

The way I worked? All I did was sit there and move every now and then. I said as much to Ellie.

"Yeah, but it was the way you moved: slowly but surely. And your profile. You have a wonderful profile."

I didn't believe a word of what she'd just said, but it didn't matter.

Lunch was delicious – and I finally had my plate of fries! – but we were on too tight a schedule for a leisurely meal. As soon as Ellie and I had had our fill, Thierry and Gilles began to freshen up our make-up. Then Murielle dressed me and I was sent to help Dom test the lighting while Ellie's hair was restyled.

One of Dom's assistants led me to a lift and we went up a level on the tower. A strong gust of wind hit me as I stepped onto the viewing platform. From this height, Paris looked like a detailed painting, the wide boulevards reduced to mere lines that dissected the little blocks of colour the buildings and parks had become. I could even see the place where I'd nearly been run over yesterday.

"Nice, *non*?" I jumped back from the railing as I felt a hand on the small of my back. "Hey, don't worry – it's only me!" Dom was smiling at me, camera in hand.

Turning my back to the view, I faced him and told myself to relax. The dizzying height was making me nervous. I took a breath and forced myself to focus on Dom instead. Quickly I brought up a subject I wanted to know more about: Rose.

Earlier I'd seen her drive off, so as an easy way of bringing the conversation around to her I asked Dom where she'd gone to.

"Spanish lesson," he answered.

"Has she always liked studying languages?"

"No. Not especially – or, rather, not that I know of.

My sister Rose is an enigma. I know she's smart and rational – she spends most of her time adding numbers – but she's also awkward and sometimes prone to hysterics. And look at her hair at the moment: one day it looks great, the next it's like a bird's nest. Why? And she's been taking Spanish lessons since last summer, but I haven't heard her say so much as *hola*. Anyway, she's a mystery to me – as if we don't have enough of those in our family at the moment." Dom broke off, head bent over his camera. He was looking at the tiny display screen on the back of it.

"Here, look. This is more interesting – you look amazing. And this one's good too. Oh, this one's beautiful… You're definitely going to get some great shots for your book," he said, as he stopped looking at his camera and focused on me.

His eyes were a dark green with flecks of gold and, despite living in the city his arms were tanned as if he spent his days outdoors. "We have a house in Normandy where I go on the weekends," he said, as if in answer to my thoughts. I quickly pretended to look at the view, hoping to hide my flushed face. "If you're here this weekend you should come with me. Ellie should come too," he said, as he moved the light meter around me.

Out of the corner of my eye, I saw Claude approach along the platform, gaze directed at me.

"Be careful, Dom," he said when he'd reached us. "We wouldn't want anything to happen to our new model, would we?"

Although Claude had directed his comment to Dom, who was still reading his light meter, he was smiling at me. Clearly his macabre joke was meant for my ears. "Why?" I asked. "Are you expecting someone else to disappear?"

"Absolutely. According to the newspapers, we're *all* doomed to disappear – so be careful when you're with us, or you might too."

Did he always speak in veiled threats?

"Speak for yourself, Claude," Dom said, as he came back to my side. "Personally, I don't plan on disappearing any time soon – and I certainly hope you don't, Axelle. In fact" – he locked his eyes on mine again – "I'm hoping you'll spend some time with me tomorrow after the Juno bag launch." He smiled as he read the stunned look on my face. "Come on," he teased, "what's your aunt going to show you: one fashion show after another with some modelling work in between? You're in Paris – there's a lot more to this city than just that. Let me show you around. We can meet at the launch and go from there. Presumably you'll be accompanying your aunt?"

The last thing I'd expected was an invitation from Dom. Caught completely by surprise, I struggled to find something – anything – to say.

"Listen, you don't have to give me an answer now," he said smoothly. "Give me your number and I'll call you later."

The last time a member of the opposite sex had asked me for my number was at Christmas. Robin Winterbottom had stopped me as we were leaving class and asked if he could call me. That evening, he did. Jenny had been beside herself with excitement when I'd answered. What with all of her hand signals and suppressed giggling, I'd had to leave the room because I couldn't concentrate on what Robin had been saying. As it turned out, the conversation didn't need much concentration: he'd called to ask if he could speak to my dad about getting some work experience at the aquarium over the holidays (my dad is head marine biologist at the London Aquarium).

Dom, on the other hand, was presenting me with an entirely different situation – one that necessitated whatever concentration I could muster. Just making eye contact was difficult – like looking into a vortex. How was I supposed to last one-on-one with him? And, if I was asking myself that question, did it mean I was already planning on accepting his date?

"Anyway, Axelle, think about it," he added. "But right now, we need to get to work."

I watched as he left to check the storyboard. Maybe, if I could manage to look at him for longer than a minute without turning bright red, tomorrow night would be the perfect time to ask him a few useful questions?

"I hope all the rumours don't scare you away before we've finished shooting today." It was Philippe de Vandrille. His voice was deep and cultured, his English perfect. He looked like a character from one of those old black-and-white films they run on Sunday afternoons: the tall, impeccably-dressed foreigner. And like in the films, I thought, he probably only said witty things.

"Not at all – I find it interesting. With such a large family full of…uh…lively characters, I think it's only natural there'd be some stories to tell." Then I added, "I'm especially intrigued by the rumours of a curse. Do you believe a curse exists?"

He seemed to seriously consider my question before slowly answering, "No, actually, I don't."

Hmm…well, that was the end of that, I thought. *Right. Change tracks, Axelle.* "Then who – or what – is making the La Lunes disappear?" Suddenly, thinking of my aunt and what she'd suggested last night, I was struck with inspiration: "Perhaps a Merlette?"

A look of surprise swiftly passed over him. "There are no Merlettes left, I believe."

I shrugged my shoulders and took a sip of water. "Can I ask you one last question?"

"This must be the last one, otherwise I'll start to think that this is a ploy of yours to charge us for overtime," he said, with a smile.

"Do you have a cat?"

He raised his eyebrows. "A cat?"

I nodded. I was thinking of the CAT I'd seen in Claude's phone and while I doubted Claude's CAT had anything to do with the four-legged variety, how else could I ask the question without raising too much suspicion? For all I knew, Philippe could have been in on CAT, too.

"I haven't. Why do you ask?"

"Just something I came across," I mumbled vaguely. My question didn't seem to illicit anything more than a cheery bewilderment from him, so I dropped it.

"Is there anything else, or may I be relieved of my interrogation?" he teased.

I thanked him, then watched as he turned and left. A moment later I was called on set.

The rest of the afternoon went by in a whirlwind of posing and face powder. Frustratingly, apart from Dom, I never got close to the La Lunes again. And even he, apart from briefly touching on Rose, had avoided any mention of his family. So much for my chance to be a detective! Argh! Maybe this whole model thing had been a mistake.

I changed into my own clothes and was standing at the bottom of the tower about to check my phone messages, when from behind me an arm reached across my shoulders and a now-familiar voice whispered into my ear, "I'll call you about tomorrow. But at the very least I'll see you at the Juno bag launch, right?"

His eyes were smiling, his mouth teasing. After a moment, I felt Dom's arm slip away. "Definitely," I answered calmly, reminding myself to breathe.

"What are you doing tonight?"

"I'm off to my aunt's."

Dom rolled his eyes. "I told you you've got to see more..."

At that moment Sebastian pulled up nearby. I waved to him.

"I thought you said you were going to your aunt's?" Dom queried.

"I am – with a friend." I quickly said goodbye and then stepped right into my next embarrassing situation. You see, when I'd accepted Sebastian's offer to come by and fetch me after the shoot, I had completely forgotten that *he rides a scooter*. And, like most scooters, his could seat two people – as long as those two people were sandwiched together. Or, more specifically, as long as the front of the back passenger was squished up against the back of the driver and the former's arms were locked around the latter's torso. And you know what that means: yours truly was going to have to press what little she didn't have against Sebastian's back – while locking her arms around him.

Ellie was laughing as Sebastian and I drove off into the sunset, my painfully hunched position ensuring daylight came between my chest and his back.

TUESDAY EVENING

Connecting the Polka Dots

We zoomed in and out of the traffic with ease. Sebastian was a confident driver and, holding onto him, I felt less frightened than I'd thought I would. Slowly I relaxed and dropped all thoughts of Dom and his family as the fresh evening air ruffled the ends of my hair and blew the back of my jacket out. Now I understood why Sebastian wore a leather jacket and biker boots.

Boots! I'd completely forgotten!

Why was I wasting my time thinking about Sebastian's boots when what I wanted was to find out about Belle's missing platform shoe? I tapped him on the shoulder and signalled to him to pull over. Thirty seconds later, he did.

"Axelle, are you okay?" He'd taken his helmet off and was looking back at me with concern.

"Yeah, I'm fine. Promise." He raised an eyebrow at me. "But you just reminded me of something. I need your help. Would you mind making a call to the La Lune mansion for me?"

* * *

"*Oui, bonjour, monsieur,* it's the cobbler here…"

We were at the small cafe around the corner from Aunt V's and Sebastian was doing his best to sound helpful, friendly and professional. "We have one from a pair of dark green velvet platform heels belonging to Mademoiselle Belle that will take longer to repair than I thought – the velvet is rather fragile. Would it be all right if I had it delivered at the end of next week?"

There was a pause while the butler called the maid, Maria, who dealt with Belle's clothes. Presently her high-pitched voice was heard on the line. "What?" continued Sebastian. "You say that you never sent in a shoe? Perhaps someone else working in the house—"

At this accusation Maria unleashed a torrent of high-octave chirps. "Well, I have one shoe," answered Sebastian calmly, "and as I told your colleague, I know it's Mademoiselle Belle's. We've worked on this pair before." The high-pitched voice became slightly truculent. "I'm sorry to bother you but perhaps it would be a good idea just to have a look and make sure that the shoe is indeed hers—"

Sebastian held the phone away from his ear as Maria lambasted him in rapid French.

"I'm sure the shoe belongs to Mademoiselle Belle. Yes, I know you've said you haven't sent anything to us – yes, I realize this isn't the season for velvet…but I don't think either one of us would want to inadvertently upset Mademoiselle Belle..."

That last bit did the trick. We waited while Maria went upstairs to have a look.

After a few minutes she came back on the line, her shrill timbre muted to a frosty acceptance that, yes, indeed, one platform shoe was missing. After a few reassurances that the shoe would be ready by the end of next week and some more of the high-pitched chirps, Sebastian hung up.

"How'd I do?" he asked, grinning.

"Perfect," I smiled – and I meant it.

"At least now we know that the shoe really is missing. Maria never sent it out for repairs and she's the only one who ever touches Belle's clothes – Belle only handles her clothes when she's wearing them. So, as it's not on its shelf in the dressing room, it has to be missing." He paused for a moment before continuing, "And surely Maria would have noticed – and said something – if the shoe had been missing for some time. It's tempting to think that the shoe must have gone missing at the same time Belle did...but why would someone need *one* green velvet platform shoe?"

I shrugged my shoulders. "That's what we've got to find out."

"Are you ready?" After the call to Maria, we'd both felt a spot of ice cream was in order, and, while Aunt V's freezer was well-stocked – giant scallops, consommé, sorbet, even a duck or two – ice cream, plain, creamy, white vanilla ice-cream, she most certainly did not have. So we stayed in the cafe.

"I'm all ears," I answered as I dug my spoon deep into the small mountain of whipped cream and hot chocolate sauce that topped the ice cream.

Sebastian pulled a small black notebook from the pocket of his leather jacket. He opened it and, from the inside flap of the tiny cover, took out two slips of paper and pushed them across the table to me. They were carefully cut newspaper photocopies. Just a few lines long, they read:

Le Figaro
Paris, France
le 23 février, 1904
16ème arrondissement – La femme d'Émile Merlette,
Thérèse Merlette, d'un fils.

And:

Le Figaro
Paris, France
le 17 juin, 1915
16ème arrondissement – La femme d'Émile Merlette,
Thérèse Merlette, d'une fille.

"Are these birth announcements?" I asked.

"Yes they are. The names of the newborns aren't given but I've confirmed the boy as being Hector Merlette and the girl is his sister. And, believe it or not, apart from his death certificate, this was the only record of his existence on file."

"What? Nothing else? No marriage licence? Or birth certificate of a child? Or divorce, even?"

"Nope. Nothing. Nada. Hector was born into wealth and privilege and then fifty-six years later he died, penniless and broken. It's just like your aunt told us. And between those two events not much happened – at least not officially."

"Hmm…and I hardly think Hector was the sort of person to do something unofficially, if you know what I mean." I sat silent, my ice cream pushed to the side.

"Axelle…?"

If Sebastian was right – that Hector Merlette died without a wife or child – then the summer love story between Hector's sister, Giselle, and the handsome imposter, Pierre Roux, suddenly took on a new importance. Because if she and Pierre had had a child…and if that child knew that the La Lune fortune was built on the back of his or her uncle's stolen designs…

I held my breath as I finished my thought. There were a lot of "ifs", but the more I turned it over in my mind, the more I felt convinced that Giselle's life held a key to the disappearances. And obviously I wasn't the only one who thought so: why else would the letters have been hidden in haste in a chimney flue?

Well, one thing was clear.

"Earth to Axelle?"

I'd better not let those letters out of my sight.

"Axelle, are you listening?" I nodded as Sebastian finished his last spoonful of ice cream before continuing. "Unfortunately, I was unable to find anything else about Hector's sister either. Like I said, I don't even know her name – that would have meant going to a different department and I ran out of time. I'll go tomorrow. I definitely think she's worth tracing—"

"Giselle."

"Giselle? Giselle what? Is that where you think she is?"

I shook my head and smiled. "No – it's not *where* she is. It's *who* she is. It's her name." I took the two letters out of my bag and handed them to him, finishing my ice cream while he read them.

"Wow," he said quietly as he leaned back in his chair and handed them back to me.

"Exactly. At the very least, it gives us something to follow up on."

We sat silently for a moment, each of us busy with our thoughts. Then Sebastian flashed me his wicked grin and asked, "Have you read the others?"

Shaking my head, I pulled the packet out of my bag and placed it on the table. "No. But I'd say now is the perfect time. Although, before we start, it might be a good idea to order some more ice cream, don't you think?"

> Monaco, 28th August, 1930

Maman,

I know you'll be shocked to read this letter – although, even you must have seen that things were bound to end this way. All my life you've called me flighty. Perhaps – but as this letter shows, in matters of the heart I am not. Despite your greatest efforts to dissuade me I've remained fast to the only person I feel has ever understood me. Monsieur Pierre Roux and I are married – there, now you know. He planned everything. Eventually I'll go back north with him to help him with his business affairs but, for now, we plan on travelling a little.

Don't try to turn back the clock, Maman – it's too late. I'm free, I'm happy, and that's all I've ever wanted. Should you insist on intruding upon our married life we'll have no alternative but to close our door on you for ever.

Anyway, be happy – if not for me, then at least for yourself. After all, you still have good, dependable Hector.

Giselle

"She really has a way with drama," I said. I couldn't wait to tell Jenny about Giselle – it was exactly the kind of story she loved.

"I'll say." I watched as Sebastian ran his hands through his hair. "I wish I could have met this Pierre, though. I'd like to know whether he really was as nasty as he sounds or just totally misunderstood."

"I'd say he must've been the nasty sort – I mean, Giselle was sixteen! Even back then that was young! I bet he thought she was loaded."

Unfortunately, the next letter confirmed my worst suspicions:

Épaignes, 17th February, 1931

Dear Hector,

My dear brother, your kind letter touched me, it really did.

I'm sorry things have turned out as they have – if only you knew how much! But I can't go back. Something in me changed for ever the day I met Pierre and it changed again the day I finally saw him for who he truly is. I'm afraid the picture isn't pretty. I know, I know – Papa and Maman tried to warn me. But, honestly, I don't believe it was him they were trying to warn me against as much as what he represented. Can you understand that distinction?

Anyway, I've made my bed, as the saying goes… But there's more to it than that, Hector (isn't there always?). Before you start thinking that your little sister enjoys wallowing in her troubles, it's not Pierre that keeps me here. I'm expecting a child, Hector – that's what keeps me here.

The baby is due at the end of March. Finally I'll have someone to share this hell with – and someone worth staying sane for. I told you that Pierre's uncle owns the inn, didn't I? The inn that Pierre claimed was his own prosperous hotel and casino. (Another lie I swallowed whole – not that it matters now.) Anyway, his uncle is unwell – very unwell. And if Pierre carries on drinking as he does, he'll no doubt be unwell soon too. But with my newly formed sense of survival, I'm pushing to take charge. My spirit isn't entirely crushed yet. You see, I'm finally that which our parents always wanted me to be: a responsible married woman.

Forgive me, Hector, for that last sentence. I don't mean to sound sarcastic, but I know you'll be kind and remember me as the carefree girl I was and not the bitter woman I'm rapidly becoming. I think you'll understand that there is no longer any possibility of reconciliation between my former life and my present one – and judging from what you've told me, our parents feel the same. The baton is in your hand alone now, Hector. You always were so kind and good, so responsible. They can count on you at least to be a solace to them in their old age.

By the way, did I ever tell you how Pierre knew about me? The Rozières' staff had stopped at his uncle's inn on their way to Deauville. To make a long story short, they *spoke loudly, he overheard, and a plan was hatched to "marry an heiress". I saw him drunk for the first time after Papa's cable reached us in Monaco. When he read that I was to be disinherited he – well, never mind what he did. It was the beginning of the end.*

I'll let you know when the child arrives.

Love always,

Giselle

The child did arrive. The next letter, dated a few months later, confirmed that. A healthy son named Jacques was born to Giselle and Pierre Roux. *You are now an uncle!* wrote Giselle to her brother. Apart from that, and the briefest of greetings, the letter said nothing more of interest. By the next letter, however, a lot had happened – not least the destructive force of World War II, the events of which couldn't help but colour the next decade of Giselle's life:

18th September, 1946

Dear Hector,

So much has happened, I don't even know where to start. I haven't heard from you in so many years… Of course, I'm not exactly the most regular letter-writer either…

I'll start with the good news: you have a niece! On April 18, 1942, I had the most beautiful daughter. I know every mother claims their daughter is the most beautiful, but my dark-haired little moppet really is. She has

enormous eyes of the most striking colour – and like a Hollywood mother, I've named her after them: Violette. Her father has eyes of a similar colour.

If you remember Pierre you'll know his eyes are not light. So I'll tell you what everyone here thinks, but doesn't dare say. Namely, that Pierre is not Violette's father. Daniel, her father, is an Englishman. He was stationed not far from here until the Liberation, and not long after he arrived he began to come round regularly with smuggled goods for Jacques and I. Of course I wasn't about to turn my back on butter, milk and fresh meat (even a ripe cantaloupe – don't ask me where he found it!). Jacques became his little shadow and I…well, I fell in love. Don't shake your head in judgement before I've stated my case – your little sister hasn't descended quite as low as you think!

Pierre's uncle died some years ago. By that time, Pierre was a complete drunkard. He's still alive – if you can call it that. He lies all day upstairs in a room I've made up for him. As long as he gets his daily ration of you-know-what and the newspapers, he's okay. By that I mean that he stays quiet and in his room. He's been like this since before Paris was invaded. To his credit, he acknowledged Violette as his daughter (not that I gave him much of a choice). And to their credit, the townspeople haven't asked any awkward questions. Truth be told, I believe the general consensus is that I've *done a good job of managing the inn. I've brought more business to the town and I think the people living here have been willing to turn a blind eye to keep Violette and me happy. Everyone bends over backwards to please her. But she's such a serious little thing – everything has to be just so.*

Her father left town soon after the war with promises to return. Of course he hasn't, but I don't begrudge him his lie, nor do I regret the time I spent with him. Violette has been a greater gift than I could have imagined… You see, poor darling Jacques is not well. The doctors say he should get better. I pray for the best, and, in the meantime, Violette adds a touch of gaiety to our lives.

Please don't worry about me. The inn is doing well, Violette and I are healthy and Pierre is too weak to be of trouble. To be honest, for the first time in my life, I'm content. I've worked hard to attain this bit of freedom and independence. It's not as bad here as you'd imagine. I'll leave you with this rustic but relatively tranquil image of your little sister!

Love always,
Giselle

"What a destiny." Sebastian carefully folded the letter and handed it back to me.

"Either that or just a lot of unfortunate choices. I wonder if Giselle is still alive?"

"If she is, she must be about a hundred by now."

"But Violette is probably alive somewhere."

"And she could be rightfully entitled to financial compensation from the La Lunes…"

"If she can prove François La Lune stole her Uncle Hector's drawings."

"Exactly." Sebastian was quiet suddenly.

"But…?"

"No buts – just something interesting. This morning, when I was going through the city records, the lady helping me said I wasn't the only one who'd been asking after Hector Merlette."

"How did she know?"

"They keep a record of enquiries."

"So who else is on the same trail?"

"Someone called…" I waited as he unfolded another slip of paper. "David le Néanar. Ring a bell?"

"Not at all. And the clerk helping you couldn't tell you more?"

"No. She wasn't on duty when this David person came through. She only noticed that he'd signed in and that his subject of search was listed as *Hector Merlette*. He was there yesterday."

"Yesterday?"

He nodded. "Quite a coincidence, right?"

"It's too much of a coincidence… It's one more question to add to the boxful we already have. Anyway, the first thing we've got to do is find Giselle's daughter, Violette. She must be alive…"

"I thought that tomorrow I'd keep digging – and don't worry, I'll let you know about every little discovery," he quickly added when he saw my crestfallen face. "Axelle, you're doing the shows, remember?"

Arghhh! *Remember?* I'd completely forgotten! Hervé would be furious that I hadn't rung him. Pulling out my phone I saw that after calling me several times and getting no reply he'd sent a text confirming my schedule for tomorrow: Lanvin in the morning at the Louvre and Chanel in the afternoon at the Grand Palais Exhibition Hall. I was also confirmed for a half-day of beauty for French *Elle* on Thursday. These prestigious jobs had clearly made him happy: he'd signed off with a row of smiley faces.

I couldn't say I was smiling, though. Again, my modelling disguise seemed to be pulling me away from the mystery – not taking me towards it, as I'd hoped. But it was too late to back out now. "You're right, Sebastian," I said as I put my phone away. "At least I might have more leads after I'm finished with the letters. Although judging by the next one, there might not be more to go on," I said as I pulled a slip of paper from the next envelope.

"What's that?" he asked as I pushed it towards him.

"*Swan Lake.* Palais Garnier. 17th April, 1961. We've gone from the war and alcoholic husbands to Paris and the ballet in the 1960s."

"Hmm. Must have been a special night," he said. Then he flashed me his smile and we got up to leave – the cafe was locking up for the night. I carefully wrapped the letters before slipping them back in my bag. I'd finish reading them as soon as I was home – I had to know the next part of the story.

Sebastian walked me to my aunt's, pushing his scooter along beside me. It was a cool, calm night. No one else was out, and, apart from our footsteps, the street was quiet. Somewhere, if they were still alive, Belle and Darius were maybe being held against their will. If so, what were they thinking? Were they nearby? Were they okay? And how did the letters tie in to it all?

"Shall we meet after your morning show? With any luck I'll have found out where Violette is by then," Sebastian said.

"And I'll catch you up to date on the letters."

"Great. I'll wait for you downstairs, in the Louvre, at the Lanvin exit. And then there's the Juno bag launch in the evening. Maybe afterwards we can go over our new leads?"

"Yeah, that sounds…" I trailed off.

"Axelle?"

I'd completely forgotten that I was thinking of meeting Dom after the launch – that hopefully I'd get him to answer a few questions. Quickly, I told Sebastian as much.

"Are you sure this is only about the case?" he asked, as he fiddled with the lock on his scooter.

I didn't know what to say. I mean, of course it had to do

with the case…but maybe a tiny bit had to do with Dom, too. So I said nothing.

I had the impression Sebastian wanted to say something, but he didn't.

He waited until I went in. A few moments after the heavy door shut behind me I heard his scooter drive off. Slowly I trudged up the stairs to my aunt's. It seemed she was still out – probably at a party – the apartment was quiet. I was tired now and longing for my bed – which, I noticed with a start when I nearly sat on her, had been appropriated by Aunt Venetia's cat, Miu Miu.

I didn't even bother moving her as I slipped under the fluffy duvet and pulled out the letters. I read them quickly, one after the other. Riddles, names, emotions and theories raced through my mind: the letters posed more questions than they answered. I turned the light out and slipped the packet under my pillow. Someone else had considered them important enough to hide – and now I was beginning to understand why.

Slowly sleep overcame me. My last thought was of Sebastian, standing downstairs, watching me leave, his light blue eyes serious. I wondered again what it was he'd wanted to say…

She'd recognized his strained breathing...
It was Darius, her brother.

She'd rolled off her bed and wriggled to his. The packed earth underneath her was cool and damp. She tried not to panic as a rat scurried over her foot.

Darius was in a deep sleep. Had he been drugged? And for how long could he breathe without his medication? What was he doing down here?

She shivered.

Had he made the same mistake she had?

WEDNESDAY MORNING

The Shows Must Go On

SHOWS GO ON, BUT BELLE STILL MISSING! screamed the morning headlines. The shows had started with a bang yesterday.

Ellie adorned the front page of *Le Figaro*. Head held high and Mona Lisa smile on her lips, she was shown bounding down the runway in a frilled pencil skirt and ultra-high stilettos. A wonderfully vertiginous and messy librarian's bun wobbled atop her head and an enormous magnifying glass dangled around her neck (all the models wore one).

Forget Hitchcock's Dial M for Murder, my aunt was quoted in the article as saying, *instead Dial D for Dior. The dynamic charge running through these separates is sure to please any modern-day Miss Marple looking for striking solutions to the mystery of the contemporary woman's wardrobe.*

Otherwise, the reviews were minimal. Uncertainty and unease loomed over the city, the glaring hole left by Belle too large to be forgotten

– no matter how nice the clothes. Where were Belle and Darius? Were they alive? And what was taking so long to find them? Photos of the La Lune mansion swarming with police did nothing to reassure the public. And the media reports that every one of the La Lunes was under constant surveillance became more farcical, as each hour passed and no real clue was forthcoming. Inspector Witt's face looked out at me from the morning paper. He was not amused.

My aunt, meanwhile, had taken no chances: she'd ordered a *Chic* company car to drive me to the Lanvin show at the Louvre (although I'd insisted that afterwards I'd get around on my own, thank you very much). In the car, my phone suddenly rang. I set the morning paper down and, without thinking, answered.

A bubbling stream of words rushed out: "Good morning, darling! How's my favourite model? I hope you got your beauty sleep. I'm going to watch the Fashion Channel later. I've invited Kathy, Annie and Camilla. I've made a delicious chicken lemon risotto which I'll heat up and then we'll sit and watch you! I'm so excited! Didn't your father and I tell you this would be a fantastic experience?"

"Uh—"

I was about to tell Mum that the line was cracking up, but, luckily for me, she had an appointment. "I'm meeting a new client with a fabulous apartment in Chelsea. They want me to decorate the whole thing. So I have to keep it short, but I'll be out on Friday to watch you in the Barinaga and La Lune shows, then I'll stay on and we can have fun all weekend – together!"

"The Barinaga show? Friday?" I hadn't heard anything about the Barinaga show.

"Yes, darling, Barinaga! Haven't you spoken with Hervé yet this morning? Axelle, honestly! It's nine in the morning your time and you haven't even called him yet! Well, don't worry – I'm here for you, darling! Right, I have to go. I'll call you later!"

Trust my mum to have already begun checking in with Hervé – on my behalf!

When I saw the mayhem, crowds and paparazzi blocking the side entrance to the Louvre, I was happy to have the car and driver. To avoid the chaos, we drove past the Rue de Rivoli entrance and around to the large glass pyramid in the courtyard of the Louvre. Here there were no crowds – for once. Today everyone was at the side entrance, hoping to catch sight of any famous models that were on their way into the Louvre. I jumped out of the car, slipped through the heavy glass door and walked onto an escalator that took me down to the level of the shows. From there I found my way to the space reserved for Lanvin. Backstage was packed. And again, just like at Miriam's, I felt I was stepping into another world.

Amidst all the chaos and excitement, Ellie stood waiting for me. She spotted me as soon as I walked in and led me through a haze of hairspray and glittering face powder to a large buffet table decked out with an amazing array of salads, quiches, cold cuts and tiny bite-sized desserts. "This is for whenever you get hungry. Why don't you load up a plate now, and then follow me to hair."

I once went with my family to Crufts, the big London dog show. I remember walking down aisle after aisle of Afghan hounds, Pomeranians, golden retrievers, etc., just before they were getting ready to judge Best in Show. The scene before me now looked similar: long tables, bright lights, intense concentration, models lined up, each with their respective hairdresser blowing, teasing, and brushing oodles and oodles of hair. Ellie took me to a wisp of a lady who had just finished with a six-foot-tall blonde. Ellie introduced her as Brigitte.

I stayed with Brigitte for an hour. My nerves, now that I was finally getting ready to walk my first show, expanded with anxiety as every second ticked past. I began to feel queasy. I longed to rip the curlers out of my hair, slip out of a side entrance and run into the fresh air. High heels, lace and accessories would be tossed by the wayside in my bid for freedom.

Calm down, Axelle, I told myself as I took a deep breath. Slowly I took another, then turned to Ellie. Her hair was still pinned up and would remain so until her make-up was finished. I watched as she devoured a plate full of goodies without moving one single hair out of place. Despite the late night and early morning (as well as the scarily hectic week ahead), she looked amazing.

For me, on the other hand, everything proceeded in a blur of nerves and distraction. I was relieved when Brigitte leaned in to my ear and said, "Axelle, *chèrie*, the curlers have to stay in your hair for thirty minutes. I'm going to finish Ellie's hair, so I'll leave you here during that time, okay? Will you be all right?"

"Absolutely," I answered. *Perfect*, I thought. Now I could turn to the one thing that was certain to distract me from my impending fashion show debut: the letters. I needed to read them through again, fully awake and with fresh eyes, to truly understand their importance.

I hung my new pea coat on my shoulders for extra warmth and popped my earphones in so that it looked like I was busy listening to music. Then I pulled the packet out of my shoulder bag and took another look at the ballet ticket. Slowly I turned it over in my hand before replacing it in its envelope. Last night, in the cafe with Sebastian, it hadn't made sense, but reading the next letter again, I began to understand...

Épaignes, 10th January, 1961

Dear Hector,
My patient brother, it has been so long...I'm not even

sure if your address is the same. I hope, however, that this long silence on your part is not due to any unfortunate circumstances?

I am writing because my daughter – your niece – Violette has asked to go to Paris. Actually, "asked" is something of an understatement. Declared is more like it. Apparently, the thought of staying on here and taking over the inn doesn't appeal to her. I can't say I blame her. Honestly, she is too clever and too beautiful for a place like this. Furthermore, having gone through what I did at her age, you know I'd be the last one to stand in her way…

So I'm sending her to Paris with a bit of money I've been putting away for something like this (if truth be told, I think that in my heart of hearts I'd always thought this moment would come). I'm also sending her off with your address. Please, Hector, would you give her a helping hand? She'll be alone and doesn't know a soul…

She'll be arriving in three days' time. Her train will arrive at midday. She'll ask for a bus that will take her to your address.

Thank you, Hector. I know she'll be in good hands. Don't worry about writing back to me – Violette will do so.

Love always,
Giselle

So Violette had decamped to Paris...and then what? The letter from Giselle was written in January 1961, just three months before the night at the ballet. I folded the letter and took out the next one...

Paris 13th January, 1961

Dear Maman,

I don't know where to begin so I'll start with the sad news: Uncle Hector is dead. Apparently, according to his concierge, no one knew that he had any living family – he never mentioned us. But before you begin to worry, I'll say that I'm all right. I'm warm, I'm safe and I've found a clean, respectable room to call my own. I'll explain...

The journey went smoothly. I had to cross all of Paris to get to Uncle Hector's. As I was scanning the list of names by the buzzer, the concierge came out to ask if she could help me. At the mention of my uncle's name she turned her small, friendly face up to me and asked if I hadn't heard. "Heard what?" I asked. "Why, heard that Monsieur Merlette died a few months ago," she said.

I thought I'd faint, Maman, when she said that. All of our planning, all of that money you've worked so hard for in my pocket, and that long journey all by myself...and then to have it all dashed by such sad news. The one person I had a tie to in this city and now he's gone. I've never felt so alone before! I could barely stand after hearing what she said. She is a kind woman, though,

Maman. She immediately took up my satchel and ignored my refusals of a cup of tea. I sat for some minutes, drinking the strong, sweet brew, until I was ready to speak. And when I finally did, I told her everything. I told her all about you too, Maman. I must have gone on for some time, because when I stopped the sun was setting outside.

After listening to my long story, Madame Fourré – the concierge – kindly offered to help. And how fortunate I am, in that she has a cousin who runs a boarding house for women! The room I have is basic – I'm in it right now – but it's clean and the landlady runs an honest and respectable house. All of this Madame Fourré arranged for me. Before leaving she also gave me the name and address of Uncle Hector's solicitor. He'd instructed her to do so should anyone claiming to be a relative of his come asking questions. I'll see the solicitor first thing tomorrow morning. At the very least he might know of someone who can be of help to me.

Despite the dramatic start I still plan on staying here. I'll begin looking for a job tomorrow afternoon. I'm sure that with some luck I'll find the job I've been dreaming of. Paris is full of the most elegant shops! Oh Maman, how I wish you were here!

Madame Fourré has said that I'm the only person whom she's ever seen wanting to visit my uncle (apart from his solicitor). She said that Uncle Hector was a very kind *man, a gentleman, very quiet. She rarely heard him speak. It appears he was something of a loner and angry about some business transaction that turned sour several years ago – it seems something was stolen from him. Madame Fourré didn't know more. I wish we could have helped him...*

I'll write to you again tomorrow, Maman, straight after I've seen the solicitor. Remember my promise, Maman: that I'll call you if I really need help. The fact that I'm writing to you with all this news should appease your worries...

I'll enclose a card of the boarding house. If need be, you can call me here in the evenings or mornings. The fixed times are noted on the card.

With all my love,
Violette

I let my breath out as I came to the end of the letter. So Hector died a lonely man and his niece Violette stayed in Paris. The ballet ticket was obviously hers, then. And the date of the letter was true to the death certificate Sebastian found yesterday. Furthermore, the concierge's description of Hector also explained the lack of a paper trail. He must have been shy and introverted to begin with, and the theft of his drawings and subsequent success of his former business partner seemed to have pushed him fully into a life of solitude and bitterness.

Again and again the same thoughts ran through my mind: is Violette still alive? And, if she is alive, is she trying to avenge her uncle's suffering by bringing the curse to life? Is she hoping to scare the La Lunes into giving her an acknowledgement of François's theft? And maybe some financial redress? And why now?

But above all, the one thought that pulsated through my mind was that I wasn't the only one who knew of her existence. Whoever had hidden the letters knew of her. And so, in all probability, did the mysterious Mr David le Néanar. The big question was: who would find her first?

The next envelope contained a short note:

14th January, 1961

Maman,
I must tell you what Uncle Hector's solicitor told me today! I'll call you on Sunday – I dare not write about it!
Love,
Violette

Interesting...

The next, and last, envelope was thick with several letters of exchange between Hector's sister, Giselle, and Hector's solicitor, confirming the small legacy that Hector had bequeathed her. After the solicitors had verified that she was indeed Giselle Roux, née Merlette, the paperwork had gone through and Giselle had taken delivery of a few pieces of furniture, some small personal effects of Hector's and several letters. A wire transfer of a small sum of money followed shortly thereafter.

Needless to say, the word *letters* caught my eye. Briefly I wondered if the letters between Hector and his sister, Giselle – the ones in the packet – were the letters his will referred to. But after Giselle inherited them, who did she pass them on to? Surely to Violette? Then why did I find them in the La Lunes' chimney flue?

"Axelle, Axelle, relax *ma petite*...you'll do fine," cooed Thierry, nearly scaring me to death. "Oh, and look how sweet you are: you're reading letters! No wonder you look so confused – nobody reads letters any more! You English are so old-fashioned!" He laughed at his own little joke. "Anyway, yesterday La Lune, today Lanvin, what next?" he asked, as I tried to drag my focus back to the show.

"Barinaga?" I answered without thinking, slipping into the chair he'd pulled out for me and submitting to his ministrations.

"Fantastic! I'll be there too!" he answered. "Brigitte has asked me to start with you and as soon as I've finished she'll brush your hair out, okay?"

"Fine. But, Thierry?"

"*Oui?*"

"Do you mind if I make a quick phone call?"

I stood up and stretched before he could complain, and

disappeared behind the nearest clothes rack. "Sebastian?" I said as soon as he picked up. "Are you having any luck?"

"No. No trace of a Violette Roux anywhere in or near Épaignes."

"Yeah, well, that's because she's not in or near Épaignes – at least I don't think so. I've done some more reading. She came to Paris and I think she may have stayed – that was her intention, anyway."

Sebastian let out a low whistle. "No wonder I haven't found anything. Do you know what part of Paris she might be in, or what she might have done as a job?"

"No, I have no idea where she might be. But she was hoping to find a job in a shop – a nice one. Oh, and I have the address of Hector's old solicitor's office. If they're still around, they might know where she went to. She met them – of course, this was in 1961…"

"Still…it's something. Text me the address and I'll check there now. I'll see you after the show."

I hung up and went back to Thierry.

By the time I was show-ready, I hardly recognized myself – and I could barely move. Putting on the amazing pink satin heels I'd been handed was one thing – walking in them would be another.

"Ellie," I said, as perspiration began to make the fluid column dress I was wearing stick to me, "what do you tell yourself…how do you just…?"

"Just walk out there, you mean?" she said, motioning

towards the stage door with her chin as she daintily popped a last forkful of pasta salad into her mouth.

I nodded.

"I block out all thoughts of fear. I listen to the music and think about how lucky I am to be able to do this. And, remember, we *can* do this. Otherwise the designers wouldn't have asked us to. I mean, look, no matter how intimidating the people in the audience may appear – they can't do what we do. *We* make the clothes come alive. *We* make the clothes say something."

"Yeah, but I've never done this before – I don't even know how I'm going to be able to walk back and forth – let alone make the clothes say something!"

"Then look out for the people you know. Use them as a distraction!" she said brightly. "Your aunt, the La Lunes – Claude will probably be here—"

"Claude? The La Lunes? You'd think that with Belle and Darius missing they'd have more important things to do – like trying to find them!"

"Shhh…not so loud, Axelle." Ellie dropped her voice to a whisper. "Don't worry – I get your point. I mean, if some of my family were missing there's no way you could drag me to a show, but…"

"But what?"

"Fashion," she mouthed. "The show must go on – no matter what. Anyway, like I said, your aunt will be here, front row. You can look for her."

"Great." I rolled my eyes as the music suddenly blasted through the speakers. Ellie gave my hand a squeeze and the show began.

I followed Ellie's advice: I shut my eyes and tried my best to relax as Brigitte gave my hair a last-minute touch-up and Thierry applied the umpteenth layer of gloss to my lips. The music was loud and that helped me to block out all of the busy preparations going on around me. As the tracks melted seamlessly from one into another the volume increased, until finally we got the cue to start. My heart was thumping so hard I thought it might burst. Following Ellie's lead, I listened to the music and placed one foot in front of the other over and over again. I was unprepared for the bright lights and flashing cameras that hit me with a jolt when I stepped out onto the runway – but, never mind – thankfully it obliterated the sight of the nearly one thousand people whose eyes were all focused on me...

"You survived the show!" Sebastian seemed happy to see me, last night's quiet goodbye forgotten. I followed him through the crowds and out of the Louvre. Finally, we made it out onto the Rue de Rivoli, where a blast of cool air swept over us. Along with the enormous sense of relief that I'd walked the show without falling down had come a voracious hunger. I was starving!

"Great. I have just the thing." Sebastian waved a brown paper bag in front of me. "Falafels from my favourite takeaway." We turned into the Tuileries Park and found an empty bench against a warm wall. I leaned back and stretched in the shining sun, happy to be out of those teetering heels.

Sebastian busied himself with the falafels and drinks while explaining how his morning had gone. "Believe it or not, Hector's old solicitor still exists – not the solicitor himself, of course, but the firm. But they had no information on Violette – or even Giselle. Once Hector's legacy was passed on to Giselle, they closed his file. Even their most senior employee couldn't remember hearing anything about the Merlettes."

"Here." I handed him the letters I'd read backstage this morning. "Read these." Then I bit into my hot falafel.

"Wow," he said, as he came to the end. "It sounds as if Hector must have been really lonely. And did Violette find a job?"

"I don't know – those were the last letters in the packet. Although" – I paused to lick a glob of falafel sauce from my fingers before it fell on my new jacket – "knowing how determined she was to get to Paris – and then to stay here all alone – I'm sure she would have been just as determined to find a job... The more I think about it the more I'm sure she must have succeeded."

"Well, we know she wanted a job in a shop but

unfortunately that doesn't exactly give us much to go on – there are lots of shops in Paris!"

"And there's no Violette Roux alive today, living in Paris?"

Sebastian shook his head. "Straight after you called I checked. There are many Rouxs – but no Violette Roux. Of course, she may have married, but without a surname we won't find her. I even asked my father to check for me. The name meant nothing to him – he's still working on the counterfeit theory. He sees the curse as nothing more than a family distraction."

"I don't believe the curse has any power either...but maybe someone is using it to hide behind? Anyway, at least your dad won't be breathing down our necks."

"True...but it seems *we're* breathing down someone's neck..."

I looked at Sebastian, not understanding.

"The mysterious Mr le Néanar. The solicitors told me that he'd called them too, asking for information."

"And?"

"And nothing. They told him what they told me: case closed."

"Hmm...interesting." A new thought began trickling into my mind. "Nothing in the packet of letters gives any concrete proof of either François La Lune stealing Hector's handbag drawings or of the curse, right? Like, even when Violette mentions the theft, it's very vague and she's totally ignorant about the context of the theft. Plus we never hear more."

"Right."

"So if someone were to just chance upon these letters, they wouldn't mean anything to them. Violette's life and these letters are only of interest if you know about the curse and if you know that she is a Merlette – because it gives her a motive to seek revenge and right a wrong. Presumably, the possibility of financial compensation could also give her a strong motive to scare and harass the La Lunes into finally acknowledging François's theft. The letters tie her to her uncle and all of the wrong-doing he suffered at the hands of the La Lunes…"

"So these letters are really only important to someone who is trying to pin the disappearances on Violette—"

"Or to Violette herself. If she's still alive, she has the strongest motive so far to attack the La Lunes…or it could be a direct relation of hers, maybe."

"But how did these letters get out of her hands?"

"And why did I find them at the La Lune house, up a chimney? And how does Belle's missing shoe and Darius's cryptic note with *Belle*, *Le Vau* and *passages* written on it tie in with everything? And what about Claude's CAT?" I stopped to stretch and suddenly remembered the tiny note I'd unfurled from the fortune cookie I'd had at my "goodbye" dinner the night before I'd left London. "Confucius says:

A man who reviews the old so as to find out the new is qualified to teach others.'"

"Well, we've certainly been reviewing the old," Sebastian said.

"Now we just need to find out something new. And we can start by finding Violette. If we can find out where she worked we'd have a good place to pick up her trail. There must be a way..." I sat thinking for a minute before my eureka moment struck. I don't know why I hadn't thought of it sooner. "I know!" I said. "Aunt V. I'm sure she'll be able to help." I glanced at my watch. "She might be in a show, but I'll give her a call now."

"Hello! Axelle, is that you?" Aunt Venetia exclaimed. Apparently I was lucky enough to catch her just as she was leaving a show by a young designer – the music was still blaring in the background. "And now I'm off to another one," she yelled. "Again, a young one. Apparently he's the next Yves Saint Laurent. Of course, they always say that, but, still, one never knows and I wouldn't want him to slip by me if he were."

Quickly I explained what I'd found out and asked if she could help.

"Finally! Progress!" she said.

"Well, I wouldn't call it progress yet, Aunt V. I mean, it may end up being nothing more than an entertaining snippet of fashion history. On the other hand, it just might shed some light on the matter."

"Well, you may as well try. After all, it's not as if Inspector Witt is making any headway with his counterfeit theory – despite interrogating poor Blossom after Harlan Forbes saw Belle's drawings fall out of her bag. I could strangle the police for leaking that information – especially as it's led to nothing but bad press. And who could imagine Blossom being involved? Anyway, listen, I'll be out of here in five minutes. As soon as I'm in my car I'll make some calls. We want employee records from circa 1961, boutiques, right? Violette Roux?"

"Yes, please."

"What kind of boutiques? Fashion? Gloves? Hats? What?"

"Hmm…I'd guess fashion." And then, following my hunch, added, "And high-end. Givenchy or something like that."

"Fine. I'll get Blossom on it right away – not that I have much hope. 1961 was a long time ago. Anyway, Blossom will be only too happy to help. Her neck's still on the line, you know. I'll call you later. We should know something by the end of the day."

We'd just stepped out of the Tuileries and onto the busy Rue de Rivoli. There were people everywhere. Some rushed past carrying packages, others wandered idly from window to window. Still others talked loudly on their phones, oblivious to anything else. And all around us, weaving their way in and out, were the fashionistas. They were as easy to spot as coloured beads in the sand.

"By the way, do you want to come with me tonight to the Juno bag launch?"

Sebastian laughed. "Does this mean I've moved up from sidekick status?"

"Uhm…maybe. But just for tonight – Ellie will be busy."

"So if I've understood correctly, what you're really asking is would I be your escort, maybe your bodyguard, and definitely your driver?" Sebastian said with a laugh.

"Exactly." He looked totally cute standing there smiling, his hair ruffled.

"Okay, I'll sign up for the job."

Really cute. Why hadn't I…never mind. Case to solve, remember, Axelle? "Great! I'll ask my aunt to have a ticket for you at the door."

"And what about Dom? Aren't you seeing him?"

Oops. I'd completely forgotten I'd said yes to some time with he of the gorgeous green eyes. He'd called this morning while I'd been backstage at Lanvin. I wasn't even sure what I'd said, but I did remember it was something in the affirmative. "I believe we're on for later."

Sebastian didn't say anything although I did see his eyebrows go up a fraction. Then he quickly shrugged his shoulders and got on his scooter. I climbed on behind him, my model bag between us, and we zoomed off to the Grand Palais, site of the Chanel show. On the way, I spotted a bookshop and got Sebastian to pull over so I could buy a book on the architect Le Vau. I was sure Darius must have stumbled across something and Le Vau was the only clue I had to his disappearance.

Five minutes later and I was at the grand exhibition hall. Sebastian slowed down just in front of the steps leading to the main entrance. Everything was cordoned off and there was security standing all over the place. The Chanel show was one of the most prestigious – lots of people tried to crash it, hence the heavy security. Sebastian waited for me to push my way to the entrance. At the top I showed the guard my ID and was whisked behind the red rope. I quickly turned to give Sebastian a last wave, and saw him speed away, before I followed the signs to hair and make-up.

It was just as loud and chaotic backstage at Chanel as it had been in the morning at Lanvin. Ellie was getting her hair done. "Oh my gosh, Axelle – look, you have to see my new website!" She whipped out her phone and I strained my eyes to look at her image on the tiny screen. Even when only a centimetre tall, she looked amazing.

"What do you think?"

"I think that if you stayed that size and we attached tiny butterfly wings to your back, you'd make a beautiful fairy."

"That's what I like about you, Axelle," she said, laughing, "you have such a funny way of looking at things! I'm going to have a link connecting my site to Alejandro's site," she said, with a nod to the hairdresser bent over her in full concentration. "Alejandro's Spanish and he's *the* best. You wouldn't know it from looking at *his* hair, but he is."

She was right: his hair was wild. He looked like a lion with an electrified mane. He also wore more silver jewellery than anyone I'd ever seen. Silver earrings, rings and bracelets covered whatever patches of skin his clothing left bare. It was a testament to his strength that even with all that silver weighing him down, he still managed to wield a heavy professional hairdryer all day long.

"By the way, Rose is here somewhere," Ellie said.

"She is? Where did you see her?" I asked.

"Hmm...she was over by the buffet table, wasn't she, Alejandro?" Ellie directed her gaze at the hairdresser's image in the mirror.

"Yes, and she's probably still there," he answered through a mouthful of hairpins.

She was. I made a beeline for her as soon as I spotted her. Or rather, as soon as I had assured myself that it was indeed her, because she looked like a totally new Rose; in fact, she looked fantastic. And it was her hair that made me say that. In place of the overgrown, tumbleweed-like growth I'd seen attached to her head before, an elegantly shaped mass of slinky, swishy femme-fatale hair swung provocatively. Dom had been right: she'd gone from one extreme to the other. Why?

I went up to her. "Hi, Axelle!" she said. Not only did she remember me from the photo shoot yesterday, she also seemed genuinely delighted to see me – almost desperately so – which I found odd considering this was *her* world, not mine. But one thing I'd noticed was that even fashion people were intimidated by fashion, so I could imagine that for someone like Rose, who was naturally shy and dealt primarily with the office side of things, fashion was terrifying. "I usually never go to the shows – except our own, of course – but Claude has too much to do, what with the launch of the Juno bag tonight, so he gave me his ticket." She was nervous, and as she twisted and shifted her weight from leg to leg she kept hitting people with the enormous bag hanging from her shoulder. "My computer," she said by way of explanation.

"Dom told me you're taking Spanish lessons. That sounds like fun," I said.

"Spanish?" she blushed. "Ah...yes. *Es muy divertido, gracias.* I'm thinking of starting German next."

"You must really like languages. But why Spanish? Have you spent much time in Spain?"

Again she blushed. "Why, yes," she said as she started searching through her enormous bag, "I'm interested in languages. But, no, I've never been to Spain – ah, maybe just once or twice." She found her phone and brought it up to her face to peer at the screen. An assortment of bracelets – including one in leather with a tiny silver heart that looked like one I'd seen somewhere before – slid down her wrist and caught on her sleeve. "Axelle, I'm sorry, but I have to make a call now. Business. But it was really nice talking to you. See you on Friday at our show," she said as she began punching in numbers.

I watched her curiously as she turned her back to me and walked away, but before I could give it more thought, Ellie came to tell me that Thierry was looking for me. It was make-up time.

Chanel turned out a collection of tweed suits perfect for an English country house mystery – although the sky-high heels and ultra-short skirts would definitely have made the local villagers raise their eyebrows.

I was prepared this time for the dozens of flashbulbs that would be waiting for me at the end of the runway. Hips thrust forward as I'd seen Ellie do, I bounded along, pearls swaying and eyes narrowed, as I looked at the crowd without noticing it (if you know what I mean). This time, when I reached the end of the runway, I heard my name called out – the photographers were beginning to recognize me. I stopped in front of them, placed my hands on my hips and shifted my weight from leg to leg. I held my head high and let my gaze settle far beyond and above their heads.

After a few moments of that I turned around and headed back towards the curtain. Fleetingly I saw my aunt out of the corner of my eye – not that she made any effort to notice me. On the contrary, she ignored me completely – just as she had at the show this morning– although I had no doubt she was scrutinizing everything I was wearing and doing. Nothing gets in the way of Aunt V's professionalism. On the runway I was just another model – nothing more.

The show went well. Or, as Ellie put it: "*You* went well, Axelle. No one could have guessed that you just did your first show this morning."

A few days ago I would have said, "Yeah, yeah, how difficult can it be to walk back and forth on a runway?" But the last forty-eight hours had taught me that modelling was tough work, and making the clothes look striking for the fashionistas sitting in the front rows was no easy task. And while I was under no illusion that I was the next big name, I was ready to admit that my long, gangly legs were better suited to this job than I'd ever thought.

Not that I'd EVER repeat that to my mum.

As soon as Chanel's head designer had walked his turn on the runway and we returned backstage, I changed into my own clothes. As I swung my bag over my shoulder, I saw Rose talking to Alejandro and a couple of the other hairdressers. She must have stayed backstage all along… and yet earlier she'd told me that Claude had given her his ticket so that she could see the show. So what had she been doing all this time? And why had she come if it wasn't to see the show?

My phone suddenly rang. *Please let it be Aunt V,* I thought as I fished it out of my bag. It was.

"I thought you did very well," she purred. She was in her car. "I would have gone backstage to say so but I have to be at the Jean-Paul Gaultier show in five minutes. That long powdery pink evening dress you wore really suited you. In fact, Axelle, if I were you, I'd work a bit more colour into my wardrobe – although, as I'm sure you're learning this week, black is best. Those schoolgirl colours you've always insisted on wearing do absolutely nothing for you. However, even an all-black wardrobe can use a bit of perking up. A scarf or a pair of shoes or *something* in a shot of colour—"

"Aunt Venetia," I said cutting her off, "have you had any feedback yet from our search?"

"Yes, I have. I was just about to get to that. Unfortunately, we haven't found a trace of anyone called Violette Roux. Blossom was very thorough and applied a lot of pressure – but nothing came up anywhere. It was too long ago. I'm sorry. For you and me. What'll you do now?"

"I don't know..."

"Well, let's talk more about it later. By the way, if you're on your way home would you please be careful with the boxes in the hall? They're some new paintings I've bought at auction. Don't touch them."

"No problem – I won't. But..."

"But what, Axelle?"

"Well, not to be nosy, but…what do you do with all the stuff – all the art you buy?"

"Haven't you noticed my walls, Axelle?"

"Your walls?"

"Yes, my walls. They're covered with art."

"Exactly. So where are you going to hang all the new stuff coming in…?"

"Don't worry, I'll make space," she said crisply. That was obviously the end of that conversation. There was a beat of silence while she geared up for the question I knew was coming next. "Oh, and, Axelle?"

"Yes?"

"What *will* you be wearing tonight?"

Some things, at least, never change…

I was happy to go home. Apart from Carmen, Aunt V's housekeeper, who was in the kitchen, the apartment was empty. I quickly said hello to her, then walked to my bedroom, slipped out of my jacket and lay on the bed. The muffled sound of the evening traffic on the Boulevard St. Germain wafted in through the gaps around the old windows. Outside, the last of the bright blue afternoon sky had faded into soft shades of purple and orange, tingeing the edges of the neighbouring rooftops with light. As I contemplated the pretty colours, a heavy, hairy weight flung itself on me and then proceeded to sprawl across my belly. It was Miu Miu. She'd decided to forgo the possibility of a tidbit from Carmen in order to say hello to me. For that she deserved a good scratch behind her ears – which I promptly gave her.

What bad luck not to have found a fresh trace of Violette… As I lay looking up at the ceiling, the various bits of information that I'd gathered weaved in and out of my thoughts. My gut told me that the clue Darius had left – his note of four words: *Belle, Le Vau, passages* – was still the strongest, even if I wasn't close to figuring it out.

Added to that were Belle's missing velvet platform shoe, the letters *CAT* in Claude's agenda, Rose's suddenly uncharacteristic (according to Dom and my aunt – and they should know) behaviour and hairstyle, and Fiona's cryptic allusion to family rifts. What had she said as I'd listened at the chimney flue on Monday evening? "Everything else must wait…we can sort things out later… between ourselves…" What did she mean by that?

Plus, of course, there was also the mysterious David le Néanar, whose tracks we seemed to be following – and there was still the issue of *how* Belle and Darius had disappeared. And the timing of the disappearances… I let my mind wander a bit more, happy to be on my bed, to just think quietly.

After some minutes, the image of the fine leather-and-silver bracelet Rose had been wearing came to mind. I sat up, surprised, chewing over my new idea. *Could it really be that?* I thought. It certainly explained a lot of things. The Spanish lessons, the slinky hair and flushed cheeks.

What was it she'd said Monday night? "We're all greedy – and our greed is waking the curse!" Yes, she'd definitely sounded guilty – and I thought I knew why. I stretched out on my bed and baited Miu Miu with my foot. *Yes*, I thought, *if what I think is right, despite what her family think, Rose's behaviour isn't erratic or strange. On the contrary, it makes perfect sense…*

Content with my theory, I leaned back against my pillows and opened the book on Le Vau. I got as far as the table of contents before the need for a nap overcame me.

WEDNESDAY EVENING

Questions and Answers

I awoke to the smell of the roast chicken Carmen had made me for dinner. She beamed with pleasure as she watched me devour half of the chicken without pausing for breath. It was served with rice and vegetables and for dessert she'd made me my favourite – île flottante: mountains of fluffy, sweetened egg whites floating in a bowl full of the palest, creamiest vanilla sauce. It may sound strange but, trust me, it tastes amazing. I wolfed down enough for two.

"Now we have to fit you into your dress – if we can!" Carmen smiled.

Aunt Venetia had obviously been worried after we'd spoken earlier, as she'd asked her office to send me a dress from the editorial racks at *Chic: Paris* to borrow for the evening. They usually had several that had either just been, or were going to be, photographed for a *Chic* magazine spread.

Carmen had already taken it out of its garment bag. It hung, freshly steamed, on a hook in Aunt V's dressing room. I quickly slipped out of my jeans and jumper, stepped into the dress, and then stood still as Carmen hovered around me, adjusting the dress so that it hung correctly in all the right places.

Aunt V's dressing room is amazing. Just standing in it made me feel glamorous. The closets are highly polished maple, while the walls are painted in subtle shades of cream and beige. In the middle of the room stands an art deco table bearing an ever-present vase of white calla lilies. A crystal chandelier sparkles above it. The room's muted luxury never fails to absorb whatever stress you walk in with. I remember my mum (who decorated it) being delighted when an interiors magazine likened it to *an urban butterfly's sleek cocoon.*

I stood near my aunt's dressing table, my arms held out from my sides, as Carmen made her adjustments. I was looking at a pair of large black-and-white photographs hanging on either side of the door on the opposite wall. They depicted Aunt Venetia's all-time favourite fashionista, Diana Vreeland, the famous fashion editor. In one her hawklike profile was captured for posterity, looking like a Japanese kabuki mask. There was absolutely nothing natural-looking about her heavily powdered skin or dark lacquered hair. *It's style,* she seemed to say, *that's immortal – not skin and hair.*

She had a point.

Carmen was now checking that no impudent bits of dust, thread or lint were still clinging to my dress.

Meanwhile I was looking at the other print of Ms Vreeland; this one showed her posing next to an enormous silk and silver dress, obviously in a museum somewhere. And, as in the other photograph, she was dressed in chic, graphic separates, her kabuki-style hair and make-up perfectly in place. For as long as I can remember these two photographs have accompanied my aunt from flat to flat.

Finally Carmen turned me around to face the three-sided mirror she had just unfolded. The dress was lovely: a one-shouldered, emerald green, bias-cut, satin show-stealer. Nothing detracted from its fluid line; there was no ruffling, pattern, trim, or contrast to distract from its clean cut and vivid colour.

It was elegant and sophisticated. It exuded glamour and urban cool…it was many things…*except me.*

I stood looking at myself the way Halley does at home when she thinks I'm hiding a biscuit in my hand: she cocks her head from one side to the other, furrowing her brows, until I open my hand and give her what she knows is there.

Now I stood, cocking *my head* from side to side, waiting for the dress to look like *me.* Carmen was getting fidgety.

"Don't worry, Carmen," I said, "I like it…it's just that it's not quite *me* enough yet." Then I remembered something Ellie had told me the other day: that style is all about contrast.

I went to my room and yanked my beaten-up leather jacket out of the closet. Ha! Now there was contrast! Next I kicked off the beautiful but painful heels I was wearing and instead donned my well-worn combat boots. More contrast!

I went back to my aunt's dressing room to have a good look. Hmm… Better…but something was still missing… Ah! That was it!

But could I?

Should I?

Yes and no were the answers to both questions. And yes won out. I walked to my aunt's dressing table, opened the top drawer and found what I was looking for. I took them out and went back to the mirror. Carmen watched in horror as I used the scissors to make a cut in the hem of the dress. Then, holding the material between my hands, I tore the silk satin to a more suitable length. The new, ragged hemline hung midway between my thighs and my knees. I liked it!

Mission accomplished – I felt like *me*! I had dressed it down, roughed it up, and – importantly – thanks to my boots, I was now also ready for action. In those heels there was no way I could have run after anyone should the need arise.

Carmen stood, mouth agape, holding the ripped-off length of the dress. Hopefully she'd find her voice by morning. Quickly I thanked her, and told her the dress now looked almost as good as her chicken had tasted. Then I looked at my watch and flew down the stairs. I could hear Ellie beeping outside – she'd offered to pick me up along with Victor the hairdresser.

The Juno bag was to be launched at the enormous La Lune flagship store on the Rue du Faubourg St. Honoré. Traffic was terrible and when we arrived I understood why: not only had all of the crème de la crème of the fashion, music and cinema worlds been invited, but hundreds of people had turned out to watch the long parade of movie stars, pop stars and supermodels. Banners with the blackbird logo lined the entire block and behind the long red ropes set up along the sidewalks security were kept busy checking invitation cards and guest lists. The paparazzi were relegated to their own area behind a red rope to the right of the entrance.

As we approached the red carpet, the paparazzi began calling out Ellie's name. I went on ahead while she and Victor answered questions and obliged the photographers. Sebastian was waiting just inside – as promised, my aunt had organized him a ticket. I was surprised to see him dressed in a shirt and jacket – although, if everyone else was dressed up, why wouldn't he be? Besides, it suited him. And it contrasted nicely – there was that word again! – with his scooter-boy hair and sardonic smile.

"You look amazing," he whispered into my ear as we walked away from the entrance. "I love your dress – and I bet you're the only girl here in combat boots," he laughed. "You're all dressed up, but you still look like you, which I like."

I quickly looked down and made as if to straighten my dress – my sidekick was making me blush. I mumbled thanks and took a hurried breath before looking back up. He was smiling at me, his blue-grey eyes dark in the evening light. For the briefest of moments, our gaze locked, and the teasing light in his eyes softened into something else. But it was gone as swiftly as it had appeared. I quickly looked away and Sebastian took a glass of orange juice from a passing tray.

"Well, what's the plan?" he asked, handing me the glass, the teasing smile back on his lips. "Are we going to set a trap and catch the culprit?"

"No." I smiled. "Tonight is an evening of quiet observation." I scanned the room but didn't see any of the La Lunes.

Sebastian rolled his eyes. "But I've been observing all day! I'm ready for some action."

"Actually," I whispered as I leaned into him, "I'm dying to tell you something – in a quiet corner."

But as we turned to move away, we bumped right into Ellie and Victor, fresh from a trip to the buffet table. "We got some for you too," said Ellie as she held out a plate of miniature savoury tarts.

Sebastian and I looked at each other and shrugged. "Mmm…thanks," I said. "But, listen, you brought the snacks – why don't we get the drinks, right, Sebastian?"

"Great idea," he said. "We'll be right back."

We'd soon found a quiet corner in the umbrella and hat section of the store.

"I don't think they'll miss us." I nodded towards Ellie. She and Victor had already crossed the room and were deep in conversation with various models and fashionistas.

We stood on our own, scanning the faces present. My aunt hadn't yet arrived, nor did I see any of the La Lunes. "You know what still bothers me?" I said, skewering a tiny meatball. "How did the kidnapper get out of the La Lune mansion, dragging Belle and then Darius with them?"

A buzz of excitement suddenly filled the air. Standing on my tiptoes I could see Philippe's head at the door. Then Rose and Dom appeared, followed by Claude. Last in was Fiona, looking aloof and icy as usual.

"And I'll tell you something else," I whispered, "I'm betting that before Friday there'll be another disappearance."

"Well, why don't we do something about it? Perhaps my father can increase the guard on the mansion? The La Lunes all have minders in order to prevent more disappearances. But still...maybe more security is needed," he said, reaching for his phone.

"Don't – there's nothing we can do to stop the next disappearance – if you can call it that."

Sebastian looked at me in total confusion, but before I could say anything else I heard that familiar voice.

"Axelle, darling, turn around – what *are* you wearing?" Aunt V was walking towards us, staring at my dress and boots. "The hemline! And please don't tell me those are your lucky boots! I wonder what could have happened? I asked the office to send a pair of Louboutins in your size together with the dress, just for you to wear tonight."

"That's right. And they did arrive," I quickly added, as I saw her about to speed-dial Blossom's number, "but..." What could I say? Then I had a sudden brainwave: I remembered a quote I'd read this morning in one of Aunt V's fashion books. It was by one of the most revered of the last century's fashion designers. It was perfect. "Well, as Elsa Schiaparelli often said, and I quote: 'In difficult times fashion is outrageous.'"

"Blithely grow," Aunt V replied as she popped a glistening olive into her mouth.

"Sorry, what?" Sebastian asked.

"Bright yellow," Aunt V continued, indicating a particularly garish shade of yellow being worn by the wife of one of France's better-known businessmen. "And people wonder why I wear sunglasses so much of the time."

"She loves anagrams," I whispered to Sebastian.

"Anyway, Axelle, darling, now where were we? Ah, yes – how right you are. These are difficult times – but that's no excuse for those boots. Although I quite think you've improved the dress with that ripped hem. I think I'll photograph it like that. Anyway, I hope you're close to figuring out this mystery." She paused and pursed her lips for a moment. "I have a trip to New York coming up in two weeks' time and I'd like to take Blossom with me, but until this mucky business is sorted out I can't. Your father," she turned to Sebastian, "has told me Blossom absolutely cannot leave the country until they have found Belle and Darius. It's most inconvenient – I have a magazine to run after all, and fashion waits for no one."

"I'm getting closer, Aunt V."

"Thank goodness." Then the editor-in-chief of one of the American magazines came and whisked her away for a chat about the new collections. "I'll see you later, Axelle, darling," she said as she left.

Sebastian and I wound our way back towards the entrance. There we were handed a leaflet describing Fiona's charity work through the La Lune Fashion Design Foundation. Donations would be accepted throughout the evening. The foundation gave prizes and scholarships to design students from underprivileged backgrounds, and every year ten winners were selected from the hundreds of designs submitted. The designs could be anything to do with fashion, from sunglasses to dresses to shoes.

"Funny to think she's so involved with this project, considering how icy-cold she seems," Sebastian said.

"It's my mother's passion. She's devoted the last thirty years of her life to it." Dom had come up to us quietly from behind – and had heard what Sebastian had said.

To his credit, rather than try to come up with some kind of excuse for his comment, Sebastian just carried on. "Well it's good of her to do it," he said with a shrug of his shoulders.

Dom ignored him entirely. "Axelle, you look incredible.

I love the boots. Can I get you anything to drink, or how about a canapé?" He waved at a waiter. "By the way, have you heard that you're on option next week for a Guerlain fragrance?"

WHAT? How did he know that? "Yes, Hervé mentioned something to me about it," I bluffed. "But how did you know?"

"Hervé also mentioned something about it to me," he answered. "I wanted to book you for a job next week but you already have several options for the whole week. That's fantastic!"

Sebastian had moved away from us and I was now alone with Dom. He offered to show me around the store. As we went from one glass-enclosed display case to another, he pointed out the various bestselling items and told me a bit about their history. Finally we came to a pale pink crocodile handbag sitting on its own. It had more spotlights on it than anything else in the store. We had to jostle forward just to get close to it. Pristine and shiny, it sat atop a glass plinth. Two security guards watched over it, keeping the crowds back. We were standing before the first Clothilde bag ever made – the very same one, in fact, that had accompanied Princess Clothilde on that fateful drive those many years ago...

"This is it – the handbag that gave my family its fame," he said.

"It gave you a curse too."

He shrugged his shoulders. "If you believe in that sort of thing."

"Don't you? Rose does. She says the curse is coming alive. She told me she can hear it moving through your house at night like a ghost." Of course Rose hadn't told me directly – I'd heard it through the chimney flue. But still, nothing ventured, nothing gained, I figured.

He laughed. "My sister Rose has a very vivid imagination. But, who knows…" Dom hesitated. "It's true that our house is a creaky old place. I've sometimes heard things at night too."

"Things? Like what? And when?"

"Now. Lately. Just bumps and things." Again he shrugged his broad shoulders. "More than likely it's my mother going through her closets late at night, preparing her perfect outfit for the following day."

"Does she do that?"

"I don't know," he laughed, "maybe. Or maybe Rose is right."

I wanted to ask him more but suddenly the lights began to dim. "Come on," said Dom, reaching for my hand and pulling me after him towards the large atrium in the middle of their store. "Juno is about to sing."

A frisson of anticipation ran through the crowd as people turned to watch a stage slowly rise from the floor. Juno, the biggest new star in pop music and the muse after whom the new bag was named, was going to perform.

"Why Juno?" I whispered to Dom.

"Because…" He leaned in close to me. He smelled good – and electric, like a summer day just before a storm breaks. I blushed when he caught me looking at his profile. "Because," he continued, smiling at me, "Belle happened to be sitting next to her on a flight to New York, and she noticed that all sorts of things were spilling out of Juno's bag: tablet, water bottle, books, clothes, you name it. It was a mess, my sister said. Anyway, Belle told her she needed to find a bag that could carry all of her stuff and look good. At that point Juno recognized her and asked her if she'd make her one – actually, from what Belle said, Juno more or less commanded that a bag be made for her. Anyway, that's how the collaboration began. And when Juno finally saw the finished product she was so delighted that she spontaneously said she'd sing at the launch – as a thank you. It's a real coup for us."

The room was now completely dark and silence had descended upon the waiting crowd. We watched as a single spotlight focused on the stage and the band suddenly appeared out of the darkness. Music filled the store. The crowds outside could be heard cheering. Now only the star was missing. Then coloured spotlights began to swirl overhead. Back and forth over our heads they crossed until one of them caught a flash of silver. It lost the flash then found it again – it was Juno. She was twirling above us on a giant purple Juno bag, silver sequined outfit glinting at us.

Once the light was fixed on her she began to sing, her glossy red mouth glistening like a jewel in the dark. Back and forth she swung on her giant handbag, arms entwined in the handles, her ruby red shoes kicking in the air. Then, ever so slowly, the handbag began to float downwards, her black hair (straightened to within an inch of its life) streaming behind her. As she landed and flung herself off the giant handbag, a team of ten shirtless dancers were on hand to catch her; within seconds she was prancing onstage, singing just beyond arm's reach. As the song came to its thundering conclusion, the room erupted.

Juno pranced a bit more, then screamed a loud thanks to the La Lunes. Dom left to join his family and I watched as Juno gave Claude, Fiona, Rose and Dom hugs and kisses when they went up onstage to hand her a new bag (Dom told me Juno had already been given one in nearly every colour of the rainbow – they had saved the purple one so that there was at least *one* to give her at the launch). Then she sang one last song – a tearful rendition of one of her slower hits. This was followed by an emotional silence. The unvoiced questions on everyone's mind, of course, were where were Belle and Darius? And would they ever be back?

After a few moments Claude walked onto the stage, a single white spot illuminating his way. There he announced that tonight he and his family wanted to recognize a certain Madame Simone Baillie for her lifetime of service to his family. She had started working as a receptionist and by the time she had reached retirement age she had been working as personal secretary to Patrick. But Simone was made of tough stuff: retirement did not entice her in the least, and so she'd asked for a new post. Something less demanding (she had travelled everywhere, and constantly, with Patrick), but, nevertheless, meaningful and challenging. After a bit of reflection, the perfect job had been found for her: she would become the company's official archivist.

Simone had apparently taken to her new job with gusto. She'd worked out an efficient new computer system for cataloguing every handbag, leather diary, dress, saddle and scarf the company had ever made. Then she'd had everything photographed and properly stored. All of this careful work had culminated in the opening of a private museum of vintage La Lune clothes and accessories. The museum was on the banks of the Seine, a stone's throw away from the National Library. It had opened a little over a year ago and, now, finally, Simone was going to have a proper, festive thank you.

We watched and cheered as she was carefully pushed onto the stage in her wheelchair and accepted her flowers and gift. She gave a short speech, her somewhat feeble voice thanking the La Lune family for all of the opportunities and excitement they'd given her over the years. It was a generous tribute to a hard-working lady and everyone was in a good mood as she left the stage and the music slowly started up again.

It was then that I had my idea…

A little while later, I found Simone Baillie in one of the smaller rooms near the central stairwell. She was in the scarf department, to be precise. Fortunately no one was speaking with her and when I went up to ask if I might have a word with her, her minder looked relieved to leave her with me for a few minutes.

Curious and chatty, she asked where I came from and what I was doing in Paris. Leaning into her so that she could hear me and I could hear her, I answered her questions as succinctly as possible. Her sparkly little eyes never left me for a moment. She was a keen listener, who didn't pass judgement but simply nodded encouragement and waited to see where you led – in short, she was the perfect secretary.

With the preliminaries out of the way, I launched into my line of questioning. "Madame Baillie, I've been trying to trace someone you may have heard of. She's a woman called Violette Roux… Have you ever met a woman by that name? I only know that she came from Normandy and arrived in Paris in January of 1961 and probably worked in one of the boutiques along this street."

She regarded me for a few moments, her tiny head cocked to the side like a little bird's. Then she looked away and contemplated the scarves for some time before turning back to me.

"Violette Roux… Hmm… Funny, someone else asked me about her just the other day…"

She was silent as she leaned back in her wheelchair and slowly closed her eyes. I watched her for a minute or two until, finally, thinking she'd gone to sleep, I lightly tapped her shoulder and whispered her name into her ear. Like an owl, she turned her head in my direction and opened her eyes, then smiled.

"I'm awake, my dear, don't worry. And yes, I knew Violette Roux. I knew her quite well, in fact. She was *très, très jolie*. She had the most amazing eyes – a deep violet colour. I suppose that's why she was called Violette…"

Violette had arrived in Paris without knowing a soul or even her way around – but she was a quick learner. And one thing that she had very quickly found out was that it was on the Rue du Faubourg St. Honoré that she would find the sort of boutique she was looking for. So, one day, not a week after she'd arrived, she put on one of the new suits she'd bought with a portion of Hector's legacy and walked into the first boutique that appealed to her. It was the La Lune boutique.

Violette got the job. She was polite, hard-working, and interested without being nosy. Furthermore, with her pretty looks and sense of style, she rapidly built up a list of clients who sought her advice. After only a few weeks, she even had a male client who regularly came by to ask for her guidance. Because he insisted on her help, Violette was instructed to make an exception and to help the gentleman in the men's department. Then, one afternoon, as she was unwrapping a new delivery, her colleague told Violette that the gentleman she had been helping these last few weeks was none other than the son of the owner of the company. The gentleman who had requested Violette's help was Patrick La Lune!

Violette was mortified. And judging from the way her colleague was talking, it was obvious her co-workers believed there was more to their relationship than just clothes. Violette couldn't sleep that night. She had worked so hard to come this far. She was not going to risk her hard-won reputation as a good employee just because the owner's son thought it was amusing to play "customer" with her. So the next time he came in – he was coming in twice a week by now – she told him in no uncertain terms that from that day forward he would have to seek the advice of one of her colleagues.

Patrick knew she was avoiding him, so he began to court her seriously – but away from the boutique. He showed up outside her lodging house, sent her flowers, and gave her – or, rather, *tried* to give her – presents. Violette refused everything, until one day he offered to take her to the ballet. Quite simply, she'd never been and had always wanted to go – so she accepted his offer...

"But then what happened?" I asked.

"They started seeing each other, and it got really rather serious." Simone paused for a moment as if she was seeing everything slowly rewind in her mind.

"So they married."

"No – their situation got sticky. When Patrick told his parents who he wanted to marry, they told him that was out of the question."

"But why?"

"Don't forget, this was 1962. Patrick's parents wanted him to marry someone 'suitable'. To them she was just a shop girl. That sort of concept doesn't exist today."

"So what happened?"

"Patrick broke it off with Violette."

I was about to call Patrick a weasel when Simone silenced me with a raised finger.

"Wait. It gets better… You see, Violette was pregnant."

"With Patrick's child?"

"Oui, oui. But still he refused to marry her, because by this time his parents had threatened to disinherit him."

"But that's horrible!"

"I thoroughly agree." She was quiet again for some moments before continuing. "But there is a happy ending of sorts."

I waited for her to continue.

"Violette was furious. She was a fiery girl, you know. Sweet as could be, but she could fight if she had to – I think she'd had a somewhat difficult childhood. Her father was an alcoholic who'd died when she was young. She'd been raised by her mother, she told me. Anyway, when Patrick refused to do the right thing she refused to have anything to do with him. But, apparently, he suggested they continue to see each other *secretly*."

"What?!"

Simone nodded her head as she looked at me. "But again she refused, and promptly accepted an offer of marriage from someone else."

"Who?"

"Another faithful La Lune client, who'd been trying to court her for months. He was older, lived on a small estate in the Champagne region, east of Paris, and he was very much in love with her."

"So she accepted…"

"She did. And her new husband never questioned the fact that the baby came a bit early."

"And she was happy?"

"Very."

"And she's still alive?"

"I have no idea. But I do know that after she was widowed she continued to live on the estate her husband left her. That was many years ago now…"

"And what was her husband's name?"

"The man Violette married was called René de Vandrille. She became Violette de Vandrille and their son was – is – called—"

"Philippe de Vandrille," I whispered. "Only Philippe isn't *their* son – he's Violette and Patrick La Lune's son."

"Exactly. Which means that by blood he is a La Lune."

Yes, I thought as I steadied myself, *Philippe is a La Lune… and* a Merlette.

For a few moments Simone and I sat in companionable silence, visions of Violette's dramatic life playing before our eyes.

Then I turned to ask her one last question. "Do you think that Philippe de Vandrille knows who his real father is?"

Again she was quiet for some time. "Perhaps…perhaps not. I doubt his mother ever told him – at that time, unlike today where anything goes, those kinds of revelations were never made. I don't know…"

"By the way, you mentioned that someone else asked you about Violette just a few days ago?"

Slowly, Simone nodded her head. "It was a phone call – I thought it might be Philippe. I thought maybe he'd guessed that I was the only person aware of his secret identity." Her eyes crinkled with mischief as she smiled at me. "Funny that two people in the same week should ask me about her."

As nonchalantly as possible I asked, "Did the caller give you their name?" I knew the answer, of course. As I waited for her to say it, the hairs on my arms slowly stood on end.

"Yes, he was called David. David le…something. I can't remember…"

David le Néanar!

Dom found me just after I'd left Simone. Once again, I'd completely forgotten about our plans and, frankly, after what I'd just learned the last thing I wanted to do was to spend the next two hours discussing fashion with Dom – regardless of his amazing eyes. Surprisingly, all I wanted was to find Sebastian and talk to him. But how could I get out of my date with Dom? I decided to take the direct approach.

"So, are you ready?" he asked smoothly as he came up behind me and put his arm around my waist. He had my leather jacket in hand and was holding it out for me to slip into.

"Uhm…actually, Dom…I'm afraid I have to cancel our plans." I felt like an idiot as I said it, but I really had to talk through the case – and not with Dom.

Dom looked taken aback but tried to make light of it. "What? Don't tell me you've decided to see Paris from the back of a scooter?" he asked with a smile. The allusion to Sebastian was clear. "You English girls have a strange idea of what is interesting."

Great. How was I going to explain that although I'd be leaving with Sebastian, my meeting with him had to do with work and nothing else – never mind that quick look we'd shared earlier.

"Yeah, well..." I said lamely as I fumbled to find the right words. Dom's eyes were a major distraction. *Come on, Axelle, focus, focus!* "Listen, Dom, I'm really, really sorry but I can't make it tonight. I've been looking forward to spending some time with you" – I felt my cheeks turn red as I said this – "but I'm afraid I have work to do and it's important." I said it with as much finality as I could muster. "I'm sorry..."

He wasn't buying it. I could tell by the way he was looking at me as he rocked back and forth on his pointy-toed shoes, his hands deep in his pockets. In fact, he looked downright angry.

"Work? Is there some show starting after midnight that I don't know about?" he asked sarcastically. "Or is *Teen Vogue* doing an early-morning shoot?"

I flushed, but less with embarrassment than anger. Out of the corner of my eye, I saw Sebastian watching.

Dom turned to leave, but before walking away he swung back to me and said, "By the way, I have a couple of options on you for next week. They could definitely help your career but, I don't know, maybe you're not so...motivated. Let's see...maybe..." He didn't finish what he was going to say. Instead he shrugged his shoulders and left.

Excuse my French, but what a jerk!

I stood staring after him practically spitting at what he'd

insinuated. He'd clearly hinted that his confirming me for the modelling options depended on whether or not I went along with his after-work plans. What an ASS! How dare he? Was this how fashion operated? Was this normal? Ughh!

"I guess your plans have changed?" Sebastian was smiling as he came up to me.

"Yes. Definitely," I answered through gritted teeth, turning to him. "Tell me something, Sebastian..."

He looked at me and raised his eyebrows.

"When I told you that I'd be meeting up with Dom, you didn't have a fit, did you?"

He shook his head. "Why should I? You're free to do whatever you want."

"Do you think you can promise me something then?"

"What?"

"That you won't change."

After that, Victor, Ellie, Sebastian and I slipped out of the crowded party as quickly as we could. Sebastian suggested that we all go out for coffee but Ellie had to get straight to Giambattista Valli for a last-minute emergency fitting and Victor had a Hollywood actress he'd promised to get colour-ready for tomorrow morning.

"I'm glad we're alone," Sebastian said as he led me past the red ropes. "I have something to tell you. My father called me..."

"Well, I have something to tell you too – something new."

"Then how about an ice cream before I take you home?"

He didn't have to ask me twice – I was always up for an ice cream. He suggested he leave his scooter where it was and that we walk to the restaurant.

Café Ruc is one of the best places to fashion-watch during the shows. Its proximity to the Louvre ensures a steady stream of models, designers, editors, buyers, hair and make-up artists and photographers. And while everything on the menu is good, I had the sneaking suspicion that Sebastian and I weren't the only ones ordering their vanilla ice cream swimming in a rich, hot chocolate sauce.

After ordering, Sebastian asked, "So who goes first?"

"You do."

"Okay. My father called me while you were talking to the retired secretary."

"Madame Baillie. And?"

"Well, it seems someone definitely planted Belle's drawings in Blossom's bag at the gallery."

"How do you know?"

"Video footage – but it's impossible to say who the person is. And no one at the party can remember. It looks like it was a woman but nobody has been able to recognize her." After a moment's pause he added, "You know, I haven't seen you look this intense since the first time I saw you and you had those ridiculous fake glasses on."

"Did they look that fake?"

"Yes they did. So what do you think?"

"Who has a solid alibi for their whereabouts on Sunday night, at the time the drawings were planted?"

"Two people: first, your aunt, obviously, as she was with you. She'd just picked you up from the station. And Philippe: he was at his office, with his partner. Otherwise, the La Lunes were at home but all in their separate rooms. After dinner that night they each went their own way, and that house is so big that you could cross Paris and come back and no one would be any the wiser. Now it's your turn."

Between mouthfuls of the most delicious ice cream, I told him what I'd learned from Simone.

"What a weasel," he said.

"I thought the same."

"It must be Philippe," Sebastian said. "He clearly has the strongest motive. Even if he doesn't know that Patrick is his father, surely Violette would have told him about the history between her Uncle Hector and the La Lunes. I mean, he'd have to be made of steel not to feel entitled to fair compensation and an apology – for his family's honour alone!"

"But if it's important to him, why didn't he do something earlier? Why wait until now? He is a lawyer, after all."

Sebastian shrugged his shoulders. "Maybe he's got some kind of long-term plan?"

We both fell silent as we finished our ice cream. Finally Sebastian asked, "When did you say your mother arrives?"

"Friday morning – but, hopefully, my aunt will keep her busy until the La Lune show – it's at six o'clock. After that, we'll be joined at the hip."

"Which means we have just under forty-eight hours to get to the bottom of this…"

"Exactly."

Sebastian offered to take me back to Aunt V's, but I said I'd prefer to walk.

"Well, just be careful," he said, "and if you think you see a black Peugeot saloon car following you – call me!"

I promised, and left. After cutting across the Tuileries Park, I crossed the river and was home in no time.

Fortunately for me, Aunt V was still out. At this late hour I definitely wasn't in the mood for one of her fashion interrogations. I quickly checked my phone for the details for tomorrow's *Elle* job: 12 p.m. at Pin-Up Studios in the 14th *arrondissement*; we'd be shooting beauty which, Hervé helpfully told me, meant facial close-ups, for a half-day only, and I was to arrive with clean hair and face. Apparently, Hervé was still waiting for the details of Friday's La Lune show.

I wanted nothing more than to go to bed, but something was bothering me. As I headed towards my bedroom I glanced at my watch and saw that it was just shy of midnight. Ellie should be finished. Quickly I wrote her a short text, and ten seconds later my phone rang.

"So what's up?" she asked.

I told her what had happened between Dom and me. "Is that the way fashion works?" I asked. "I mean, he clearly threatened to confirm me or cancel me depending on whether I went out with him!"

Ellie was silent for a moment.

"Listen, Axelle, I'm sorry that had to happen to you... and I'd be lying if I said that sort of thing never happens. It does. But – wait, wait – let me finish before you get mad. It happens, *but you have the right to decide whether you want to play along with it or not.*"

"But isn't what he did illegal or something? I mean—"

"Illegal? I don't know," Ellie said, interrupting me. "There are those – like Dom – who try to play that game, especially with the new girls – but the majority don't. You can't be professional and a perv at the same time! Talk to Hervé about it. It's the agency's job to protect us and to see that things run smoothly. We pay them for that, remember?"

She had a point.

"And a woman can come up against that kind of thing no matter what kind of job she has. I have a cousin who works in the City, in banking, and she gets crap thrown at her all the time. Talk to Hervé about it. It sounds like Dom should have his wings clipped. He's a spoiled brat who thinks the rules don't apply to him."

"Thanks for telling me."

"I thought you were seeing him because of the case..."

"I was, I think. Maybe a bit for his eyes, too."

"Yeah, well, pretty is as pretty does, don't you think?"

"Absolutely." I hung up with a smile. Talking to Ellie had helped.

My last thought of the day was of Belle and Darius. Belle had been missing since Saturday, Darius since Monday. How was Darius holding up without his medication? Were they eating? Drinking? Would they be alive by the time I found them? The thought of finding two dead bodies was gruesome.

Hurry, I told myself, *hurry, hurry*.

*B*elle was alone again.

She'd wriggled to Darius to check his breathing. It was shallow, but he was alive, thank God – but then their captor had come in before she'd made it back to her bed. Not a noise had been made, no threat given. She'd simply been dragged across the room, then pulled through a door and left on the damp floor of the room next door.

A silent tear made its way down her smudged cheek. She was beginning to lose hope…

THURSDAY MORNING

<u>Secrets</u>

Grrr…grrr…grrr…

Miu Miu was awake. Her blue-grey whiskers tickled my exposed ear and when she saw my eyelids slowly open her purring went up a few decibels. It reminded me of Halley at home. As soon as I so much as crack an eye open her tongue is all over my face, her smelly breath drying so quickly that by the time I make it to the bathroom I can hardly stand the smell of my own face.

At least Miu Miu doesn't lick.

I got out of bed and walked to the large window overlooking the awakening street. The heavy blue silk curtains shimmered in the early morning light and as I opened the window wide a fresh spring breeze blew some of my notes off the desk. It was another capricious spring day and it seemed more than likely that a storm would break by midday.

I'd just sat back down on my bed and had taken out the packet of letters – I continued to reread them in the hope of finding something important

I'd missed – when I heard Aunt V outside my door. "Axelle, I know you have a late start this morning and that you'll be shooting for *Elle* this afternoon. Is there anything else you plan on doing?"

"Good morning, Aunt V!" I crossed my room and opened the door.

Aunt V gave me a quick peck on the cheek then pulled away. "I'm running late. Ooh… And what kind of pyjamas are those?" She was looking at my pink PJs as if they were some kind of contagious disease. "Aren't you a little old for hearts, Axelle?"

I admit my PJs are a little on the corny side – and, as Jenny likes to point out, they look similar to ones I had when I was six. But they're super-soft and, well…I like them for that. "They're soft," I answered with a quick shrug of my shoulders before changing the subject. "Anyway, I thought I'd do some research this morning. Then I'll meet Sebastian after *Elle*."

"What'll you do then?"

"I don't know. It'll depend on what we find today."

"Good." There was a pause as she looked at me, her eyes unblinking. I stood riveted in my doorway, nearly flinching under her relentless stare. My aunt can look pretty intense sometimes – scary almost – and this morning was one of those times. Finally she spoke.

"Well, I hope you're getting closer. We've got to get *Chic's* name cleared."

Whew. I let my breath out and slumped against my door, relieved her stare had broken, relieved that she was leaving.

Or so I thought.

Suddenly I saw her eyes flicker over my slumped shoulders and towards my bed. Quickly I straightened back up, turning slightly to block her view, but I was too late! "Since when do you write letters, Axelle?" she asked.

Stupidly I'd left the packet of letters – with one unfolded – on my bed. "Uhm…since…always."

"Always?" She fixed her gaze on me.

"Uhm…yes. It was Gran's idea. She…uhm…thought it might be a good exercise for me to imitate as many kinds of handwriting as possible. To get inside the minds of different personality types."

I stood calmly, hoping she'd buy my story. I didn't want her reading the letters – it would lead to too many questions, primarily about how I'd found them. Although…although why was Aunt V even curious about them? I mean, it could be any kind of paperwork on my bed, right? Since when had she ever expressed any real interest in me beyond my wardrobe?

As I shifted my weight she brought her eyes back to me, the letters apparently forgotten. "Uhmm, Aunt V?"

She arched an eyebrow at me.

"Your bag. It's leaking." Strangely, from one corner of her blue crocodile-skin handbag liquid was dripping.

"Ah." She looked down. "So it is. It must be my water. Hydration – important, you know, during the shows."

I bent low to wipe it with a tissue.

"Don't bother, Axelle," she said quickly. "Carmen will clean it up."

"Okay." I stood up again. "By the way, last night—" I wanted to tell her about Simone Baillie's revelations, but I was cut off.

"I'm sorry, Axelle, but I'm running late. I have to go. Tell me later. I'll be home late again tonight, so if I don't see you this evening, I'll see you tomorrow. Call if you need anything..." she said with a quick wave of her fingers.

Whatever.

One thing was for sure though, I thought, as I stood watching her leave, bag clutched tightly – if *I'd* had water dripping from *my* bag, she'd have had a fit!

I went back into my bedroom and fetched the book on Le Vau before heading into the kitchen for breakfast. As I munched on my fruit salad, I delved into the world of Louis Le Vau. Apparently, King Louis XIV was his greatest patron and the royal palace of Versailles his crowning achievement. But, apart from that, it seemed he'd worked for everyone who was anyone in seventeenth-century Paris. As I flicked through the pages, a black-and-white photograph of a large stone mansion caught my eye. The caption underneath said it was the *Hotel de Buismont*. I knew that *hotel* in French meant "mansion" but who or what was *de Buismont*? And why did the mansion look so familiar?

Of course! I nearly upended my bowl of fruit salad as I pushed my chair back from the table and ran to my aunt's sitting room. I sat at her desk and flicked her computer on. And there it was, on Wikipedia, in the first sentence: *The Hotel de Buismont, designed by Louis Le Vau, and better known today as the La Lune mansion, was built in 1665 for wealthy financier, Salatin de Buismont.*

No wonder it looked familiar – the Hotel de Buismont and the La Lune mansion were one and the same! Presumably Darius knew this too...

But what about the word *passages* in his note? What did it mean? Or could *passages* really be as straightforward as it sounded? Like the passages in a house? Or, more specifically, the passages in a house designed by Le Vau?

Back and forth I flipped through the pages of the book, hoping my hunch was right. I scanned the dense text until I found the words I was looking for: *secret passages*. According to the book, the houses Louis Le Vau designed were full of them.

And what was easier than disappearing via a secret passage?

"Well done, Sherlock." Sebastian had just arrived.

"That's Holmes to you."

He laughed. "I thought you might say that."

"If I didn't have to do *Elle*, I'd follow this lead myself."

"I know. But don't worry, I'll dig – hard. And I'll keep you posted."

Great. I'd just noticed I'd put my jumper on inside out. Not surprising, considering that after calling Sebastian I'd realized I was still in my heart PJs. At least I'd managed to brush my teeth and hair. I stretched and poured myself another glass of orange juice. I still had half an hour before I had to leave.

"By the way," I said, as I handed him the day's *Figaro*, "did you read your horoscope yet? Apparently you're going to make a major discovery today."

"And according to your horoscope, romance is in the air for you this week." He was grinning.

"Yeah, right," I said, recalling Dom's anger last night. "Fat chance."

"Are you so sure?" He was leaning back, still grinning, but his eyes didn't leave mine.

I quickly turned back to the computer, hoping I looked sufficiently absorbed by the Wiki entry on Le Vau. *Come on, Axelle, focus, focus. Ignore your sidekick's broad shoulders and killer smile.* Easier said than done. Somehow my annoying sidekick had morphed into a distraction – of the cute kind. I wasn't sure when or how it had happened but, honestly, I'd need a blindfold to ignore Sebastian now – which, incidentally, wouldn't have been a good thing on the clue-gathering front. *You have a case to solve, remember, Axelle? I told myself. Besides, you're working with him – you have a working relationship with him. And that's how you need it to stay – I mean, imagine if...no, don't go there. Not now, anyway.Argh! I have to solve this case.*

I took a breath, turned, and met his stare. Shrugging my shoulders, I said, lightly, "Who knows? Anything could be possible this week."

"I guess time will tell." He was still grinning at me, a teasing glint in his eye.

"Uh-uh," I mumbled and quickly turned back to the computer.

After a moment he said, "What I don't understand is that my father and his team searched the entire La Lune mansion and didn't find any sort of secret passage, and yet..." He hesitated as he grappled with filial loyalty. "And yet I'm sure you're right – there must be a secret passage in that house. It would certainly explain the noises Rose has been hearing."

"Yeah, and Dom too. Anyway, while a secret passage in the house might explain how the kidnapper moved within the house without being seen, it still doesn't explain how the kidnapper has been able to get in and out undetected."

"Unless..." He was looking out the large open window towards the river.

"Sebastian...?" He'd stepped out onto the narrow balcony.

"What did you say my horoscope said?" he asked.

"That you'd make a discovery today?"

"Well, I think I've just made it." He stepped back in and turned to leave. "I'll pick you up after *Elle*," he called over his shoulder. The door shut with a bang as he ran down the stairs.

I arrived at Pin-Up Studios in time to join the *Elle* team for lunch in the studio cafe, and by five o'clock the shoot was finished. It was a beauty shoot, a gold and shimmery summer make-up story. We shot three different photos, each one focusing on a different aspect of my make-up: eyes, lips and skin. This meant that my make-up was changed three times. I'd asked the digi-tech guy to take a photo of me (with my phone) in each of the different make-up looks I'd worn. I'd show them to Hervé when I saw him next. Apparently, bookers love to see whatever images a model can bring back from a shoot. The afternoon went by quickly, but, still, not quickly enough: by the time we'd finished I was itching to follow up my clues.

Sebastian picked me up outside of the studios and drove towards the Seine. However, along the way he suddenly motioned to me with his hand that he wanted to stop. He zigzagged through the traffic, then zoomed up the Boulevard Saint-Michel. A few moments later we parked on a tiny side street tucked away in the residential part of the sixth district behind the Luxembourg Gardens.

"I need to show you all that I've found out and we need to do it somewhere quiet…somewhere we're not likely to be overheard. And, anyway, we have some time to kill," he added mysteriously, as he led me to the park, "because what we're going to do is better done in the dark."

I followed him to a small space enclosed by trees and crawling vines. Opposite us, against a backdrop of spring green, a large fountain was set into a high wall. A Greek god hovered on top, surprising the lovers underneath. Water cascaded gently into a long, narrow basin. The air was quiet and humid, twilight on its way. "It's the Medici Fountain," Sebastian said, as he dragged a second chair to one of the small metal tables flanking the water.

He loaded our table with folders and maps.

"Your idea this morning about the possibility of secret passages was spot on. And your comment last night about getting out of the mansion while dragging Belle and Darius didn't go unnoticed," he added with a smile. "In fact, it's what triggered my idea this morning as I looked out from your balcony towards the river. I'll show you what I mean." He struggled to get one last folder out of his sack. "*Et voilà!*" Excitedly he laid a floor plan of a house out on the table.

"It looks old," I said, as I scanned its sepia-toned lines and elaborate handwriting, "really old…"

"It is. This is a copy of the 1665 original. It's the floor

plan of the La Lune mansion. Fortunately for us, most of Le Vau's work is well documented – even if it's sometimes difficult to get hold of. With a bit of help from a friend – he's a history geek – I found all of this at the *Bibliothèque Nationale*. And I was told that all of Le Vau's big projects have secret passageways."

Slowly, I traced what appeared to be one of them with my finger.

"What you're running your finger along is the longest secret passageway in the house," Sebastian said, "but it's so well concealed that unless you happened to have been there when the construction work was going on, you'd never know it exists. That passage connects with another one in the opposite wing, via a secret door in the library. It ends in this passageway, then connects to a hidden staircase which runs the entire height of the house from cellar to attics. It also connects to another secret passageway which runs the length of this wing."

"Why so many?"

"Because Salatin de Buismont was a bit of a shady character. By the time he had this house built he was one of the wealthiest men in France – he even loaned money to foreign governments – but there are no clear traces of how he gained his fortune. And apparently, he also had a rather complicated private life. His diaries are full of escapades – including, if he's to be believed, a long affair with the king's wife…"

"No wonder he needed to move around the entire house without being seen."

"Exactly. But there are two things that really interest me about this map."

"And they are?"

"Firstly, that according to the records at the *Bibliothèque Nationale*, about a year ago a Mr le Néanar asked to see this plan. And the second thing is this," he said, pointing to a minuscule circle on the basement level of the house.

"What is it?"

"Well, if it is what I think it is, then you're looking at my clue."

He unfolded another large sheet of paper and laid it on top of the floor plan.

He was right beside me, our arms touching. "This one looks old too," I said quickly.

"That's because it is."

Carefully he turned it so that it faced me. I couldn't really make sense of it. It was a map with double lines that obviously delineated paths or roads of some sort. But where was this place, and where did the lines lead?

"Is this the river?" I asked, pointing to a thick wavy line that divided the map in two horizontally. "And this map is dotted with the same circle that you just showed me on the house plan." I peered closer, excited now. I didn't yet know what it all meant but something was connecting.

"Yes, that's the Seine and, yes again, that's the same circle that we saw on the floor plan."

"Do they signify the same thing?"

"I hope so..."

"And that is?"

"An entrance to the catacombs." He took a breath. "Every circle on this map," he continued, "represents a direct entrance to the labyrinth of underground tunnels collectively known as the Catacombs of Paris."

"Catacombs? Isn't that where dead bodies are buried?"

He nodded.

"I didn't know that Paris had catacombs..."

"And I'd forgotten them until this morning, when you said 'secret passages' just as I was standing in your aunt's sitting room looking at the river. There used to be a public entrance to the catacombs there – I went one weekend with my father, a long time ago. But that entrance was closed a few years ago. I think the entrance is now in the 14th *arrondissement*."

He stopped to point to a spot in the middle of the Left Bank on the catacombs map. "If you look here, this circle – see how it's off the tunnel route – seems as if it could correspond to where the La Lune mansion is. And if that's true...if it matches with the circle on the house plan..."

"It means we've found a way on and off the property—"

"That connects directly with the secret passages in the house."

"But why would the house have direct access to the catacombs?"

"Well, the catacombs were created at the end of the eighteenth century, which means the house predates them by nearly one hundred and twenty years. Now, as we know, Salatin de Buismont asked Le Vau to design the house with a complex passageway system – but it was Salatin's *grandson* who had the entrance to the catacombs excavated."

"Why?"

"Because, according to my research—"

"You shouldn't believe everything you read on Wikipedia," I said.

Sebastian rolled his eyes. "I, *mademoiselle*, have sources in high places. This information comes directly from the *Bibliothèque Nationale*. Anyway, as I was saying, de Buismont the grandson was a clergyman – a very high-ranking one and, as such, he was involved in the removal of the human bones from the old city cemetery at les Halles to the newly excavated catacombs."

"Yuck! Why did they have to move the old bones?"

"I believe it was a case of overcrowding. It got to the point where there wasn't enough room to properly bury them – the bodies, I mean."

"Gross!"

"Yeah, well, all those exposed rotting bodies were becoming something of a health risk – hence the need for the catacombs: lots of space and all underground. Anyway, apparently, clergyman de Buismont often accompanied the black-veiled wagonloads of bones during their midnight procession through the city – the wagons were always accompanied by priests who sang a burial service – and it was he who blessed the catacombs when they opened. Now, like his grandfather, he had a complicated private life – even more so because he was a clergyman. And because he had ambitious plans for himself, there was only one thing to do about his private life…"

"Hide it."

"Exactly. And what better way than with a secret entrance into the catacombs? So he had an entrance built, linking his house to them directly. And that," he continued in a whisper, "is what I'd like to go and check out now."

I was speechless. History and high fashion on an underground collision course – literally. If these maps and plans were right, then the how and where of this mystery were well on their way to being solved.

"Wait a minute… You said the mysterious Mr le Néanar had checked out the floor plan of the house. But what about it?"

Sebastian nodded. "I asked my friend if he could look up Mr le Néanar in the sign-in record books for the maps of the catacombs, going as far back as possible. His name was listed – from about eight years ago."

"Wow. Eight years. So this guy has known about the secret passageways and catacomb entrances for a long time."

"It seems so."

"Do you think he's been using them?"

Sebastian shrugged his shoulders. "Well, I don't think he's been looking this stuff up just for research."

We sat in silence, the fountain gurgling gently beside us, until after few moments I suddenly sat up. "CAT!"

"Where?"

"No, no. Not that kind. I mean Claude's CAT. The C-A-T from his agenda for Saturday, remember? I bet it refers to the catacombs!"

"You might be right. But if so…it means he knows about the secret passages too. And, if he did go into the catacombs on Saturday night…"

"It was either because he'd kidnapped his own sister…"

"Or, like you," he teased, "maybe he was just following a hunch and hoping to find the perpetrator of the crime."

"Hmm…maybe." I glanced at my watch. My mum would be arriving tomorrow morning. And Belle had been missing for five days, Darius for three. I didn't have time to waste. "Shouldn't we get going?" I asked Sebastian, but he was already packing up. Two minutes later, we were back on his scooter, heading towards the river.

The humid stillness of the park was quickly forgotten: by the river, the air was fresh and brisk. Sebastian parked and locked his scooter. Then we walked quickly along the quayside until we turned down a staircase that led to the cobblestoned bank of the Seine.

When we reached the bottom he stopped and quickly scanned the bank – it was deserted. We walked along for about a hundred metres until we were standing directly underneath the Pont de la Concorde. Sebastian turned to an iron door set into the base of the bridge. It was painted black and looked as if it hadn't been used in years. Long rust stains ran from its top edge down to the ground – even its bolts were rusty. It reminded me of Erik's underground world in the Phantom of the Opera.

"Is this the entrance we're looking for?" I asked Sebastian.

"Uh-huh."

"How do we get in?"

He smiled at me as he reached into one of his jacket pockets. "With this." He pulled out a large, black, iron key and showed it to me before sliding it into the lock. "It's a master key."

"Where did you get that?"

I didn't get an answer because at that moment the key clicked into place and turned, surprisingly easily. The door swung open with an unexpected speed. We nearly fell in.

Sebastian quietly shut the door behind us. We were engulfed in total darkness. I heard him rustling in his rucksack and a moment later the bright beam of his torch lit the ground. "Here, take this," he said, as he handed me a torch, a box of matches, a thick ball of string, and a small compass. "Unwind the string behind you. I'll do the same

– that way we'll know if we're going round in circles and, if we get separated, we might have a chance of finding each other. The La Lune mansion is lying south-east from us. If you get lost and want to get back to this entrance, head north-west. Got it?"

I nodded.

"Good. Let's go and find out if this idea works as well in real life as it does on paper." Then he turned to me and smiled. "Holmes?" He was holding his hand out. I placed my hand in his and followed him in.

While I can highly recommend the Eiffel Tower as a destination for the entire family, I'm not sure a visit to the catacombs is to everyone's taste. Although, having said that, they're definitely…interesting.

The door we went through led immediately to a slippery stone staircase that took us down for quite some way. At its base, three tunnels met. Sebastian led us down the one which, according to his map and compass, would lead us to the La Lune mansion – not that the tunnels travelled in straight lines. We knew we'd have to keep our wits about us. There are apparently lots of stories of people breaking into the catacombs just for the fun of it, only to end up getting lost and dying. There are so many tunnels covering so much ground that without a way of tracing someone it is nearly impossible to find them – even if you know where they started out from. Apparently, most die of thirst… With that encouraging thought in mind, I quietly followed Sebastian and concentrated on not losing him.

We were only about a kilometre from the La Lune mansion. If we moved quickly and managed not to get lost, we'd need about half an hour to get there. The air was heavy and thick, stale with age; it felt as if it stuck to my lungs as I breathed it in (a bit like my mum's home-made hummus). I was trying to breathe as calmly as I could, but the narrow passages and damp darkness made me feel claustrophobic. As I was concentrating on breathing – one in, one out, two in, two out – I suddenly slammed into Sebastian's back. "What—"

"Shhh…look…"

Following his torch's beam, I nearly screamed as it alighted on a skeleton.

"Do you think he died here?" I asked.

"I have no idea. Maybe…"

"Are we going to see many of them?"

"I'm afraid this one is the first of many…" he said, taking out his map. "You see this, here where it's marked *the Crypt of St. Geoffroi*? Well, I've heard that the skeletons of his followers *line the walls and ceiling*."

I really didn't know what to say to that.

We carried on silently for some time. It was rough, slow going through the tunnels. Most of the passages – in fact, all of them in the area we were covering – hadn't been used in a very long time. I kept slipping on the slimy stone surfaces and the constant crunching underfoot did nothing to up the comfort level. "What do you suppose all the crunching could be?" I finally asked Sebastian.

"Oh, that? Here, I'll show you," he said as he stopped.

A second later and I wished I'd never asked. Trust me: on occasion, ignorance is bliss. Sebastian moved the beam of his torch, turning around so that it shone on the wall between us. Then in one slow movement he lowered it to the ground. To my amazement the floor was a moving, heaving sea of black. Back and forth, left and right, the slick viscous liquid rolled in gentle waves around our feet.

But after a few moments I realized that it wasn't some thick liquid after all; it was too noisy for that. Besides, it was *dry*. As we stood quietly looking down, a hard metallic sound, something akin to banging cutlery – only muted – emanated up from the ground. I stared down more carefully and, to my utter disgust, it slowly dawned on me that it was definitely not liquid swirling around my feet. quite simply, the tunnel floor was thick with cockroaches. Large, black, cockroaches, their hard shells shining in the light.

AHHHHHHHH!

Sebastian quickly clamped his hand over my mouth and told me to shush, in case someone heard us. I promptly bit him. As he stood shaking his hand, I tried to calm myself down as much as possible.

"*Mon Dieu*, you bite hard! Haven't you ever seen a cockroach before?" he asked.

"Of course I have – BUT I'VE NEVER WALKED THROUGH A RIVER OF THEM!"

"Trust me – you have them in London, too."

"Thanks, but knowing that doesn't make this any easier!"

"I think it'll get better once we're further along."

"How do you know? Maybe they get larger the further we go."

"Ah…actually, I believe the higher we climb, the less of them there are."

"Great. So you knew about this and didn't even tell me!"

"If I had, would you have come?"

He had a point. At that moment I could feel the cockroaches beginning to crawl up my trousers. "Uh, Sebastian, do you think we could do some running? Like, now?" They were going up his trousers now, too.

"Trust me, I don't like them any more than you. Let's get out of here!"

We ran like I've never run before – at least it seemed like that, although it was so dark and slippery that I don't know how fast we were actually going. The horrible crunching underfoot gradually diminished, but we didn't let up speed or stop until we no longer heard it at all. As my breathing returned to normal, I looked around and realized that we were no longer in a tunnel, but rather in quite a large chamber.

It was dry, appeared to be cockroach-free, and had far higher ceilings than any of the passages we had seen so far.

There were nine pillars in the room, and everything looked as if it had been carved out of the bedrock. Chisel marks covered every surface. And although there had been attempts to disguise them with decorative carving, neither the stone nor the ambience in this part of the catacombs lent itself to delicate artistic endeavour; the chamber looked crude and sinister.

"Where are we?" I asked as I peered over his shoulder at the map.

"Here..." he said, dragging his finger under the elaborate script. "The Tomb of the Hidden Heart."

"Is there really a heart hidden here somewhere?"

"According to legend, yes. Although I've been told it was actually a finger."

"Tomb of the Hidden Heart definitely sounds better than Tomb of the Hidden Finger," I said, laughing.

Together we eased ourselves down onto the floor, leaned our backs against the same pillar and took a long drink from our water bottles (another of Sebastian's good ideas).

"Isn't it strange," I said, "to think that two hundred years ago de Buismont's grandson was using these very tunnels as his private escape route? I mean, he was probably in and out of this creepy place every day – and night."

"Yeah, but don't forget that at that time the passages would have looked fresher – if you can apply that term to a cockroach-infested tunnel. What I think is more weird is that someone is using them now to destroy the La Lune family. I wonder how they even got the idea of coming down here?"

"Well, presumably the mysterious David le Néanar could tell us. But what about a key? How easy is it to get a key to the catacombs? And does one key open every entrance?"

"The master key—"

But I didn't hear any more, because at that moment everything went black.

THURSDAY EVENING

The Caribbean

I could hear the gentle lapping of water all around me. Everything else was quiet. As I lay on my back, breathing quietly, my eyes shut, I was reminded of pirates. I've always liked pirates. Pirates never wear much clothing – or at least in the films I've seen – presumably because where they are it's always *warm*.

And it was just that thought that woke me up to the fact that perhaps I wasn't a pirate after all and that the water gently lapping all around me couldn't possibly be the Caribbean. It was icy cold – definitely more English Channel than Sargasso Sea. *How odd*, I thought. But I was having trouble waking. It just seemed so much easier to go back to sleep – and I no doubt would have if a particular image hadn't come to mind. It was of a black, long-tentacled, fast-moving torpedo of filth and disease – and it was heading my way. That got me awake.

Good thing, too, or we would have drowned. Because, wherever we were, the water level was rising – *fast*.

I couldn't see anything except for a silvery reflection far off to the right somewhere. My arms were stretched out at my sides as if I'd been dragged here by my feet – which I probably had been. I smiled to myself. For some reason I found it highly amusing, imagining that this was how shipwrecked pirates must feel. I don't know how long I lay there smiling stupidly to myself, but once I could feel the water lapping up around and into my ears, I figured it was time for a pep talk. *Okay, come on Axelle*, I told myself, *forget Captain Jack Sparrow and his crew and concentrate on getting up and finding out whether Sebastian is nearby. Get moving! Wake up! You're going to drown if you don't.*

This was, of course, easier said than done. My eyes were doing a fine job of resisting all attempts to keep them open. I willed myself to force them wide open for thirty seconds. To my delight, there really did seem to be a spot of light far to my right. Finding a way out suddenly seemed like a possibility – or so I hoped. I slowly turned my head to the other side and could just make out a shape sprawled in the water next to me. *Good*, I thought, *at least Sebastian is all right. Or is he?* By increments I forced myself towards full consciousness so that I could help him. Why was he still asleep? And why couldn't I wake up properly?

Even on Sundays I didn't have this much difficulty getting up. Taking a deep breath, I turned on my side, much as I imagine an inebriated sloth would. From that position I managed to lift myself so that I was leaning on my elbow.

That lasted for about two seconds before I lost strength and splashed back down into the water. Now *that* did wake me up. I began the process all over again and finally achieved a sitting position. Then I called Sebastian's name. He didn't seem to hear me, but the act of sitting up and getting a few good gulps of air into my lungs enabled me to drag myself to him. I shook him and yelled into his ear for good measure and finally he woke. Within seconds he was coughing – he'd actually had his head to one side and had swallowed some of the water as he'd woken. With my help he pulled himself up into a sitting position.

We both splashed some water on our faces. Our clothes were soaked through.

"Somebody hit us," he said between coughs.

"And then left us here to..." A cold shiver ran through me as I left my thought unfinished.

"Don't say it," he answered.

We both attempted to stand. The water was now up to our knees. I'd woken up just in time – a minute later and we would have drowned.

"They've taken all of our things!" said Sebastian as he slogged lopsidedly through the water, looking for his rucksack in the tiny bit of light afforded by a small torch he pulled out of his jacket pocket. "Do you see yours anywhere?"

I didn't.

"What about the map?" I asked.

Sebastian lifted his wet shirt to reveal a secret inside pocket. "I still have it! And the key too. The map may be a bit wet but it's in one piece. Anyway, we need to get to that spot of light on the water. There must be an opening somewhere above it for the light to shine through," he continued, as he began wading out. The water now reached our waists.

The cold water and fear of being trapped motivated us into action. Slowly, we made our way through the black swirling water to the other side of the chamber.

"Don't get caught in an undercurrent!" yelled Sebastian. "It's coming in fast now!"

We didn't know yet if the water was being fed into the room through a sluice, or rushing in from an underground source. Either way, we had to be careful of the current. Standing as firmly as I could on one leg, I cautiously swiped my other foot in front of me to find the next safe foothold. It was very dark, even with Sebastian's torch, but as we neared the spot of light bobbing on the swirling surface, I was able to see the far wall. We were in a chamber that seemed to be about the same size as the Tomb of the Hidden Heart. Here, too, the space had been carved out of solid rock. In panic, I noted that the ceiling wasn't very high – how were we supposed to get out of here?

"There's an opening above," Sebastian said, as he swept the torch beam overhead, "but I can't reach it. Axelle, here, climb onto my shoulders and take a look."

I put one of my feet into his cupped hands and laid my hands on his shoulders. The water was now above our elbows.

"I'm going to kneel down, then you can step onto my shoulders, okay?"

I nodded and watched as he took a deep breath and went underwater. It took a few seconds for Sebastian to steady himself; the ground was uneven and the current was strong at floor level. Finally, after some moments, I hoisted myself onto his shoulders. He clamped his hands down over my feet and rose out of the water in one smooth movement.

"There's some kind of iron grille here, but I can't make it move. It must open from above," I said, as I tried pushing it upwards. "I'm not having any luck!"

"Hold on," said Sebastian, "I'll look for my pocket knife – I still have it – but I'm going to have to let go of your legs in order to get it." I held my hands against the ceiling to balance myself while Sebastian fumbled beneath me. Finally he got it.

I reached down for his knife, then brought it up over my head and ran it along the edge of the grille, hoping to loosen it from its iron frame. Repeatedly I jammed the blade between the grille and frame. Finally it started to loosen. I handed Sebastian back his knife and used my hands to push against the door.

"The water is getting pretty high…" Sebastian said nervously.

"Sebastian, do you think you could push me up somehow? Hold me firmly by my shoes and push me up against the grille. I can feel it budging but I need more weight behind me!"

Grabbing hold of my shoes, he shifted his weight and then pushed me against the grille with all of his strength. He repeated the action again and again, until I began to feel the grille give way to my shoulder. Finally, with one last push, it broke open. The water was now nearly at Sebastian's mouth. I felt him gather his strength and thrust me upwards and through the opening. I pulled my legs up behind me, then turned around and lay on the floor facing him so that I could extend my arm to him.

"Ouch. My shoulder!" I winced in pain as he grabbed my hand. Yet somehow I pulled him up and through the hole. But there was still no chance to catch our breath – just as he landed beside me, an enormous wave of water crashed through the opening.

"Come on! We have to move – now!" I screamed. Then taking hold of his hand, I helped him to his feet. We sprinted down the tunnel as water rushed in from behind, nearly carrying us along with its force.

I'm not sure how long we ran for, but it was a good while. The water gained on us until we reached a crossroads. Sebastian led us sharply to the left – the right decision, because we hadn't gone twenty metres before we came upon a staircase. We sprinted up it and at the top found ourselves underneath a busy street. There, finally, we fell to the ground and savoured being alive and safe.

After a few minutes of just breathing, I opened my eyes to a greenish glow streaming in through the grates over our heads from the street lights above. I also made out a slinky shape off to my side. No doubt it was a rat, but after what we'd just experienced, I couldn't have cared less.

Then I felt something warm close on my hand. I opened my mouth to scream and tried to yank my hand back but I couldn't – it was held fast.

"It's me," Sebastian whispered. "Are you okay?" His profile was backlit, his forearms were scratched and his shirt torn. His chest was still heaving as his breathing slowed. I relaxed my hand in his grasp while I caught my breath.

"You know," he said, turning his face to me after a few minutes, "you look quite sweet with your hair wet and a cockroach on your shoulder."

I screamed and sat up, only to hear him laugh as I frantically slapped at my shoulders with my hands. There was no cockroach.

"Very funny. Does swallowing sewage water always have this effect on you?"

"No. Just you have this effect on me," he answered.

How was I supposed to take that?

He peered up through the grates above us and then looked back down at the map open in his lap.

"Amazingly," he said, "we're not that far off course… that's the Boulevard Raspail just above us. And, if we have a bit more luck this time around, I think we can be at the La Lunes in about ten minutes."

He stood up and reached down to me. "Ready?" he asked, as he pulled me to my feet.

We went down yet another stairwell to a tunnel, which would lead us in an easterly direction. The passageways were again narrow, but less slippery here.

"Well, the further we are from the river…" Sebastian said. At the next fork in the tunnel we turned north onto the path that would take us to the La Lune house. "I think the kidnapper has to be Philippe. He clearly has the best motive and he's strong enough to drag people around these tunnels."

"And he drives a black Peugeot. He's probably been following me since trying to run me over. He easily could have followed us in here."

"Exactly."

"But still, like I've said before, why didn't he do something about it years ago? I mean, he's a lawyer – surely he could have found a legal way to punish the La Lunes."

"Good point. So maybe your aunt's right – maybe it is Claude. Everyone says he's super-jealous of Belle and, if *CAT* means what we think it does, he knows about the catacombs."

"And I wouldn't put it past him to hit us and leave us—"

Sebastian stopped abruptly and pointed upwards with his torch. In the dim light I could just make out a circular shape about a metre in diameter, snugly encased in the ceiling directly above our heads.

"This should lead us into their house."

Sebastian pulled a rickety collapsible ladder down from overhead and climbed up it. Then, gathering his strength, he pushed against the trapdoor. Despite appearances to the contrary, it lifted easily and quietly.

"This has definitely been used recently," he said as he poked his head through the opening. After listening carefully for a moment, he pulled himself out of the catacombs and into the house. A moment later his hand reached down, searching for mine. I climbed the ladder and, placing my hand in his, let him lift me out.

With intense satisfaction we looked at each other, our eyes blazing with the same sense of victory: we'd found the secret entrance! We were in the La Lune house.

The kidnapper must have used the catacombs to go in and out of the house unseen. But how and where had they taken Belle and Darius? Could *they* be in the catacombs? But how would they survive? Or maybe Belle and Darius had been smuggled through the catacombs and were now somewhere else entirely?

Questions whizzed through my mind, but however much I wanted to go back down to the catacombs and search for more clues, I hesitated. I felt I'd already pushed my luck more than enough for one evening – furthermore, the water would be high now. Who knew how we'd be able to find our way around?

At least we'd solved a key riddle to this case: how did the kidnapper get in and out of the La Lune mansion – and on and off the grounds – undetected? Answer: the catacombs!

As for searching for more clues in the house, we could hear footsteps coming and going. The house was clearly full of people, and therefore too risky – no matter how tempting. In fact, I was starting to ask myself how we'd get out.

Carefully we crept along the corridor, following the beam of the torch, looking for the door.

"Sebastian?" I asked, as we shuffled along in the dim light.

"Yeah?"

"If we can't get back through the catacombs now the water's risen, how are we going to get out of their grounds?"

"That's exactly what I'm asking myself…"

Sebastian eventually found the door leading out of the room we'd climbed into. Fortunately he remembered the way the passages ran and, without too much trouble he led us into some kind of laundry room. There he pulled out his floor plan of the house.

"We're here," he said, pointing to a small room on the basement level. "If we take this passageway to the secret stairwell, we can get up to the ground floor. From there, we can try going out through one of the terrace doors like we did the other night."

"And if we position ourselves by the hedges again…"

"We can follow someone out… That's the advantage of trying to break out of a fashion family's house," he said, as he looked at his watch. "They always have fashionable events to attend. It's nearly eight o'clock now. They should start leaving at any moment for some dinner party or more fashion shows."

When you knew it existed, the labyrinth of secret corridors was easy to move around in. Dry and well ventilated, it was a luxurious treat after the catacombs. The doors all opened easily and quietly, testifying to their recent use. They operated with a variety of spring mechanisms, all still original, all still functioning.

"The architect sure— Argh! That hurts!" Sebastian hissed. He'd stubbed his toe on something hard. "Wait. I need a moment," he whispered as he hopped on one foot.

I stooped to the ground and ran my hands over the dark floor, searching for whatever he'd stubbed his toe on. I picked up a bulky wooden shape; running my hands over it, I touched velvet… I'd found the shoe!

"But why here?" asked Sebastian. He was leaning against the wall now.

"That's what I've got to figure out. Would you mind carrying it for me? I don't have a pocket or bag."

"Here." He lifted it from my hand and tucked it inside his shirt.

Then we slipped along the secret passageway until we

reached the hidden staircase. From there we went up a floor and into the main part of the house.

We entered the large drawing room; it was dimly lit and quiet – or so I thought. Once we'd caught our breath and our eyes had adjusted to the low light, we realized we could hear voices. Looking at Sebastian, I put a finger to my lips and tiptoed to the chimney. As I bent my ear to the flue, Sebastian came to my side. Together we listened as upstairs, in the library, Claude and Rose were talking.

"I've never seen your hair look so messy," Rose was saying.

We listened as Claude poured himself a drink. "Just because your hair – for once – isn't looking like a rat's nest is no reason to get catty. Besides, I've had a long day."

"And you're white as a ghost. Maybe *you're* the one making the noises I hear at night?"

Claude didn't answer.

"What? You're not going to tell me that it's my *imagination*?" Rose continued. "Beginning to believe in the curse, are we?"

After a moment's silence, Claude said, "If you don't mind, I've got to bathe." We listened as he poured himself another drink and left.

"After leaving us for dead, I'm not surprised he wants to wash the evidence away," Sebastian said.

"I'm not sure it's him," I answered as we pulled away

from the chimney. "The more I think about it, the more I don't think he'd leave so obvious a clue as *CAT* in his agenda."

Sebastian and I crossed the room. It was dark outside; moonlight splashed the terrace with a yellow glow. But beyond the terrace, near the bottom of the lawn, a well-lit construction site was buzzing with activity. Workers were laying down some kind of flooring while many more were busy attaching long sheets of canvas to a large metal frame that had been erected on the grounds. Furthermore, potted topiary in all shapes and sizes was being unloaded from a florist's van that was parked not far from the house, to the right of the terrace.

"They must be putting up the tent for tomorrow's show," Sebastian whispered. "This could make it easier for us to get out of here."

"Let's hope so," I said as I unlocked the terrace doors and put my head out to listen. The sounds of music and a lone hairdryer floated out from the upstairs windows; from the lawn, the sounds of hammers, drills and shouting drifted towards us.

"I think it might be best to make as if we belong here," I said quietly. "The workers, if they notice us, will hopefully think we're a part of the family or close friends, or something…"

"And the family will think we're with one of the crews."

I nodded.

Sebastian and I stepped out and shut the doors behind us before retracing our steps from Monday night. Silently we weaved our way around the patio furniture, careful not to hit any of it. I didn't want a noise to bring Claude or Rose to their windows – from this distance they might easily recognize me! Of course, I couldn't be certain that we were going unnoticed from above, but that was a risk we had to take.

We moved as stealthily and as quickly as possible until we reached the side of the terrace. Once there, and with the florist's van parked only a few strides away, we relaxed and simply walked quietly along the side of the house and towards the courtyard at the front. Once we'd arrived at the courtyard, we hid behind the bushes bordering it. Contrary to the scene in the garden behind the house, here there was little outside light – and most of it was directed at the courtyard just in front of us. The gate stood open to the street – but there was a security guard with a walkie-talkie posted at it.

"We should make a run for those tall bushes near the gate," said Sebastian. "And then from there we can hide alongside a car as it exits. Surely one of the La Lunes will be leaving soon…" We waited, our weight on the balls of our feet, ready for action. After a few moments we heard the security guard's walkie-talkie crackle to life. "Ready to run?" Sebastian asked.

I nodded, and taking a deep breath, sprinted across the courtyard, Sebastian by my side. We were halfway across when a car came in from the street. "Get down and roll!" Sebastian hissed.

We dropped out of sight just as Fiona drove in. "Her hair looks too perfect – there's no way she could have been the one who hit us in the catacombs," I pointed out from behind the safety of the low hedge lining the driveway.

Sebastian shrugged his shoulders. "Her hair is like a helmet: it could probably withstand a tornado. A trip through the catacombs would be nothing for hair like that. But I doubt she has the strength to drag unconscious bodies around."

From the house, the sound of clicking high heels was followed by the opening and shutting of a car door. An engine revved and gravel crunched as a car turned to drive out of the courtyard. It was Rose. I had the feeling she wasn't the best of drivers even during good times, but now, with her fear of the curse hanging over her, she looked so nervous behind the wheel I was surprised she didn't just call for a taxi.

Carefully, we climbed over the low hedge and waited for Rose to drive up beside us. The security guard was again busy on his walkie-talkie (and, fortunately, on the other side of the gate from us). As Rose slowly eased forward towards the opened gate, we crept to the side of her large car and crouched low beside the back door. I could see her taut features reflected in the wing mirror. The darkness hid us well and, careful not to get our toes under her wheels, we followed her as she nudged her car out of the gate and onto the street. When we reached the sidewalk, we quickly stood up, looking as if we'd been politely standing and waiting for her to drive out before continuing on our leisurely evening stroll. She was so distracted that she even lifted her left hand off the steering wheel in a quick gesture of thanks!

From the La Lunes, we'd walked to the river to fetch Sebastian's scooter, and from there he'd taken me home to Aunt V's. We now stood outside her building, our day over. The street was quiet, the sky cloudy – the only light came from the lone street lamp on the corner. I shifted my weight from foot to foot, Sebastian fiddled with his helmet, neither of us sure how to say goodbye after the day we'd had.

"We have a lot going on tomorrow," I said finally.

"Yeah...plus," he smiled widely, "your mother arrives." His blue-grey eyes crinkled at the corners as he teased me. After the afternoon we'd had, his hair was more tousled than ever. At least Sebastian still looked cute, his ripped shirt and the brown guck smudging his face only enhancing his looks. I curled my toes thinking about what kind of vision I presented. Good thing the street was dark.

"Thanks for reminding me."

"Lunch after Barinaga?"

"Uh-uh. Perfect."

"You still have fifteen hours – more if your aunt can keep your mother busy." He was smiling.

"Yeah, well, I'll need every minute," I said as I stretched my back.

"Are you sure you're okay?" I watched as he slowly looked me up and down before his eyes settled on my face. "Your shoulder's not too sore?" His eyes and voice were serious, the light, mocking tone gone. "I'm sorry, you know, about… about dragging you down there and nearly getting us killed. If I'd known or thought—"

"Forget it, Sebastian – how could you have known? It was my fault. I'm the one who's dragged you into this, remember? Anyway, look, I'm fine," I said as I slowly rotated my shoulder. "I'll be good as new tomorrow."

Carefully, he reached out with his right hand and slowly ran his finger from my left shoulder across my collarbone to my right shoulder. "Sure?" he asked again softly.

"Sure." I stood quietly as he gently pushed the ends of my hair behind my shoulders. *Who cares about our work relationship?* I thought, as the moonlight threw his strong features into sharp relief. Surely weak knees and thoughts that had nothing to do with the mystery wouldn't change anything between us? Would they?

His finger traced the contours of my jaw, then the outline of my lips. I leaned against my aunt's door, our eyes locked. Again I had the impression that he wanted to say something, but just as he ever so slightly leaned in to me, a group of dinner-party guests tumbled out of the building next door. We pulled back, the noise catching us by surprise, and watched the lively party until they'd turned the corner.

"Right," I said as I took a deep breath. My hands were in his and he was smiling at me. Why did we have to do anything tomorrow – or now, for that matter? Why couldn't we just keep looking at each other in the warm night air?

Because you have a case to solve, remember, Axelle?

Slowly I pulled one hand away from him. Smiling, he refused to relinquish the other. Finally, he took it to his lips and kissed it. "À *demain*, Holmes." The teasing light was back in his eyes.

"À *demain*, Watson."

He opened the heavy wooden door and held it as I went in. But just as the door shut behind me, I heard my name called. I turned around and pulled the door open again.

"You forgot Belle's shoe – the velvet platform," Sebastian said, handing it to me.

Then he smiled and left.

In a warm, fuzzy haze I quickly changed out of my wet, dirty clothes and gratefully ate the club sandwiches and warm soup Carmen had left me, then scooped up Miu Miu in my arms and went to the balcony off the sitting room (carefully sidestepping yet more expensive art deliveries) for some fresh air – it was time to start thinking straight. I let the cold night air sweep over me until, finally, I felt my old self ticking again – without distraction. My sidekick was cute – gorge really – but I had a mystery to solve.

Taking a deep breath, I stood with my hands on the railing and tipped my head back. Somewhere in the back of my mind a niggling thought was slowly forming itself, but I couldn't quite figure out what it was…nor was I sure I liked it. But the thought was there, quietly turning over on itself, waiting until the moment when I'd finally pluck it out and make sense of it… It was as if I *knew* it already, but just couldn't remember it.

I didn't have time to think further, though. A car came to a halt down below and Miu Miu stood with a start. After a quick stretch, she left in a hurry and with her tail straight up in the feline form of a happy greeting. At this hour that could mean only one thing: Aunt Venetia was home.

Peering over the railing, I saw Aunt V down below; a minute later she was inside. "Axelle, darling, are you here?" This was followed by the clicking of her heels as she made her way down the corridor. Stopping in the doorway, she looked in. "Oh, you're here," she said. She seemed surprised to see me. "I thought you'd still be out…"

"Actually, I've had a long day. I came home as soon as I could."

"I see… Anyway, how nice you're still up. Why don't you follow me to my dressing room and tell me about your day while I step out of these shoes – they are killing me!"

I accompanied my aunt into her dressing room. As she set down her handbag (a La Lune Clothilde bag in lilac ostrich – drip-free tonight, I noted) on the polished surface of the round table that stands in the middle of the room, I padded across the plush cream-coloured carpet to one of a pair of delicately carved chairs set against the wall and perched myself on its edge. My aunt, meanwhile, slipped behind a tall upholstered screen to undress.

Not ten seconds later came The Question: "Axelle, darling, what *are* you wearing?"

For once I actually felt the question was justified: I was wrapped up like a mummy. I was wearing a few layers of mismatched jumpers, together with baggy tracksuit bottoms. Slouchy socks covered my ankles, my hands were tucked into my sleeves, and I had a scarf tied loosely around my neck. Even I had to admit the effect wasn't especially alluring.

"Uhm...I've had something of an adventurous day, so basically I just wanted to slip into something warm and comfortable when I got home."

She stepped out from behind her screen. "An adventurous day? What did you do?" Through her sunglasses, I could feel her eyes boring into me as she stood, tying the heavy sash around the waist of her dressing gown.

Changing the subject, I asked, "Aunt V, wouldn't you be more comfortable without your sunglasses on?"

"More comfortable? Axelle, darling, after a night like tonight, preceded by a full day of shows, I'm feeling half blind. Anyway, after a good night's sleep I'll be like new.

So, tell me, what did your adventurous day entail? Are you getting any closer to finding Belle?"

"Actually...yes." Unfortunately I'd reached a point where I didn't have much I could share with her – and I was lucky she hadn't insisted on seeing the letters this morning. But most of all, my common sense told me not to say anything to anyone about our visit to the catacombs or even about the maps and plans that Sebastian had found. We had, after all, broken into the La Lune mansion...and, unless I found Belle, I didn't think my attempts at deduction would amuse anybody.

Plus – for whatever reason – my intuition seemed to be on red alert. I suddenly felt edgy and uneasy, so I kept my thoughts to myself.

Instead, I went into the details of the *Elle* shoot. I even showed her the photos on my phone of the different make-up looks. She was sitting at her dressing table, removing *her* make-up – she'd finally slipped her sunglasses off – with something she'd poured out of one of the many bottles standing on the mirrored tabletop.

"So you're not really any closer then? To finding Belle, I mean?"

"Well...some things are beginning to come into focus."

"Such as?"

"Well, did you know that Versailles and the La Lune mansion were designed by the same architect, Louis Le Vau?"

She was now standing in front of her hidden safe, putting the bits of jewellery she'd worn that night carefully away into their respective boxes.

"Hmm…yes, I do seem to remember reading something about that – I studied interior architecture for a few semesters here in Paris, you know. Before I moved into fashion."

After shutting the door to her safe, she turned to face me. "Why? Do you think that has any bearing on the case?"

The stress of being a suspect was clearly wearing on her. She stood still, head high, arms calmly folded in front of her like always, but, for once, she seemed to be posing. Her soft cashmere dressing gown and the thick cream covering her face did nothing to lessen the impression of a very brittle twig on the verge of snapping.

"Are you ready to give Inspector Witt the helpful nudge he so obviously needs? Can we call him? Do you know which La Lune it is? Or have you found a Merlette?"

"Like I said, I'm getting closer," I answered slowly. "By tomorrow at nightfall, I'll know… I…I have a plan." I surprised myself when I said this. For, until a few minutes ago, I'd had no plan. But suddenly an obvious idea had come to me. I needed to call Sebastian.

"Well, just be careful that whoever is behind all of this doesn't feel that you're too close on their tracks. If something were to happen to you…"

"Don't worry – nothing is going to happen to me. Besides, wherever I go I'm always either with Ellie or Sebastian. We're always together."

"Good."

I watched as she screwed the lid back onto her eye cream. "Uhmm…Aunt V?" I asked, as I stood before the photograph of Diana Vreeland with the silver dress.

"Yes?"

"What is this dress made of? It looks amazing."

"It *is* amazing – I've seen it at the Hermitage in Russia. It's Catherine the Great's wedding dress. It's made of silver – *real* silver – thread embroidered on silk. It shimmers like the moon."

"Has Diana Vreeland always been an inspiration to you?"

Aunt Venetia was now standing beside me, looking at the photograph. "Yes, she has – for her sense of style, anyway, if not her lifestyle."

"Why not her lifestyle?"

"She died quite penniless and, to my mind, had become rather tiresome towards the end – which was why she was pushed out of magazine editing and given a job as curator at the Metropolitan Museum of Art in New York City." Aunt V stopped for a moment of pensive reflection. "That's certainly not how I plan on ending my days."

Then she turned and walked to her dressing table, where she picked up her latest anagram puzzle book before coming to give me a kiss goodnight.

"I probably won't see you in the morning – I've promised Miriam I'll look at a young designer – this one is supposed to be the next Valentino," she said with a roll of her eyes. "Anyway, these young guys only get the very early or very late time slots, so I'll be out of here by seven. But I'll see you at the Barinaga show and then the La Lune show. Oh, and I'm going to have someone fetch your mother from the Gare du Nord. Thereafter she'll be accompanying me. I thought that might be easier for you," she added with a smile. "So you'll be quite on your own for the entire day."

"That's fantastic, Aunt Venetia. Thank you." What a relief! I'd be able to put my plan into action without any trouble now…

"Goodnight, Axelle darling."

"Goodnight, Aunt V."

Back in my room, I picked up the book on Le Vau and read for a while. Finally, I drifted into a fitful sleep, during which I slipped from one dream to the next. Dom, Rose, Fiona and Claude – even Philippe de Vandrille – flitted in and out of my mind without any pattern or message I could fathom. Frustrated and angry, deep sleep eluded me. And then, in my last dream, my gran appeared. We were sitting at our kitchen table in London. "Ah," Gran said as she looked at me, eyes twinkling, "always remember to follow your intuition, Axelle, follow your intuition…"

Yeah, thanks, Gran, but where to?

I awoke at this point. Through my open window I heard

the faint beginnings of the gradual crescendo of morning sounds that would peak at about nine o'clock: the dry-cleaning van picking up laundry, the owner of the corner bistro whistling as he swept the pavement, my aunt's concierge chatting with a neighbour, the occasional jogger, and a varied assortment of scooters, motorbikes, vans, cars, trucks and taxis zooming along the surrounding streets.

I stretched a bit and turned to lie flat on my back, the image of Diana Vreeland's portrait returning to my mind. I lay in this relaxed state for a few minutes – until, cursing my stupidity, I sat up with a jolt, kicked back my duvet and grabbed the nearest pencil and scrap of paper. As quickly as I could I wrote the following:

DAVID LE NÉANAR

The thought that had been trying to form itself in my mind last night was now crystal clear…and surely, I thought, surely it wasn't just a coincidence?

It was hard to imagine the world teeming, alive, around her. Even fresh air had become a distant memory.

An incessant dripping came from somewhere in the room. Otherwise, there was nothing but silence and the occasional scuffle of a rat. Since she'd been dragged into the other room, she'd heard nothing more from her brother.

How much longer could they last?

FRIDAY MORNING

Rambling Rose

The La Lune Curse Strikes Again! screamed the morning headlines.

Rose was missing.

Anonymous sources implied she'd left a letter behind, assuming blame for the disappearances. The same sources claimed that her highly-strung nerves had buckled under the weight of her guilt – but was it true?

According to the newspapers, Fiona was beside herself, her third child missing. And, if the front-page photos were anything to go by, her icy façade was rapidly melting. Even Claude looked scared.

I finally set aside the papers and answered my ringing phone.

"This is what you meant, isn't it? When you said there would be another disappearance?" It was Sebastian. I felt groggy and tired. My head hurt – and his accusatory tone did nothing to help.

"Axelle? Aren't you awake yet? Don't you have to be at the Louvre for Barinaga in twenty minutes?

And what about Rose? It's what you meant, isn't it? And you didn't want me to call my father! I shouldn't have listened to you! I'm going to call him now."

"No, wait, Sebastian, don't! You're right – I was talking about Rose. But she's okay."

"How do you know? Did she call you just after she'd disappeared?"

"Isn't it a bit early for sarcasm?" I got up from the kitchen table, where I'd been sitting in my PJs, and walked to the bathroom to get the shower started. "Listen, yes, it was Rose I meant. But I know she's okay. I…" I didn't really have a good reason – at least nothing I could explain logically. "Look, I can't really say why… Can you just trust me on this? I'll explain straight after the show, promise."

"Yeah, but maybe you're wrong! Maybe she's—"

"Please, Sebastian, just trust me, okay?"

He was silent for a moment. "Okay – but you'd better explain at lunch. I'll meet you at the Rue de Rivoli exit straight after the show."

"Wait! One more thing…bring the map, would you please? The one of the catacombs…"

"And I suppose you'll explain that later too?" he said, the teasing tone sneaking back into his voice.

"Maybe." We said goodbye and I rushed to get ready.

David le Néanar, David le Néanar… His name raced through my mind. I could have kicked myself for having missed it!

I had ten minutes to get to the Louvre. I'd told Aunt V not to order me a taxi, saying I'd walk across the river and through the park. Why hadn't I accepted her offer? With the shows going on, I'd never find a taxi on the street. At this point I had no choice but to run through the park.

Pulling my bathrobe on, I bounded into my room and grabbed a new little top that Aunt V had given me. I was about to pull it on but then decided otherwise. *Today*, I told myself, *I'll need all the luck I can get*. I dug into the back of the wardrobe and pulled out my lucky jumper. Then I slipped into my most worn pair of jeans and my motorcycle boots. My two concessions to fashion were the long scraggly scarf and my H&M jacket. A quick glance in the mirror told me I looked fine – and I didn't care who thought otherwise. As I ran out of the apartment I stopped long enough in the kitchen to grab a croissant and a banana. Carmen shook her head as I ran out of the door. Then I flew down the stairs and out onto the street. After running all the way, I reached the Louvre only ten minutes late.

"Make-up artists and hairdressers to the left, please." As I walked into the space reserved for Barinaga, a large hand suddenly stopped me in my tracks.

"Buhh I'm won om dhe bodels!" I said as I searched in my bag for my ID.

"*Excusez-moi, mademoiselle?*"

Pulling the banana out of my mouth, I showed my ID and said, "I'm one of the models. See?"

The security guard eyed me suspiciously until suddenly a familiar voice rang out: "Axelle! There you are! Come on! You're late!" It was Ellie and she was waving frantically at me from behind the rope.

"*Humpf!*" He still didn't believe I was one of the models. He shook his head and grudgingly let me past. "*Allez-y, allez-y*, but if you get caught it's not my fault."

"And a good day to you too," I murmured as I squeezed past him. But, then again, I thought as I caught sight of myself in a mirror, I wasn't looking especially fantastic this morning. That was confirmed to me when I saw Ellie's face as she greeted me.

"Uh...Axelle? What's happened to your hair?"

After four days of professionally-done hair, I'd forgotten what it was like to have a bad hair day. I peered into the nearest mirror again. Was that really me?

"Yes, it's you," laughed Ellie over my shoulder. "What did you do?"

What I'd done was have a night of vivid dreams, got dressed really late, then run through the park with wet hair. I had to admit that, even for me, the end result was not pretty. "I was trying to go for a natural look," I said to Ellie.

"Well, it worked! Most trees don't have as many leaves. Let's hear what Benoit has to say."

Benoit was the Barinaga hairdresser-in-chief. To his credit, he didn't scream in horror at the sight of my hair. In fact...he kind of *liked* it.

"Wow. *Intéressant, non?*" he said as he circled around me. He acted as if he was seeing someone's hair for the first time in his life. Of course, he probably was seeing hair *like mine* for the first time. "You know, I kind of like it," he finally pronounced. "It's, like, wild. Like a forest fire. Like those Jean Cocteau profiles. And so seventies at the same time. Would somebody get me Alexander, please. Now!"

Alexander was the creative director of Barinaga. As I stood in place, a small crowd began to gather around me, but they all parted like the Red Sea when the creative director Alexander appeared. Judging by the look on his face he, too, was surprised by the apparition growing on my head. But after walking around and listening to Benoit's sales pitch, he suddenly broke into a smile and pronounced it to be "*Superbe!* But maybe we should exaggerate it even more..."

Suddenly a beehive of activity broke out. "This is it!" yelled Benoit as he pointed at my hair. "This is it! *This* is Barinaga Autumn/Winter! This is what I want you all to look at!" he told the assembled hairdressers on his team. "It's sexy, it's wild, it's *très différent!* Come on, let's get going! We haven't got time to waste..."

And that's how I inspired a look...

"Gosh, Axelle," Ellie said a while later, as we were getting our make-up done. "Your jumper really is lucky. Imagine that you just walk in like that and inspire the hair for the entire collection – even I've never done that! How fantastic. Where did you say you got that jumper?"

The show went without a hitch, ran on time, and my hair was the undoubted star of the event. It was odd to see all the models with "my" hair. But what I'd found really amusing was when Benoit sent all the hairdressers and their assistants on a leaf-foraging expedition in the park. Who would have thought that a bunch of fashionistas would still have their hunter-gatherer instincts intact? But back they came, one by one, each with an assortment of fashionable bags stuffed with leaves. "Hurricane chic" was the new term coined for my hair.

After slipping out of my last Barinaga outfit – rock-star leather trousers with a long, sparkly jersey jumper – I signalled to Ellie and together we left for lunch. Miraculously she had the afternoon free, so she'd be able to help me later.

As planned, Sebastian was waiting at the Rue de Rivoli exit. After walking the five minutes to Cafe Ruc, we were shown to a cosy corner table. Immediately Sebastian and I ordered our burgers and fries, Ellie her salad.

"So what happened to Rose?" whispered Sebastian.

"She's gone to Spain with Alejandro – the hairdresser." Looking at Ellie, I said, "The one who did our hair on Wednesday at the Chanel show."

"What?! Alejandro?" Ellie said. "How do you know?"

"Because of the bracelet."

Sebastian rolled his eyes. "Could you please explain what a bracelet has to do with Rose running away with a Spanish hairdresser?"

So I explained, beginning with the bracelet, then continuing through to the Spanish lessons and erratic hairstyles.

"I thought she was just odd," Sebastian said.

"Yeah, well, you're not the only one, but that's the thing, isn't it? People are constantly misreading each other – especially family members. Often they don't even notice what's right under their noses. And that's the case with Rose. Think about it: new hairstyle, sudden interest in Spanish lessons, then going to a fashion show – something she normally doesn't do unless it's a family show. And, then – instead of watching the show – she hangs out backstage! Something had to be going on. And hair like hers can't just be straightened at home – it needs the help of a professional. And why Spanish? Especially when the little I heard doesn't lead me to believe she has a talent for languages."

"Yeah, but how did you go from Spanish lessons and blow-dried hair to a long-distance love interest?" Sebastian said.

"Observation," I answered. Quickly I gave silent thanks to the many hours I'd spent since childhood "spying" (as Mum called it) on friends and neighbours. "I've noticed that when someone suddenly starts paying attention to their appearance or changing their normal routine it's often because of a new interest – be it another person or a job... But because no one has ever seen Rose with a boyfriend, because everyone always thinks of her cosying up to a calculator in some dark office, it's been impossible for anyone to imagine what's been going on, let alone see it."

"But it's not like she's been showing up everywhere with him on her arm."

"You're right – she wasn't flaunting him – but she wasn't hiding him either. If her family had paid a bit of attention to what she was doing and asked themselves why, instead of just assuming her new interests were more odd behaviour, they'd have figured it out... Plus, like I said, there's the bracelet. That little silver heart screams romance. Once I realized it was the same one that Alejandro was wearing, everything sort of clicked."

"I have to say," Ellie said, "it was pretty sharp of you to see that. I never noticed..."

"What confirmed it for me was that she stayed backstage during the Chanel show, even though she'd told me she planned on watching it. What made her change her mind? Or had that been her intention all along? And, if so, then why? What was she doing all that time?"

"Actually, while I was changing, I did notice her backstage talking to the hairdressers – or maybe it was just Alejandro," Ellie said.

"I saw that too. And as you'd mentioned to me that Alejandro was Spanish, another piece of the puzzle clicked."

"Well," Ellie sighed, "she'll never have a bad hair day again if she marries him."

"Okay. But, still, if she's not guilty, why run away?" Sebastian asked.

"I think she has no idea how to talk to her family about the new life she wants. I mean, I've seen how they treat her. And remember Monday night, when we were climbing the rose trellis to get into their house? At one point Rose heard us and opened the terrace door to listen. Claude said sarcastically, 'Don't be silly, Rose, it's only your imagination – as usual.' I mean, they all talk to her as if she's twelve years old. Plus the fact that she showed up at the shoot on Tuesday – crying – shows she's clearly struggling. And I don't think it's only because of the disappearances – horrifying as they are. And now…"

"And now you think she wants her own life independent from her family," Sebastian said.

"That's sad…" Ellie said.

"It is…but…" I paused as I took a few sizzling hot fries and dipped them in the mayonnaise and then the ketchup. Why do French fries in France taste so yummy? "But I think that after tonight the La Lune family dynamics are going to change drastically…and Rose will be happy again."

"Why?" Ellie and Sebastian asked.

I kept eating my fries.

"You know who's behind the disappearances, don't you?" Sebastian leaned back and watched me.

I nodded.

"So are you going to tell us who it is?" Ellie asked.

I thought about it for a moment before answering, "No, not yet."

In order for my plan to work, I couldn't risk Ellie and Sebastian giving anything away – the element of surprise was necessary. They'd have to wait for the answer.

After lunch we headed straight for the La Lune mansion. My mum, thank goodness, was busy seeing the shows. Apart from a call before lunch to tell me that she'd arrived and was SO looking forward to seeing me on the runway later, I hadn't heard any more from her. The show was to begin at six, hair and make-up at four. I wanted to be early, though, so that I could put my plan into action.

I gave my aunt a quick call to see if she could meet me backstage before the show started, saying I had something to tell her.

"Does this mean you've finally found the culprit? That my magazine and I will have our reputations restored?" she asked excitedly.

"I hope so, although, to be honest, Aunt V, the desire to find Belle and Darius – and see them alive – is uppermost in my mind right now – but I'd be delighted to have you and *Chic* in the clear once again."

"Yes, well, me too." Then, after a pause, she added, "You know, I'm very curious to see what the culprit wears…"

After having cleared security at the gates (Aunt V had sent an invitation for Sebastian), we made our way to the tents Sebastian and I had seen being set up in the garden yesterday. The large one was reserved for the runway and to the right of it, connected by a short covered walkway, was the hair and make-up tent.

I went straight to hair and make-up – I wanted to meet with the La Lunes, Aunt V and Philippe *before* the show started. Ellie told me that normally all of the La Lunes made an early visit backstage to check on hair and make-up – especially when it was held at their home. And, hopefully, with a bit of luck, Aunt V would show up at the same time. I needed to have a quick word with all of them – preferably together.

The tent quickly filled. The din of hairdryers, gossip and loud music reverberated within the white canvas "walls". I was sitting, eyes closed, as the last touch of glitter powder was brushed on my face and shoulders, when Ellie said, "They're here. All of them. And your aunt's just showed up, too."

Perfect – the moment I'd been waiting for. I thanked the make-up artist as I got up and grabbed my shoulder bag. Then, I crossed the tent and went straight to Aunt V and the La Lunes.

"Oh, Axelle. There you are," Aunt V said. I air-kissed her, then said hello to the La Lunes. Not that they noticed – Dom, especially, acted as if he'd never met me before.

Whatever. Then again, Hervé had promised me that he'd speak with Dom the next time he saw him in the agency. Dom's petulance seemed to confirm that Hervé had had his chance. And, frankly, I preferred this muzzled version of Dom to the aggressive one I'd encountered Wednesday night. Hopefully he wouldn't try that again.

"Shall we go to the corner for our chat?" Aunt V asked.

I shook my head. "Actually, I need to speak with all of you – now, preferably. It's about Belle," I added, when I saw them hesitate.

"Sorry, Axelle," Claude snapped, "but this isn't really the moment – you're here to walk, remember? And I've got a show to put on."

"Surely, this can—" Fiona started.

"Easy, Claude, Fiona," Philippe said. "She's just trying to help. Surely we can spare a few minutes." Turning to me, he said, "Axelle, why don't you start? There's a free table just here."

"Honestly, Philippe." Claude turned to leave but my aunt stopped him.

"I want to hear what my niece has to say, Claude. And as it concerns your siblings, I suggest you listen."

Before anyone else tried to leave, I cleared my throat

and pushed all thoughts of failure out of my mind. Out of the corner of my eye, I saw Ellie give me the thumbs up.

"I'm sorry to interrupt your busy schedules. Thank you, but you needn't worry – I'll need less than a minute."

I stopped for a moment as I rummaged through my bag. I could see Claude and Fiona rolling their eyes. Dom was looking at his camera screen and Philippe and my aunt sat very still in their chairs.

"Ah! Here it is!" I said as I pulled out a small wrapped package. Slowly I peeled off the two layers of paper covering the object and then set it on the table. I heard a sharp intake of breath all around.

"It's Belle's missing shoe. I found it yesterday. It was in quite a strange place...but I'm planning on going back to that same place straight after the show – and I believe that if I look further, I'll find Belle and Darius... But I'm afraid one of us sitting at this table is behind the disappearances."

Everyone was quiet.

Finally, Philippe spoke. "And what about Rose?"

"Don't worry about Rose – she's fine. Right now, we have to concentrate on Belle and Darius."

I moved my eyes slowly from face to face. Nobody moved, nobody said anything.

"Anyway, like I said, I'll be looking for Belle and Darius straight after the show. And if everything goes as I think it will, I'll see you all later tonight."

Needless to say, I wasn't allowed to leave that easily. After a moment of shocked silence, the questions and comments came:

"Who are you to get so involved?"

"I'm innocent!"

"Great. A model policewoman!"

"Where are the police?"

Without another word, I turned and left.

The show tent looked amazing. And, presumably, because it had been set up in the garden, Belle (who, according to the gossip circulating, had planned the show's decor weeks before) had opted to bring the garden theme inside the tent. What she'd done, however, was to make it surreal. Everything was white. The topiary bushes I'd seen being transported across the lawn yesterday from the florist's van were in fantastical shapes: some clipped like peacocks and rabbits, others into cylinders, cones and balls. Everything was coated in glittery, white "snow" and the special lights gave the scene a magical iridescence. It was like stepping into Alice's Wonderland.

The clothes were also white. Long white evening dresses, white trouser suits, white blouses, skirts and jackets. White handbags, shoes and scarves. It was bewitching and beautiful – Belle had done an amazing job designing it all. The only question on everyone's lips was: would she ever come back? Or was this the last Belle La Lune collection there'd ever be?

The show ran smoothly and as soon as it was over Ellie and I changed into our own clothes with lightning speed.

"I refused to give *Modelinia* a quick interview," Ellie whispered. "If only they knew what we're about to do."

"And I'm supposed to meet my mum back here in ten minutes. Obviously that won't be happening. How do I look?"

"Like a fashion ninja," she answered with a smile. "It suits you."

I was dressed in layers of soft black cotton, dark jeans and black trainers. It was comfortable and practical. I rolled up my lucky jumper and combat boots and put them into my work bag. Ellie and I then hid our bags under the floor of the tent. With what we were about to do, we didn't need the excess weight. Hopefully the tents wouldn't go down until morning. We quickly said goodbye to the other models, the hairdressers and make-up artists, then left.

Sebastian was waiting for us near the bushes, as planned. He handed us each a water bottle, torch, string, copies of the floor plan and catacombs map, and a walkie-talkie.

"In the house they should work fine. Of course, once we're deep in the catacombs they'll lose reception, but they'll work for longer than our phones."

Then, when the coast was clear, we ran across the open gravel to the house.

"We can't go in from the terrace," whispered Sebastian as we crouched low. "There's too much security on that side of the house. But I've had a look around, and there's an open side window in the study. From there we can access the secret passageway."

Carefully we snuck along the wall to the study window and climbed in. It looked much as it had on Monday night – only without Inspector Witt asking questions. On the off chance that luck would strike twice I couldn't stop myself from closing and opening the fireplace damper – but nothing fell out.

It didn't take us long to find the small lever that, when pushed, opened the hidden door that led to the secret passages. Both the lever and the door were extremely well concealed in the wood panelling that lined the room – without the old architectural plans of the house, we'd never have found either. Pushing on the lever released the first spring, which in turn released the weighted lever that kept the door shut. We made sure to shut everything again from the inside – just in case the person we were looking for was behind us. As it was – they weren't. They were ahead of us.

We stood whispering as we discussed which route to take through the house and into the catacombs. Suddenly Sebastian put his finger to his lips.

"Shhh," he said as he nodded his head upwards.

Holding our breaths, we listened. From the far end of the passageway above, we heard footsteps. Softly and stealthily, they crept along the length of the secret corridor, pausing for a moment directly above us. A few seconds later we heard a door open into the spiral staircase just near us. The footsteps quickly descended, pausing again on our floor before continuing down the stairs.

"Come on," whispered Sebastian as he started to move forward, "they're on their way into the catacombs!"

Together we moved down the passageway. The chase was about to begin.

I insisted on going first – after all, it was my plan. And I didn't want to put Sebastian or Ellie in more danger then necessary. I would lead, Sebastian would follow me as closely as he could without being seen, and Ellie would stop and keep watch at the first fork in the tunnel. From there she could easily hide and go for help if she needed to.

Whoever we were following made quick time in reaching the catacombs entrance. In their hurry, they'd left the trapdoor open and the ladder unfolded. One by one we climbed down, then stopped to listen for the footsteps. Quickly we followed their sound – if we lost them we'd lose our chance of finding Belle. Together we followed the twists and turns of the tunnel until we came to the first fork. Here we left Ellie, with instructions to call for backup if we didn't return within the hour. Then I loosened my ball of string and left. From here on out I'd leave a trail behind me. Sebastian would follow me in ten minutes.

For some time all was well: the footsteps padded steadily ahead of me. I stayed just far enough behind that I could turn my torch on. I stopped to look at the map every so often to orient myself. It seemed we were going in circles, or maybe just taking the long way around. The kidnapper must have known I was down here. After all, just before the show, when I'd shown my aunt, the La Lunes and Philippe de Vandrille Belle's shoe, I'd also clearly announced my plan to find Belle and Darius by returning to where I'd found Belle's shoe and then *going further*. The kidnapper must have understood I meant the catacombs, so the circular route they were taking was either to find me or lose me. I was careful to stop whenever the footsteps did. I was also careful to keep my torch on low beam. I even had a scarf twisted around it to lessen the glow.

After a while the footsteps slowed down a bit, their even patter echoing like a softly ticking clock. Maybe it was the lack of fresh oxygen – we'd gone down several staircases – but a wave of dizziness and nausea washed over me, leaving me momentarily dazed. I was no longer sure if the footsteps were in front of me or behind me. I turned my torch off and stopped to listen. I could hear them, but I couldn't pinpoint them. They seemed to bounce off the walls and come at me from all directions.

I took a deep breath, the muggy air sticking in my throat, then unscrewed the cap of my water bottle and took a sip. I could hear something scurrying beside me – probably rats if my last visit was anything to go by – but dared not turn my torch on for fear of giving myself away.

I stood, ears straining for the slightest sound, my weight balanced on the balls of my feet, ready for a quick getaway. What had happened? Where were they? Had I lost them? How? And yet the hairs on the back of my neck were standing; I could sense someone nearby. But where? I was in total darkness; a slight draught ruffled my hair from behind. Somewhere not far from me water dripped, its regular splatter echoing like an underground heartbeat. I checked my walkie-talkie but I'd lost reception.

And then I heard it: a sharp whizzing sound slicing through the air. Instinctively, I ducked. Something smashed on the wall just behind me, shattering like china. I covered my head with my arms as the bits fell around me. The footsteps started again, their pace urgent. I followed, and, after a few minutes, suddenly heard something like a bowling ball rolling on the tunnel floor. Too late I realized it was headed for me.

My foot hit it straight on; I stumbled and fell forward, my knee cracking against the rock floor. Argh! I lay sprawled on the ground, my face and shoulders in a pool of water. My knee burned with pain. I was dizzy, desperate for fresh air. *Come on, Axelle, get up, get up!* With one of my hands I fumbled near my ankles until I found the ball – only it wasn't what I'd thought.

It was a skull.

Exhausted, I let it roll out of my hand. I lay on my back, catching my breath. I tried forcing myself to concentrate, to get up. Suddenly one of my fingers smarted with pain, as if something was biting it. What was it? I lifted my head, stagnant water dripping down my cheek, and shook my hand. But as I reached with my free hand to turn on my torch, I heard another whistle through the damp air. I rolled over, but not quickly enough – this time the flying skull grazed my head. I caught my breath as another sharp spasm of pain shot through me.

As I turned onto my side and sat up, I felt something grab at my hair. I shook my head in an attempt to loosen its hold and heard its high-pitched squeal fill the blackness. I grabbed it with both hands and pulled its writhing body. It jumped and jerked in my hands but wouldn't let go. Its sharp teeth tore at my skin, and still it continued to shriek its horrible, high-pitched, fevered squeal. I wanted to cry out, disgust making my stomach turn. As I opened my mouth to yell, no longer caring who heard me, its long scaly tail brushed the inside of my mouth.

I kept screaming. I figured whoever it was knew I was here so I had nothing to lose. At the same time I also realized that the person throwing the skulls must have night-vision goggles on. I cursed my own stupidity for not having thought of that and bit my tongue as another rat scurried across my lap. In a fury I grabbed the skull lying at my feet and flung it blindly out in front of me, not caring whether it hit its mark or not. A grotesque little laugh echoed down the walls as the patter of the footsteps resumed.

I got to my feet. The chase was back on.

The person I was following seemed to be losing patience: they kept stopping to hear if I was behind. After the third pause, I heard them resume their stride with a new, more urgent cadence. Now, the footsteps seemed to say, it's time to get serious.

Well, fine. I was ready. As I moved along I checked to make sure my string was still unwinding and reached for my water bottle. Drat! I'd lost it when the first skull had been thrown. Plenty of time to worry about that later, I told myself – and pushed forward, intent on keeping up.

After some time the footsteps suddenly slowed, then turned up a stairwell. Quickly and quietly I followed. From above I could hear a key being inserted into a lock, the metal scraping as the lock was turned. Then the door slowly swung open, its hinges rusty with age. These hinges, unlike those in the mansion, had been neglected, presumably because no one had been expected to hear them. I increased my speed – I had to catch the door before it shut. There'd be more passageways beyond – and if I didn't get through this door now, who knew when I'd find my way out – or if? Surely the person on the other side was hoping I'd make a mistake, hoping they could lock me up here too. With a last burst of energy I bounded up the final steps and, with my foot, only just managed to stop the door from shutting. I slipped through it and crossed the chamber beyond to another door.

From behind the door I heard a familiar voice barking orders, presumably to Belle and Darius.

"Shut up, you idiot," the voice cackled, "I've brought you some company!"

Throwing my weight against the door, I pushed it open and skidded in. What I saw shocked but didn't surprise me. I held my ground as a face contorted with rage and hatred turned to me. Quickly I moved my hand to my belt and unstrapped the small can that was attached to it.

Fortunately, the night-vision goggles were pushed up on the hair I knew so well – the way was clear. Although she'd known I was coming she obviously hadn't expected me to come prepared to attack.

In that second I shot the pepper spray full into the face of my Aunt Venetia.

FRIDAY NIGHT

Clear as Perspex

From the catacombs I was escorted directly to the police
station – Inspector Witt's office, to be precise, where I'd
been just last Monday. It already felt like ages ago.

After a doctor had thoroughly cleaned and checked my
head, wrists and hands, I locked myself in the bathroom
and gargled with the most powerful antiseptic at hand. But
no matter how much I gargled, the feeling of that rat's tail
in my mouth wouldn't leave.

Meanwhile, a team of forensic specialists were
dispatched to Aunt V's to pack my things up while
Inspector Witt organized a hotel for my mum and me.
Staying at Aunt Venetia's was clearly out of the question:
it was now an official crime site – as was the La Lune
mansion.

Sebastian and his father had arrived about two
minutes after I'd found my aunt. Inspector Witt had
been in on our plan although he'd forbidden it at
first, deeming it too dangerous. But who knew how
long it would take to find Belle and Darius if Aunt

Venetia didn't lead us to them. Finally, for this reason, Inspector Witt relented and agreed to be on alert outside the mansion, waiting for Sebastian's call. And it was he who had given me the pepper spray.

After temporarily blinding Aunt V, I'd tied her up with my belt, and then freed Belle and Darius. Both were terribly weakened. Aunt Venetia had given them soup – but not quite enough. She'd had no plan in mind for their care when she'd caught her two surprise charges. Once a day she'd taken them some thin bouillon she'd made at home with powder. She'd carried it in her handbag – that was the liquid I'd seen dripping from her bag, what she'd claimed was water. If something had happened to Aunt V, Belle and Darius would have starved, their skeletons for ever lost to the catacombs. As it was, they were carried out on stretchers and taken by ambulance to the American Hospital in Neuilly. The initial feedback for Belle was positive. Apart from dehydration, and a couple of bumps on her head, she was all right. Darius required more supervision – although, it was a miracle he hadn't suffered a severe asthma attack.

I, on the other hand, was not all right. While I'd had the whole of a day – ever since my nightmare had led to the truth dawning on me – to come to terms with what my aunt had done, I still hated myself for having trapped her. Because of me, she'd be in prison. Because of me, her life was shattered.

"It's not because of you!" Ellie insisted.

"It's because of her greed that she's going to prison. It's because of her ruthlessness that her life is shattered," Sebastian added.

But they hadn't seen her face. A face twisted in such anguish! A face poisoned by an uncontrollable desire for more! Apparently, it knew no bounds. By the time I'd left the catacombs, there were already search teams trawling through the cavities near where Belle and Darius had been held. The few that had been looked into were a treasure trove of art. Sculptures, paintings, furniture – even jewellery; anything that was easy to transport through the vast underground network that she'd mapped out as her own. She'd been at it for a long time and, with her practised eye, she'd chosen only the best. And, just like in her apartment, many items were packed in cartons and packages wrapped with tape displaying the logos of some of the finest art dealers in Europe. I supposed we'd later read in the papers that she'd stolen the tape too.

The worst thing for me, however, was the one horrid phrase that wouldn't stop replaying itself in my mind since I'd heard it: "Shut up, you idiot – I've brought you some company!" For her, I, like Belle and Darius before me, was simply an obstacle that needed to be pushed to the side. So she'd taken me up on my pre-show challenge and gone into the catacombs to lead me to her lair. What she planned on doing with me after she'd trapped me was anyone's guess

– including her own. I honestly believe she hadn't thought things out further than that.

Of course, I'd sprung my plan on her just before the show, knowing that she wouldn't have the time to prepare for the chase without missing the La Lune show, which, in turn would raise a lot of questions about her whereabouts – something I was certain she'd want to avoid. My hunch had paid off. She'd been fidgety during the show; I'd noticed that from the runway. But still, pro that she was, she insisted on performing her role of front row fashion-editor-supreme – chase or no chase.

One thing was certain, however: she'd already admitted to Inspector Witt that she'd planned to pin the disappearances on Philippe de Vandrille. She'd intended to use the packet of letters she'd hidden in the chimney flue – the very ones I'd found – to identify him as a vengeful heir. Whether this plan would have worked or not we'll never know, but, at some point – if I hadn't taken the letters – she'd have planted them on Philippe.

And as for me? *Why* had she asked *me* to find Belle?

I'd asked her as much as she was led out of the catacombs. "I just wanted to keep you occupied, out of my hair, out of my apartment! Who'd have thought you'd actually figure out my plan? Or find Belle?" she'd spat at me. "Most days you can't even find something smart to wear!"

It was a sad climax to a brilliant career and a pathetic end for the aunt I'd respected. She'd always complained that as a child she had wanted for more material comfort than her detective father could afford. But with the successful careers she and her sister, my mum, had forged, who knew she was still harbouring such fear of having too little?

How, I wondered, would Mum react?

I think my mum wanted to take it well, and even tried to… but her efforts fell flat. Annoyingly, the only thing that seemed to lift her spirits was my modelling. My dad, bless him, hadn't been at all surprised – at least, not by his sister-in-law's thieving.

"I told you it was impossible that even with her enormous salary she could afford all of the stuff that was constantly going in and out of her apartment."

Of course, he'd never imagined anything like the scope she'd achieved. And certainly he'd never imagined she'd try to catch me – or, as my mum preferred to think of it, hold me for ransom. (I refrained from pointing out that she'd never asked for money for Belle and Darius. She'd just wanted them out of the way.)

Miriam offered a shoulder for my mum to cry on – Venetia, her friend of many years, had deceived her too. Not once had Miriam suspected that her close friend had been stealing from the very same fashion designers they worked together with and gossiped about. Aunt Venetia had hidden her double life well.

"If only I'd known," Miriam cried, "I'd have done something, helped her...but I never guessed! All this time Venetia's been criss-crossing Paris underground, using the catacombs, *and I never guessed*. For years she's been going in and out of the houses of some of the biggest names in fashion – undetected! – to steal art. *C'est incroyable!* And then she's been stashing the stolen art in the catacombs *underneath her apartment building*. And I never suspected anything..."

But no one could have suspected anything without regularly visiting Aunt V's apartment. Only by actually seeing the quantity of packages that came and went through her home could anyone have had an inkling. It was now clear those packages were all filled with stolen art. She'd always maintained they were deliveries of art she'd just *bought* – and, granted, every wall of her apartment was hung with amazing paintings...but, the fact was, she'd *lied*. Those packages that she claimed were "deliveries" had never been delivered to her. They were packages that *she* was *sending out*! Art she'd stolen, then kept in the catacombs until she'd found a buyer with an illegal collection in some faraway place. At that point she packed the art and carried it directly through the catacombs into her apartment building's basement then into her apartment. From there they'd get picked up by some very discreet and expensive couriers.

This, of course, explained why my aunt had stopped entertaining in her apartment several years ago.

"And I thought it was because she preferred the Ritz," Miriam said.

My aunt had studied interior architecture during her pre-fashion days. It was during this time that she learned about Le Vau and his secret passages. However, it was only much later, when she'd decided to fluff up her retirement nest egg with stolen art, that – using the pseudonym of David le Néanar – she began to seriously research Le Vau's buildings, with the intent of perhaps using the secret passages she'd read about as a student. She struck gold, however, when she stumbled upon the little-known fact that some of Le Vau's grandest mansions had direct points of access into the catacombs. This, then, became the inspiration for her ultimate plan.

"It's quite amazing," Sebastian pointed out. "Not only did you find Belle and Darius, but in the same stroke you found one of the greatest art thieves Paris has ever known."

I wouldn't call that amazing...but I'd certainly accomplished what I'd set out to do – and paid a much steeper price for it than I could have imagined.

A strong pair of arms suddenly enfolded me from behind. I turned and faced Sebastian. His eyes were smiling as he tucked my hair behind my ears. "How did you know it was your aunt?" he asked.

It was late by now – nearly midnight – and Sebastian

and I were at my hotel. We sat downstairs in a small wood-panelled reading room off the main lounge, cosy and dark, with heavy curtains and rich fabrics. Rain lashed against a window that looked over the private courtyard garden, while a large fire blazed in the fireplace. We sat in deep armchairs we'd pulled up to the fire. A pot of hot chocolate sat on a warmer on the low table in front of us.

Mum was still with Inspector Witt and Miriam – it seemed she'd be occupied for a good part of the night. Together with the *Chic: Paris* press office, they were now working on a plan for the various press announcements that would have to be made – and not just concerning Aunt Venetia. Apparently, my life wouldn't be the same after tomorrow morning either. Details about my hunt for Belle were beginning to leak out, and it was only a matter of time before the mainstream press started asking questions – questions I'd have to answer. It seemed the fashion press wouldn't be far behind.

"Enjoy being incognito tonight," Miriam had said to me. "It'll probably be your last night of anonymity. And once this story breaks, every magazine and designer will want to book you, so you can give some thought to your modelling career as well…"

That was a ramification I hadn't even BEGUN to think about – nor did I want to. At least, not now, tonight.

I was exhausted, but too wound up to feel sleepy. Occasionally, feelings of angst and guilt overwhelmed me.

A part of me felt like a traitorous bounty hunter: after all, even when I'd realized it was my aunt behind the disappearances and I'd had the chance to back down, I hadn't. I'd chosen to go on to the end. Yes, she was a criminal, yes, I'd saved two lives…but, nevertheless, she was – is – my aunt… As a sort of anti-venom to my self-hate, I regularly reminded myself that she wouldn't have hesitated to trap me if I'd given her just a few more seconds. That helped… but still…

"So how did you know it was your aunt?" Sebastian repeated.

"I wish I could claim a clear line of logical deduction, but actually I ended up bouncing from one hunch to another; and these hunches led me to my dream…"

"David le Néanar?" Ellie had just walked in. After Sebastian's father had gone into the catacombs, she'd left for a fitting. That was a supermodel for you: super-focused – on work. Even while catching criminals. Ellie had just finished and had come straight to the hotel to hear everything.

"Right. You know my aunt loves anagrams – she's addicted to them, actually. Well, David le Néanar is an anagram of Diana Vreeland. It was under my nose the entire time, but it wasn't until last night, after I'd had a good long look at the portraits of Diana Vreeland hanging in my aunt's dressing room, that the name stuck in my mind… And then later, when I saw the same prints in my dream, it all clicked. Funny how a little thing like that can make all the difference…"

"It's also funny that she'd choose such an obvious name," Ellie said.

"Obvious to you, because you're in fashion," I answered. "But most people have never heard of Diana Vreeland."

"It's also typical for…criminals," Sebastian said slowly, looking at me.

"It's all right, Sebastian. She is one. I have to get used to it."

"Criminals often like to work with inside jokes, so to speak. They're often vain and like to think of themselves as clever. What your aunt did is quite typical."

Needless to say, it was my aunt who'd left Sebastian and me to drown in the catacombs. And I suppose grazing me with her car on Monday had been a way of warming up – maybe deep down she already knew I'd be breathing down her neck by the end of the week. Like she'd told me earlier, by asking me to find Belle, she'd hoped to have me running around Paris searching for clues she thought I'd never find, rather than right under her nose figuring things out. As it turns out, I did figure things out – something she'd never expected. So she had to get me off her trail. Leaving me in the catacombs had seemed like a good way. A shiver ran down my spine as I remembered how surprised she'd been to see me last night. I'd thought it was because I was still awake – in fact, it was because I was still alive.

"But how did she learn so much about the curse?" Sebastian asked.

"Good question. I still don't know exactly how. But my aunt always seems to know everything, so it didn't really surprise me – until I spoke to Simone."

"Simone Baillie?"

I nodded. "While I was talking with Simone it suddenly dawned on me that perhaps my aunt knew the La Lunes – or had known them – better than she let on. So as I turned to leave I asked Simone one last question. I wanted to know whether my aunt and Patrick had ever known each other well."

"And she said yes…" Ellie said.

"Actually, no – she's too discreet for that. What she said was that she was aware that not long before he married, Patrick La Lune had spent quite a bit of time with a certain well-known magazine editor. She said they'd been passionate. But after a while they cooled, and then Patrick married Fiona. My aunt can be very nosy and persuasive. I'm sure she got the entire story of the curse out of Patrick – simply out of curiosity. I think the idea of using that information only occurred to her after kidnapping Belle."

"*After* kidnapping Belle? Why not before?" Sebastian asked, surprised.

"The need only came up after she encountered Belle and Darius."

I took a sip of my hot chocolate before continuing. "My aunt has been stealing for years, right? And she's never bumped into anyone before – I mean, that's the point of using the catacombs and the other secret passages she's found out about. Well, late last Saturday night or early Sunday morning, while trying to steal a tiny Giacometti sculpture from the La Lunes, she was caught by Belle – I heard Belle tell your father this," I nodded to Sebastian, "as she was put into the ambulance.

"And then, on Monday, my aunt was cornered by Darius – alone – and found out that he knew she used the secret passages. He accused her of kidnapping Belle, so now she had to get Darius out of the way as well. She did it very quickly – he has the wound on his head to prove it – just before the five o'clock meeting. She hit him, then tied and gagged him so that during the meeting she could safely leave him in one of the house's secret passages. After the questioning by Inspector Witt, but before we had dinner together, she dragged him into the catacombs."

Sebastian's phone rang.

"Yes? We're in the reading room...uh-huh, she's still up," he said, looking at me. "Good. We'll wait. À tout de suite." He put his phone away before saying, "That was my father. He's on his way. He wants to explain everything."

Inspector Witt came alone – my mum and Miriam were working at the agency and Thomas, Inspector Witt's assistant, was with my aunt and her lawyer. Sebastian's father seemed relieved to have finished for the night. He ordered a whisky from the bar before joining us.

"Fortunately, your aunt has made a full confession," he said. "That'll help her – and *Chic*. We'll move things along as quickly as we can, but, unfortunately, there's no way of avoiding the press...*c'est la vie*."

He took a swallow from his drink and leaned back before continuing. "First, let me say, thank you." He was looking straight at me. "I underestimated you, Mademoiselle Anderson. You were right to follow your instincts. Keep doing it and I can retire sooner than planned. But the case is quite complex and your aunt was a clever adversary. Finally, however, her luck ran out...Belle caught her with the statue and Darius confronted her about the secret passage. And, then, of course, she never imagined her niece would catch her."

I flushed, as guilt washed over me.

"Don't forget," he continued, "that you've helped Philippe, too. Your aunt had hoped to frame him as the nephew who avenged his wronged great-uncle."

I nodded. "Straight away she hinted – strongly – that I should look into the possibility of there being a living Merlette."

"By the way, she learned of the letters' existence years ago. While confessing earlier, she told me that one afternoon – this was when she was dating Patrick – she stumbled upon the letters while searching for an earring that had slipped beneath Patrick's bed. They were in a small ribbon-tied box underneath the mattress – just like in a clichéd police movie. Of course, she read them."

"After hiding Darius, she remembered the letters, and formed the idea of pinning the disappearances on Philippe – but for that she *needed* the letters, both as proof of who Philippe really is, and of his strong motive. As luck would have it, when she searched for them before I arrived to interview them all on Monday, she found them, again, in a box under Patrick's bed – with Patrick fast asleep in the bed." The inspector shook his head. "Hard to believe that Patrick never put them somewhere safer.

"Incidentally, that was her one big mistake – hiding the letters in the chimney flue, I mean. The clutch handbag she was using that day was too small to accommodate the bundle of letters – besides, she'd just dragged Darius into the secret passage – *he* was her main concern at that moment. She quickly hid the letters behind the flue and figured she'd fetch them later – but then you found them."

He smiled at me before continuing. "And her proof was gone. So, going on what she remembered from the letters, she began, using her David le Néanar alias, to search for Violette. She needed proof that Philippe was the heir she knew him to be."

"And Fiona? Did she know about any of this?"

"She'd heard of the letters, years earlier, from her husband – although she didn't know if he still had them.

After Belle disappeared, she started looking for them. The noise Rose and Dom heard at night was Fiona looking for the letters."

"But why was it so important for her to have the letters?"

"Fiona knew that her father-in-law François had stolen the designs for the Clothilde bag – Patrick had told her as much. So the chance that the letters might contain even the slightest allusion to that was enough to scare Fiona. Remember, the La Lune Fashion Design Foundation is her life's work. And imagine: they hand out prizes for design – but their company's success was founded on design theft. She'd never live it down! It would be ruination for her and the foundation and a huge blot on the family name.

"Furthermore, the letters were proof that Hector Merlette had an heir – and over the years her husband had hinted to her about Philippe being related to the Merlettes. She was worried that with the letters he might demand financial redress and rake up a scandal long-buried. For her children's sake, she was willing to thwart him in any way she could. She was sure he was behind the disappearances – his motive was strongest. So Fiona's foremost thought was to destroy those letters. It was imperative that she find them – but your aunt beat her to them."

"Who planted Belle's drawings in Blossom's bag?"

Inspector Witt shook his head. "Fiona. It was a stupid ruse to lead the police away from the rumours of the curse and family scandal. By the time she realized Philippe wasn't responsible for Belle's disappearance, she regretted what she'd done.

"Darius came closest to solving the whole thing. Some time ago, in the course of his reading, he'd learned about the secret passages in the house, but didn't really believe they existed – until Belle disappeared. Darius was exploring the passageway – *at the same time your aunt was in it.* Venetia was back in the house on Sunday night to steal a couple of small paintings. Don't forget that Belle had interrupted your aunt's foray the night before so Venetia went back the next night to finish the job, so to speak. Darius saw her – although your aunt didn't see him – just as she disappeared into the catacombs with the paintings. The next day, Monday, he found her on her own and confronted her before the meeting. She immediately felt cornered by him and lashed out. Without wasting a moment she grabbed the nearest heavy object – a paperweight, Darius told me – and hit him hard. She then hid him in the nearest secret passageway before calmly joining the others for the five o'clock meeting. Darius had known her for years, of course, but only as a chic and professional editor. Her swift and violent action took him completely by surprise.

"Their violent confrontation," continued Inspector Witt, "culminating in Darius's disappearance, was a real blow to us because Darius was the only one who'd made the obvious connection between Belle's disappearance and Venetia's suspicious presence in the passageways."

"But Claude knew about the catacombs – he must have known about the secret passageway, too. Have you asked him about *CAT*?"

"I'm afraid *CAT* is simply the nickname of someone he'd been interviewed by for a job. Contrary to his original police statement, tonight he told me that, in fact, last Saturday night he'd slipped out of the mansion straight after dinner to meet *CAT* – Catherine Lafont, the well-known fashion headhunter. But because of his family's paranoia with the curse, Claude wasn't ready to say anything about looking for a new job. Hence, the mysterious *CAT* – for Catherine. By chance, Philippe had seen him, walking home."

"Which is why Claude was so edgy at the casting. He'd lied." I refrained from mentioning that Claude had also been cross because I'd looked at his phone.

"*Oui.*"

What about Rose?" Sebastian asked.

"Ahh, *la Rose*," answered Inspector Witt. "Again, Mademoiselle Anderson was correct: love, and a certain amount of desperation, pushed Rose to flee to Spain. According to the letter we've found, she and Alejandro had planned this split from her family many months ago. Of course, she never could have guessed how unfortunate her timing would be. I have spoken with her – she's on her way back – and through her sobs she said she'd felt that if she didn't go through with this break now, then she never would. Apparently, she's always felt like an outsider within her own family – and she'd finally had enough."

We fell silent for a moment. Rose's sadness felt nearly palpable after hearing about her desperate attempt to flee.

"And Venetia's definitely the one behind the other so-called 'fashion crimes'?" Ellie asked, breaking the silence.

Inspector Witt nodded. "Although it's not yet officially confirmed. But Venetia had been in and out of the homes of the fashion world's elite so often that she knew exactly what they owned – and, as you know, many of the top designers and fashion brand owners have amazing art collections. Unfortunately, she used her privileged access for more than just networking."

"By the way," Sebastian asked as he stood and stretched. "Why the shoe? Did your aunt use it to hit Darius or Belle?"

I shook my head. "Not at all. While we were waiting for the paramedics, Belle told me that *she'd* taken it. She'd heard someone moving around the house and, after having quickly grabbed the nearest heavy shoe, went to investigate. She found my aunt downstairs, stealing the small Giacometti sculpture. But unfortunately, my aunt lured Belle into a secret passageway, hit her, then quickly tied and gagged her. Belle never had a chance to use the shoe. It was dropped where Sebastian stubbed his toe on it yesterday."

Ellie suddenly stood up. "I think it's time I got some

shut-eye. I've got Saint Laurent first thing tomorrow morning."

"And I'm sure my father has some questions he'd like me to answer," Sebastian whispered as Inspector Witt stepped out of the room to take a call. "At least I have someone I can blame for my illegal behaviour." He was grinning right at me.

"Go ahead, Watson. If I can take some cockroaches and skull-flinging, I can certainly take on your father."

SATURDAY MORNING

Rhymes with Bliss

"Good morning, Axelle! Axelle, wake up," my mum commanded as she finished drawing open the curtains. "It's such a bright, sunny morning, and listen – aren't the church bells wonderful? Come on now, we have a lot to do. The press conference begins at ten, followed by various interviews. I'll get you some tea," she said as she disappeared behind the adjoining door.

Miu Miu was on my bed. She hadn't been allowed to remain in Aunt V's apartment either. In fact, it seemed that she would be going back to London with us. I'm not sure she'd be kneading my stomach with such enthusiasm if she knew what was awaiting her across the Channel.

"Axelle, darling, I know you'd love to sleep longer but we have to get you ready," my mum said, as she came back into the room and handed me a cup of hot tea. "*The Times, The Guardian, Le Figaro, Paris Match, Washington Post, The New York Times*, papers from Italy, Japan, Australia… They all want to see you. There is so much to do. Plus more will be waiting when we get back to London tomorrow. And just think: all of this press about finding Belle is bound to give your modelling career a boost."

Great, I thought, *my modelling career. Exactly what I don't want, exactly what I'm not interested in.* The only thing that stopped me from venting was the sight of my mum's red-rimmed eyes. Yesterday had taken its toll. Her carriage was as upright as usual and she was elegantly dressed, but her eyes were full of worry and anxiety. Of course, who could blame her? It's not every day that your sister is revealed as a kidnapping art thief. I watched her as she moved about the room straightening out my clothes, pouring my tea, shooing Miu Miu off the bed. The fog of doom hanging over her only lifted when she talked about my modelling. The fact that I'd spent so much time and effort solving this case – and that I'd only used the modelling as a sort of entry ticket – hadn't yet registered.

In fact, I thought with a sigh, it seemed as if all of my plans for credibility and independence had come to nil.

Again I bit my tongue. For the moment I'd let my mum amuse herself with my modelling. I'd also do the minimum required of me for the press and then, when things had calmed a bit, I'd tackle the issue of my career as a detective.

The press conference went okay. Miriam had kindly given us use of one of the conference rooms at her agency. Like my mum, she too couldn't move out from under the shadow caused by last night's revelation.

"Of course," she said to me, "I saw she'd been buying a lot, but she did earn a very good salary, and I thought that she'd perhaps invested wisely – or so she'd always implied. Never, ever could I have imagined her capable of stealing from the designers. I mean, she *loved* the designers! She had the utmost respect for them and their work. It's so sad, because she's a very, very good editor. She changed the look of the entire magazine business, you know. And she had such an eye for detail…"

So she did – and apparently, when it came to solving mysteries, I did too, according to the journalists. Maybe it was an inherited trait. From Gran probably. I was happy that Gran hadn't lived to see her eldest daughter go to prison – especially after having been caught by her granddaughter.

Belle La Lune had invited Mum and me for lunch.

As the butler ushered us into the same grand drawing room where I'd last seen the family gathered, on Monday night, I wondered why it felt so strange to be back in the La Lune mansion. After all, it was hardly my first time – I'd been in and out any number of times over the course of the last week – not to mention that I'd seen every floor and at all hours. Then it dawned on me: this was the first time I had actually been *invited* in. Until this moment, every time I'd been into this house, I'd snuck in.

Belle was waiting for us when we walked in, and despite her time in the catacombs she looked stunning. Her long blonde hair was the colour of fresh corn and hung like spun sugar down her back. A tiny black jumper was layered over a transparent long-sleeved T-shirt and tight leather jeans hugged her long slim legs. A pair of high, high leather and chainmail boots finished her ensemble. Even sitting down, with a cashmere throw over her lap and a nurse at her elbow, that palpable fashion vibe – an intimidating mixture of innate style and originality with a good pinch of insouciance – came off her in waves: she was a star and she knew it.

Darius was still in the hospital – and would be for a few more days. Otherwise, he was in good spirits and hoped to personally thank me for saving his life once he was out.

Lunch was delicious. We began with white asparagus accompanied by a mousseline sauce. By the time we got to the second course (*poussin de la ferme* and spring vegetables) I began to relax, because I'd noticed that while my mum tried repeatedly – in her usual toe-curling fashion – to push the conversation towards the subject of my "modelling career", Belle steadfastly refused to be lured in. Much to my delight, the more my mum pushed, the harder Belle resisted. She didn't want to hear about my options with *Teen Vogue* or for the new L'Oréal hairspray. At one especially low point in the conversation (my mum was banging on about how Hervé believed I had the most amazing eyebrows he'd ever seen) I caught Belle's eye – and in a sign of tacit complicity, she winked. I could have got up from the table and kissed her. Instead I tried to transmit a look of boundless gratitude, but for all I know she might have thought it was for the delicious strawberry soufflé.

Finally lunch came to an end, and Belle led us back to the drawing room for coffee.

And that's when she dropped the bomb.

She motioned for us to sit down. No sooner had the coffee arrived than my mum began informing Belle, yet again, about how many requests I'd been receiving through Miriam's agency for magazine photo shoots – only this time Belle cut her off.

"That's wonderful, Mrs Anderson – and while I can understand your pride in Axelle's potential, I'd be curious to hear what Axelle has to say about her future."

My mum and Belle sat waiting for me to reply. Belle was calm, but my mum looked at me like an X-ray machine.

I decided to go with the truth.

So, taking a deep breath and with a quick glance at my mum, who was perfecting her X-ray glare, I said, "Actually, Belle, I don't mean any disrespect, but fashion – and modelling in particular – just doesn't interest me that much.

I did get a real kick out of finding you, though – even if it means I'll have to visit my aunt in jail for the next twenty years." My mum's eyes were searing into me now. "However," I continued, "I'm going to stick to detective work… I think I might even try solving some more mysteries."

"Oh, Axelle," my mum interrupted, "you don't really mean that. What do you think she should pursue?" she added coyly, turning to Belle.

"It is my belief, Mrs Anderson, that people should pursue their dreams."

"Yes, but, Belle," my mother insisted, as she leaned forward and sweetened her voice, "from one woman who values her independence to another – let's face it, this modelling career is a once-in-a-lifetime opportunity that should be taken! Axelle will never be able to earn an income from sleuthing, and where will she be then? Modelling – especially with your help – could be a stepping stone to many opportunities."

"I agree that she is on the cusp of a once-in-a-lifetime opportunity with regards to the modelling…" My mother visibly preened in my direction as Belle said this. "However, as to her inability to earn an income as a detective – I'm afraid you're wrong about that, Mrs Anderson: your daughter's just earned half a million euros."

You could have heard a pin drop on the thick carpet. Slowly, like a small fish making its way from the ocean's depths to the surface for air, a dim memory of the first time

I'd seen Claude came to mind. He'd been on television the night I'd arrived...

"I asked you to lunch to thank you again for rescuing me," Belle said, as she looked at me, "and to ask you for your bank account details. I don't know if you watched my brother Claude's press conference the Sunday night after I'd disappeared, but he did offer a half a million euro reward for any information leading to my safe return and, as he said it on national television, we can hardly renege on our offer, can we?"

She was smiling now. "However, Axelle, should you decide to accept the reward, I have two conditions I'd like you to honour: one, that you'll set aside the bulk of it for your education and risk-averse investments, and two that you'll use what's left to pursue your mystery solving."

The shock of having so much land in my lap at once took my breath away. I couldn't even yet find my voice.

As I sat blinking, Belle added, "And, by the way, with the experience you've garnered this week, you might want to consider specializing in fashion mysteries. I'm not saying it would be easy...but I think you'll find this business could use your help. Although," she said, looking intently at me, "give it serious thought before you jump in. The fashion world is glamorous and glitzy, and fun, too...but, like all businesses involving big money and big names, it has an underbelly of jealousy, secrets and cut-throat competitiveness. If you choose to specialize in fashion mysteries you'll have to remind yourself that a criminal is a criminal – no matter how stylish they may be or how beautiful they may look."

Belle reached for the telephone and within thirty seconds Philippe de Vandrille had whisked me away to the small study Inspector Witt had used for questioning last Monday night. As the attorney to the La Lunes, he was responsible for handing over my reward. He'd prepared most of the necessary documents so that I could sign them before leaving, speeding up the process. Calmly and clearly, he explained the general gist of the deal, including the conditions set by the family. I wasn't entirely free to do with my reward what I liked. It was on paper now: Belle's conditions were to be met. But as long as I met them, I was one lucky girl.

He really does have an elegant profile, I thought as I watched him, *like something from an old coin.* The family resemblance stood out. Of course, it had been there all along: the tall, slim build, well-drawn jawline and cheekbones, even something about the way he moved. It had been there all along…and yet not many had noticed. A different name and childhood had put him in a particular box. Only Patrick's old secretary, Simone, had known without a doubt. Fiona had heard but had never seen real proof. And Aunt V had first surmised, then hoped. Otherwise, no questions asked. His secret would go no further – or so I thought.

He caught me by surprise when, after I'd signed the papers he'd prepared, he confessed to me that he had guessed some time ago that his father was Patrick. "And knowing you, you've probably also guessed," he said with a smile.

I flushed, not sure how much to admit to. My discomfort only made him smile more.

"Philippe," I finally said, "would you mind if I ask you a last question?"

With a smile, he looked up from his papers spread across the desk. "Of course not. After everything that's happened, I rather feel you're entitled to ask me whatever you'd like."

"Why have you never said anything? To the family, I mean…about being Patrick's son and Hector Merlette's heir?"

"You mean why keep it a secret, when it seems I could so clearly profit from being acknowledged as a La Lune and Merlette heir?"

"Yes."

"I'll answer your question with a question," he said. "If you were given the chance to let the world know that *you*, Axelle Anderson, were in fact Belle La Lune's half-sister – that your father was Patrick La Lune and that your mother was Hector Merlette's niece; that, in fact, you had more right to own the company than anyone else – would you take the chance? Would you want to be acknowledged as such?"

"You mean live in this mansion? And Fiona would be my stepmother?" (Now there was a thought!) "And I'd have siblings who wouldn't try searching for me if I disappeared? And I'd be at every fashion show and live, dream and breathe fashion?"

He nodded.

"Hmm… And I could go to the Café Ruc for French fries whenever I wanted and have all of the clothes I wanted?"

Again he nodded.

"Well," I answered after a short pause, "I'd have to say no – no way."

"And why?"

"Because living with the La Lunes, I'd go bananas," I said with a laugh. "No, seriously, my answer is no, because from what I've seen the La Lunes are way too dysfunctional. Well dressed, but dysfunctional – and cold like ice (except Belle). Most of them seem incapable of being even friendly with each other. I mean, I don't care how extravagant the lifestyle, living here with them would be a nightmare – to me anyway. Plus, fashion isn't really my thing."

"Well, that's my answer to your question," Philippe said. "When I found out – I'd long suspected, by the way – and finally confronted my mother with the truth, she asked me what I'd like to do. Did I want to pursue the matter legally? Did I want to confront my father Patrick about it? Did I want my mother to do it for me? What did I want?"

Turning out towards the garden he continued, "I decided

to follow in my mother's footsteps and let sleeping dogs lie. I like my life, I loved my father René, and I'm happy being Philippe de Vandrille. I'm not sure that being known as Philippe Merlette-La Lune would really make me any better or happier."

I can't say I remember much of our meeting with Belle after that. I know I was finally able to emit some appreciative squeaky sounds, which Belle graciously accepted. She then hugged me and said goodbye, with one last entreaty to call her any time I needed help – fashion or otherwise. She also said that she expected us to keep in regular contact and then kindly offered to send us back to our hotel with her chauffeur, but Mum and I wanted to walk home. After the shock we'd received, we needed to feel the earth under our feet.

As we stepped out onto the Rue de Varenne, the sun hit my face with a sharpness my mind lacked. Quietly I mused on the fact that so many conflicting emotions and experiences, good and sad, new and bewildering, could happen within the span of a week. I wondered how long it would take before everything felt "normal" again. Would life revert to its pre-Parisian rhythm once I was back in Notting Hill? Or was I now on some kind of fashion fast-track?

Shielding my eyes with my hand, I tilted my head back

and gazed up. I thought of Gran and wondered if she was watching...and if so, whether she'd ever forgive me for turning her daughter in...

"Axelle?"

"Yes, Mum?"

"Don't you think fashion people are just so clever and kind? I really think you should stay in close contact with Belle. She wants you to. And, by way of celebrating, I might get you a few new dresses. The spring sales will be on when we return and I..."

Like I say, some things never change.

Sebastian and I had made plans to meet in the afternoon. Because of my morning press conference and long lunch, we decided on something easy and close-by: ice cream.

Unfortunately, when his call came through from reception it was my mother who answered. With a cheesy knowing look in my direction, she said we'd be right down.

"*We?* But, Mum, you don't have to come down."

"Axelle, don't be silly, of course I do. I'm your mother – and this is your first date. Sebastian has to know that I'll be looking out for you."

"You're joking, right? I mean, Mum, Sebastian is my friend and we're going out for an ice cream – not a date!"

"Of course you are, darling," she said, that look still on her face as she locked our door behind us.

Thankfully, Sebastian didn't seem surprised to see my mum. He politely said hello and explained our plans. My mum, who wishes I was full of raging hormones and really thought there would be more excitement to our "date" than just ice cream, looked slightly deflated.

Sebastian and I walked to the small park in the middle of the Place des Vosges. Happily, today I had no fashion show or photo shoot to rush off to, no cockroach-infested tunnel to explore. The rest of the day was mine to enjoy as I saw fit. It was still, warm and windless, not a cloud in the sky, although the night's rain had left large puddles. They lay like mirrors in the sandy gravel of the pathways, reflecting the tidy shapes of the clipped trees and the impressive facade of the old buildings surrounding the square. Silently we continued, our steps falling into an easy rhythm, as we headed towards the cathedral of Notre Dame.

I was thinking about when I'd see Sebastian again. I'd been so focused on solving the mystery that I hadn't thought further than last night. But now, mission accomplished, I suddenly realized that I had no reason to see him after my train pulled out tomorrow. A feeling of emptiness hit me with a force that took me by surprise. We'd become friends, so of course I'd miss him – and I'd come to depend on him. But…was there more to it than that?

"Are you okay?" He was smiling at me, blue eyes crinkling at the corners. Did he have to look so gorgeous?

"I'm fine. Just thinking."

"Seriously, Axelle, don't you think you've done enough thinking for one week? Just relax. Look," he said, pointing to the river.

The Seine was moving rapidly, the dark, swirling water slapping against the side of the stone bank with reassuring enthusiasm. Seagulls screeched and swooped above us while tour boats chugged slowly past, their modern white shapes barely fitting under the centuries-old bridges spanning the river. When we reached the Notre Dame we stopped to admire its romantic bulk from the quayside. Finally, we climbed back up onto the road, crossed the nearest bridge, and joined the queue at Berthillon, the famous ice-cream maker. As we crossed back over the bridge, ice creams in hand, Sebastian suggested we stop midway to look at the view.

The sun was beginning to drop, its late afternoon light bathing the stone bridges and buildings in a soft yellow-orange haze of warmth. Sebastian was surprisingly quiet, and it dawned on me that since we'd left the hotel he'd been watching me in a funny way. Well, maybe not funny, but differently, anyhow, to the way he normally looked at me. Not that it was uncomfortable or anything…it was just…I don't know…different.

I tried to look discreetly down at my chest, thinking that maybe I'd spilled some ice cream. Slowly, though, a funny, fuzzy feeling at the back of my brain started to kick in and my palms began to sweat. Pulling my eyes away from his, I quickly turned back to the water.

"Axelle?"

I began to panic. I mean, like, what if he wanted to kiss me or something? This was one scenario I was absolutely NOT prepared for. Not at all. I mean, of course I liked him, but I'd had so much on my mind all week that canoodling with a hot French guy just hadn't really entered into it.

Okay. Maybe that was a tiny lie. I mean, there'd been a few moments, in between the cockroaches and rats, when I'd thought...

"Axelle, I've had an amazing time with you this week," he began, hastening to add, "solving this mystery and all..."

Okay. I was seriously panicking now. Questions raced through my mind: what did he want? What did I want? Did I want to kiss him? Why was I so sure that he wanted to kiss me? *Don't think so much, Axelle,* I could hear Jenny saying, *just go with the flow.* Yeah, easy for her to say! His hand was coming towards me...gently he swept back the hair from my right cheek and pushed it behind my ear.

Taking my chin in his hand, he turned my face back to his and leaned in. I began to hyperventilate. This hadn't been part of my plan, this had nothing to do with anything, this was just... Hmmm...this wasn't so bad. Cautiously, once my body had told my brain to stuff it, I leaned forward and kissed Sebastian back.

Everything slipped from my mind: the La Lunes, the

cockroaches, my sore shoulder – even my mum. All I was aware of was the feel of his lips, his smell, his hands on my waist and back. Every caress, every nuance in his movements shot through me till I was dizzy, until all that mattered was him.

His hands slowly moved up my back to my neck. If he hadn't been holding me, I think I'd have fallen into the river.

And then my phone rang.

And rang.

And rang.

WHY NOW? And who was it?

Shut up! Shut up, I told myself. *You're going with the flow, remember?*

I ignored my phone and leaned harder into Sebastian. Kissing him felt amazing. He tasted good and smelled good and I could have kept kissing him for hours – and maybe would have if my phone hadn't rung *again*.

ARGH!

It couldn't be my mum. With romance on the cards she wouldn't have rung me even if Ralph Lauren, Giorgio Armani and Coco Chanel, back from the grave, had called her asking to speak to me. It couldn't have been Jenny, we'd spoken this morning, and Ellie was doing the Sonia Rykiel show...so it must be someone else...it must be *work*. Hervé, maybe? During the shows the agencies were open on the weekends too. It must be Hervé.

355

I reached into my jacket pocket and pulled out my phone. As unobtrusively as possible, I switched it to silent – and saw the tiny blinking screen. It was *Miriam*. What could she want?

I felt Sebastian laugh as he pulled away.

"Go on," he said with a grin, "answer it." Unlike Dom, he seemed to find the interruption amusing. "It's probably important."

"Axelle, is that you? I'm sorry to call you today, you must be exhausted," Miriam said in her usual breathless, upbeat manner. "But listen, the phone has been ringing non-stop with questions about you. The fashion brigade is desperate to work with you, but we can discuss all of that on Monday." There was a short pause before she continued. "There was a call, however, which was just put through to me…and I thought you might be interested to hear about it *now*." I heard her reshuffle the notes on her desk. "It was New York calling…"

Oh no, I thought, *more photos*. I was just about to say that this could wait until Monday too, when Miriam continued:

"Have you ever heard of the 'Black Amelia'?"

"No."

"It's the most famous black diamond in the world. *Chic: New York* is – was – using it on a shoot, but…" Her voice trailed off.

"But?"

"It's missing…"

The End

And don't miss Axelle's
<u>third case</u>, coming soon...

Fashion's most stylish detective just
can't resist tackling another glitzy
mystery - especially when it lands on
her own doorstep!

Look out LONDON,
<u>Axelle's</u> back in town

HOW TO SPEAK SUPERMODEL

Axelle's guide to surviving in the world of fashion

If you want to blend in with the fashion set, it's worth learning the lingo. HERE'S A HANDY GUIDE:

* BOOK: This is another word for the all-important portfolio models have. A book or portfolio is used to show clients and designers both how a model looks in photos, and what kind of work they've done.
* BOOKER: A staff member at an agency whose job is to handle requests from clients and to represent and set up appointments for models.
* CLEAN CLEAN: This is how a model should show up for a photo shoot: with freshly washed hair and a clean, make-up free face. Clients often specify clean, clean.
* FITTING: A session that may take place before a fashion show or photo shoot where the clothes to be modelled are fitted onto the model.
* GO-SEE: An appointment for a model to see a photographer or a client. Unlike a casting, there is no specific brief.
* HAUTE COUTURE: Pronounced "oat-ko-chure" this phrase is French for "high-fashion". Couture is extremely high-end, tailor-made designer clothes that only a few dozen people in the world can afford.

✳ <u>LIGHT METER:</u> A device used to measure the intensity of light for a photo. Photographers or their assistants will hold a light meter up in front of the model before taking the photograph.

✳ <u>LOCATION:</u> Any place, other than in a studio, where a shoot takes place.

✳ <u>NEW FACES:</u> Models who are new to the business.

✳ <u>OPTIONS:</u> An option is put to a model by a client to see if he/she would be available for their shoot. Options are then either confirmed as a booking, or released.

✳ <u>STORYBOARD:</u> A comic-like piece of artwork that shows a frame-by-frame depiction of a photo shoot in drawings.

✳ <u>TEAR SHEETS:</u> These are photos which are literally torn from magazines, and which a model can use in her book. Tear sheets from magazines like *Vogue* and *Elle* are what every model hopes to have in her book.

✳ <u>ZED CARD OR COMPOSITE CARD:</u> This is basically a business card for models. A5 in size, zed cards or composites normally show at least two photos, as well as basic info such as a model's hair colour, eye colour, height and agency contact details.

And if anyone's still suspicious that you don't belong, just throw in one of these handy phrases...

"I love those boots! Whose are they?"

"Wow, you're really working that hat!"

"Feathers are a must have this fall."

"It's all about accessorizing right now."

"I'm loving emerald green."

"Punk is so of the moment."

"Neon just screams 1999."

"Grey is the new black."

"Velvet is so important this season."

NOW DON'T FORGET THE AIR KISSES, DARLING!
MWAH, MWAH!

Carina's favourite places to visit in the city of romance and fashion

"I absolutely love PARIS and had a blast living there. The city's ARCHITECTURE, HISTORY and CULTURE never fail to amaze me. Of course, the WONDERFUL food might also have something to do with it! I'm often asked for my FAVOURITE PLACES to visit - so here they are."

THE LOUVRE: As one of the world's largest museums it would take weeks of visiting to do the LOUVRE justice. But when the culture junkie in me needs a quick fix I head straight to THE FOUR SEASONS by NICOLAS POUSSIN (they hang in their own room). Totally uplifting!

MUSÉE DE LA CHASSE ET DE LA NATURE: I love dogs! And was therefore delighted when I discovered this QUIRKY little museum that is definitely off the beaten track. Housed in a GORGEOUS seventeenth-century mansion, and located in the lively Marais, this museum is jam-packed with animal portraits.

SENNELIER: I often think that if Harry Potter's Diagon Alley had an art-supply shop, it would look like this.

Established in 1887, and still run by the Sennelier family, every nook and cranny of this creaky, wood-panelled shop is stocked with the PRETTIEST, YUMMIEST, most SCRUMPTIOUS collection of pastels, pencils, paper, feather quills, Japanese watercolours, exotic papers and anything else your artistic heart could possibly desire.

BERTHILLON: If you like ICE CREAM, this is it. And while the weekend queues wind around the block, no worries. With a view of the Notre Dame and the Seine River swirling past, the time will fly! Located on the ENCHANTING Ile St. Louis, take a walk around the island as you finish your ice cream.

LADURÉE: A peek at the windows of this YUMMYLICIOUS patisserie alone are a treat! And while Ladurée shops now dot many cities worldwide, the original at 16, rue Royale is the one I like. Their MACARONS are my favourite: I find it impossible to leave Paris without a BEAUTIFUL Ladurée box filled with a selection of colourful macarons. And if I'm really hungry I'll go upstairs to their pretty little salon for tea.

THE TUILERIES GARDENS: As far as I'm concerned, a visit to Paris isn't complete without a walk through the Tuileries Gardens. Either end is a good place to start. Walk all the way through, the palace courtyards included. The views, <u>SPLASHING FOUNTAINS</u>, and elegant design make it <u>LOVELY</u> any time of the year.

<u>PLACE DES VOSGES</u>: Known as the oldest planned square in Paris, the Place de Vosges <u>OOZES</u> history – and the prettily planted centre of the square is a lovely place to catch some <u>SUN</u>. Just don't forget the <u>ICE CREAM</u>.

HAVE FUN!

www.usborne.com/fiction